NEW YORK REVIEW BOOKS
CLASSICS

PARIS VAGABOND

JEAN-PAUL CLÉBERT (1926–2011) ran away from his Jesuit boarding school at the age of seventeen to join the French Resistance, serving undercover in a Montmartre brothel to gather intelligence on the patrons who were German soldiers. After the liberation of Paris he wandered through a catalog of odd jobs including boat painter, cook, newspaper seller, funeral director's mute, and café proprietor. For many months he lived with the city's down-and-outs, though without losing touch with some of Paris's literary figures, notably Blaise Cendrars, and gathered the raw material for this book, first published in 1952 as *Paris insolite*. In 1956 he moved to Provence, where he remained for the rest of his life, writing many books, including a classic firsthand study of Gypsy life, originally published in 1961 and translated by Charles Duff as *The Gypsies*; and the encyclopedic *Dictionnaire du Surréalisme* (1996).

PATRICE MOLINARD (1922–2002) began his career taking stills for Georges Franju's legendary documentary on the Paris slaughterhouse at La Villette, *Le sang des bêtes* (1949). As a film director, he is best known for *Fantasmagorie* (1963), *Orphée 70* (1968), and *Bistrots de Paris* (1977).

DONALD NICHOLSON-SMITH was born in Manchester, England and is a longtime resident of New York City. He came across Clébert's *Paris insolite* as a teenager and has long wished to bring it to an Anglophone audience. Among his many translations are works by Paco Ignacio Taibo II, Henri Lefebvre, Raoul

Vaneigem, Antonin Artaud, Jean Laplanche, Guillaume Apollinaire, Guy Debord, Jean-Patrick Manchette, Thierry Jonquet, and (with Alyson Waters) Yasmina Khadra. For NYRB Classics he has translated Manchette's *Fatale* and *The Mad and the Bad*, which won the 28th Annual Translation Prize of the French-American Foundation and the Florence Gould Foundation for fiction.

LUC SANTE is the author of *Low Life*, *Evidence*, *The Factory of Facts*, *Kill All Your Darlings*, *Folk Photography*, and, most recently *The Other Paris*. He translated Félix Fénéon's *Novels in Three Lines* and has written introductions to several other NYRB Classics, including *Classic Crimes* by William Roughead and *Pedigree* by Georges Simenon. A frequent contributor to *The New York Review of Books*, he teaches writing and the history of photography at Bard College.

PARIS VAGABOND

JEAN-PAUL CLÉBERT

Photographs by
PATRICE MOLINARD

Translated from the French by
DONALD NICHOLSON-SMITH

Foreword by
LUC SANTE

NEW YORK REVIEW BOOKS

New York

DEER PARK PUBLIC LIBRARY
44 LAKE AVENUE
DEER PARK, NY 11729

THIS IS A NEW YORK REVIEW BOOK
PUBLISHED BY THE NEW YORK REVIEW OF BOOKS
435 Hudson Street, New York, NY 10014
www.nyrb.com

Text copyright © 1952, 1981 by Éditions Denoël, Paris
Photographs copyright © 2009 by Éditions Attila
Translation copyright © 2016 by Donald Nicholson-Smith
Foreword copyright © 2016 by Luc Sante
All rights reserved.

Library of Congress Cataloging-in-Publication Data
Names: Clébert, Jean-Paul, author. | Nicholson-Smith, Donald, translator. |
  Sante, Luc, writer of introduction. | Molinard, Patrice, photographer.
Title: Paris vagabond / Jean-Paul Clébert ; translated by Donald Nicholson-
  Smith ; introduction by Luc Sante ; photographs by Patrice Molinard.
Other titles: Paris insolite. English
Description: New York : New York Review Books, 2016. | Series: New York
  Review Books classics | Translation of Paris insolite, co-authored with Patrice
  Molinard (photographs), published by Denoël, 1952, and reissued by Attila in
  2009.
Identifiers: LCCN 2015038075 (print) | LCCN 2015044381 (ebook) | ISBN
  9781590179574 (paperback) | ISBN 9781590179581 (epub)
Subjects: LCSH: Paris (France)—Description and travel—20th century. |
  Paris (France)—Pictorial works. | Clébert, Jean-Paul. | Authors—France—
  Biography. | BISAC: FICTION / Biographical. | FICTION / Action &
  Adventure. | FICTION / Literary.
Classification: LCC DC707 .C537913 2016 (print) | LCC DC707 (ebook) |
  DDC 914.4/360483092—dc23
LC record available at http://lccn.loc.gov/2015038075

ISBN 978-1-59017-957-4
Available as an electronic book; ISBN 978-1-59017-958-1

Printed in the United States of America on acid-free paper.
10 9 8 7 6 5 4 3 2 1

CONTENTS

FOREWORD

PARIS VAGABOND, first published in 1952, is one of the most extraordinary books ever written about that city. It follows in the lineage of great narratives by champion walkers—Louis-Sébastien Mercier's *Le tableau de Paris* (1781–88), Nicolas-Edme Restif de la Bretonne's *Les nuits de Paris* (1788–94), Alexandre Privat d'Anglemont's *Paris anecdote* (1854), Léon-Paul Fargue's *Le piéton de Paris* (1939), among others —although its focus is more pointed and specific. Had a translation come out in the 1960s or '70s heyday of budget travel guides, someone might have been tempted to call it "Paris on Nothing a Day." It is primarily concerned with all the ways in which people managed to survive in the city on no money at all, a lifestyle shared by Jean-Paul Clébert himself. As he told the journalist Olivier Bailly in a 2009 interview:

> It was not a reportage but a personal investigation; it was me in the streets of Paris, rediscovering a city that was still as it had been during the Occupation, which is to say that in some ways it was still the pre-war city, that of the Surrealists and of [Pierre Mac Orlan's concept] *le fantastique social*, which lived on.... It was a clandestine Paris that I came to know as a clandestine myself.

Clébert was born in 1926 to a bourgeois family (whose identity remains unknown) in the wealthy suburb of Neuilly-sur-Seine and educated in a Jesuit boarding school in Passy, from which he ran away at age seventeen and joined the Resistance. Somewhere along the line he shed his surname and became Clébert, a relatively uncommon name that I can't help but think he chose because of its proximity to *clebs*, argot for "dog." At loose ends once Paris was liberated, he took on a variety of jobs, including hauling produce crates at Les Halles, hawking the newspaper *L'Intransigeant*, and more colorful employment he describes in the book, such as the inimitably French and positivistic task of taking measurements of random apartments all over the city. From there he slid into living as the lilies of the field, who neither toil nor spin. Between 1944 and 1948 he spent time with the ragpickers in the Zone (the roughly thousand-foot-wide ribbon of land that surrounded the city's former military wall and for a century served as refuge to marginals of all sorts), with the Roma of the Maximoff clan at Porte de Montreuil, with the surviving Jewish community on Rue des Rosiers, with the clochards around Place Maubert and Rue Mouffetard, with hoboes and lamsters and eccentrics and living ghosts all over the city. The whole time he took notes, with any available pencil on any available paper, such as restaurant place mats and bits of newspaper. He kept a sack of these, and when around 1951 he came to write his book he drew them out one by one at random, the shape of his text thus determined by a venerable Dada chance operation.

He sent his manuscript to Blaise Cendrars, one of his two professed literary forebears (the other was Henry Miller). Cendrars was a pioneering modernist poet ("The Prose of the Trans-Siberian and of Little Jeanne of France," 1913), novelist (*Sutter's Gold*, 1925; *Moravagine*, 1926), reporter, librettist, filmmaker, and, maybe most important, the author of a quartet of rollicking, shape-shifting memoirs: *The Astonished Man* (1945), *Lice* (1946), *Planus* (1948), and *Sky* (1949). That they are adventurous and poetic perhaps at the expense of factuality would not have disconcerted Clébert, whose own book was eventually described in a review by Georges Arnaud (author of *The Wages of Fear*) as "a travel narrative in which everything is true, even the legends. And what of it?" And while Clébert's long, rolling, jangling sentences are akin to Jack Kerouac's spontaneous bop prosody—the tone of *Paris Vagabond* eerily prefigures *On the Road*, for all that Clébert's book takes place entirely within one city and its only means of locomotion is shoe leather—in fact both Clébert and Kerouac took inspiration from Cendrars, whose sentences can cascade for half a page, veering left and right, dropping introspectively and then rising anthemically, without drawing breath.

Recognizing a literary heir, Cendrars arranged to have *Paris Vagabond* published by his own house, Denoël. The book was a sensation, and narrowly missed obtaining a major literary prize (it got four votes for the Prix Renaudot, eight for the Sainte-Beuve). Two years later, the book was issued in a deluxe hardback edition by Le Club du Meilleur Livre, which requested illustrations. Clébert was close to the photographer Robert Doisneau, one of the book's dedicatees, but couldn't afford his rates, so he turned to Patrice Molinard, a street photographer he met at the fleamarket who at the time lived in a former brothel near the Opéra that had once been frequented by Toulouse-Lautrec. Molinard's 115 photographs, which to an extent were directed by Clébert, form the perfect visual analog to his text. (The published photos are perhaps roughly executed, but they are all that we have. Molinard destroyed his archives in the late 1960s, so that there are no surviving negatives, and no one has succeeded in locating original prints.)

Paris Vagabond led directly to the publication by Denoël of two other books, written by friends of Clébert: Jacques Yonnet's *Rue des Maléfices* (1954; originally entitled *Enchantements sur Paris*; in English translation as *Paris Noir*), a dizzying chronicle of occult forces along the clochard corridor on the Left Bank during the Occupation; and Robert Giraud's *Le vin des rues* (1955), an affecting survey of clochard life in Paris. The three books are often considered together as a trilogy, a record of the fragile and impoverished but nonetheless incandescent postwar years. Yonnet had been an active Resistance fighter, a reporter (he broke the story of Dr. Petiot, a mass murderer who preyed on Jews during the Occupation), and eventually a chronicler of bistros for the trade journal *L'Auvergnat de Paris*; *Rue des Maléfices* was his only book. Giraud, who had also been in the Resistance, was an inveterate barfly, sporadically a *bouquiniste* on the quais, and eventually a prolific author of books, some of them in collaboration with Doisneau, such as his pioneering study of tattooing (1950), and many on the arcana of argot, a subject on which he was a recognized expert. The three along with Doisneau hung out heavily at Chez Fraysse on Rue de Seine, the local of Jacques and Pierre Prévert, the antiquarian Romi, and many other raffish personalities of the period.

Clébert also spent time a few streets away at Chez Moineau, a much cheaper establishment that attracted penniless bohemian youths and was documented by the Dutch photographer Ed van der Elsken in his fictionalized chronicle *Love on the Left Bank* (1956). Among the habitués was Jean-Claude Guilbert, who appears in these pages as "the Shepherd" and who went on to act in Robert Bresson's *Mouchette* and *Au hasard Balthazar*. Also frequently present were Guy Debord, Michèle Bernstein, Gil J. Wolman, Ivan Chtcheglov, and the other members of the Letterist International. Although Debord never made any written mention of Clébert or his book, his half brother, Patrick Labaste, told Debord's biographer Christophe Bourseiller (*Vie et mort de Guy Debord*, 1999) that Debord had "loved" *Paris Vagabond*. And although Bernstein told Bourseiller that the word "psychogeography" had first been uttered by a North African with whom they smoked kif at a café on Rue Xavier-Privas, it is notable that that concept and its twin, that of *dérive*, or "drift," both entered the Letterist vocabulary after the publication of Clébert's book. In fact the circumstantial evidence is strong that Debord drew from *Paris Vagabond* the whole idea of the drift, defined as

> a technique of forward movement through a variety of ambiances.... One or several persons, giving themselves over to the drift for a period of variable length, dispense with the usual reasons for moving about, and with their relationships, jobs, and leisure activities, in order to let themselves follow the pull of the landscape and the encounters that come from it. ("Théorie de la dérive," in *Les Lèvres Nues*, November 1956)

This sounds like nothing so much as a description of Clébert's book, even if Debord later credited Thomas De Quincey and his *Confessions of an English Opium-Eater,* with its account of night wanderings in London, as the inspiration for the drift. And how else but by way of *Paris Vagabond* would the Letterists have come to know of the obscure and remote Rue Sauvage, the destruction of which is mourned in the seventh issue (August 3, 1954) of the Letterist International organ *Potlatch*?

A year after *Paris Vagabond* Clébert published a sort of companion volume, *La vie sauvage* (Denoël, 1953), which sets him adrift in the countryside, a lovely book that has sadly never been reprinted. He wrote a few largely uninspired texts on Paris—a photo book aimed at tourists, again with Molinard but to quite different effect; an update of a 1910 walking tour by the Marquis de Rochegude—and was courted by the major magazines of the period, but he was sick of city living and made his way south to the mountainous Luberon region of Provence, which was dotted with abandoned stone villages, in one of which he lived for a decade without water or electricity. In 1968 he moved to Oppède-le-Vieux, a ghost village turned into a sort of artists' commune during the war, where his neighbors included the American photographer Alexey Brodovitch and Consuelo de Saint-Exupéry, the widow of the aviator. He spent the rest of his life there. He wrote thirty-three books in all, many on the history and lore of Provence, his most celebrated volume being *Les Tziganes* (1961), published in English the following year as *The Gypsies*, which is arguably the finest work for a general audience on the subject. He died in Oppède on September 20, 2011.

—Luc Sante

TRANSLATOR'S NOTE

I FELL in love with this book as a teenager and owe a joint debt of gratitude to a lucky star and to Edwin Frank and all involved at New York Review Books for giving me the opportunity to translate it half a century later.

I should like to caution readers (or perhaps defend myself) with respect to the translation of slang in Clébert's book. My aim has been to avoid verbal anachronisms in view of how tightly the work is anchored to place and time (Paris circa 1950). In my choice of English vernacular terms, I have tried, but failed, to embrace the stated goal of Christine Donougher when translating Jacques Yonnet's *Rue des Maléfices* as *Paris Noir: The Secret History of a City* (2006): "to capture the flavour of the argot...without resorting to a vocabulary too suggestive of a non-Parisian environment—American or Cockney, for instance." This is, I believe, impossible; for one thing, "suggestive" is subjective. American readers may find some of my words too British; British readers vice versa. But I want slang to remain slang—and slang possible around 1950. With this in mind, I have referred frequently to Lester V. Berrey and Melvin Van den Bark's monumental *American Thesaurus of Slang* (1947).

I must thank the following for their generous and indispensable advice: Alain Chaillat, T. J. Clark, Brigitte Dieu, Emir Harbi, Claire Labarbe, Cathy Pozzo di Borgo, Florence Sébastiani, and Alyson Waters.

A very special thank you is owed to Luc Sante, a fellow lover of *Paris insolite* and the author of what is almost a companion work: *The Other Paris* (2015).

Yet again I have a debt to Mia Nadezhda Rublowska that I can never repay for endless linguistic help along with support of every imaginable kind.

—D. N.-S.

PARIS VAGABOND

To Robert Doisneau, photographer, whose magic eye captures reality and for whom life is thus stranger than fiction.

To Robert Giraud, visionary, explorer, meditator, chronicler of the city's lower depths and great harkener to the bells of Paris.

And to Patrice Molinard, whose clear-eyed images in this new edition [1954] offer proof of authenticity.

PREFACE
To the First Illustrated Edition

So, over a year after my *Paris insolite* appeared, and therefore two years after I wrote it, I once again pulled out the pile of notes taken randomly during my wanderings, a voluminous paper bag stuffed with a hopeless conglomeration of used envelopes, newsprint edges, unfolded Gauloise packets, and multicolored and multifarious scraps of paper on which I had penciled, inked, erased, scrawled, corrected and inventoried all manner of leads, addresses, names of people, store signs, street names, and sites of great poverty or cheap debauchery in an unknown Paris. I soon noticed that amidst the mass of jottings in their incredible muddle there were plenty of stories, landscapes and character sketches that I had not used. Once written, in its haphazard way in bistros and in public places, indeed at sidewalk level, where the action was (if such everyday doings may be so described), my book, I realized, had left out a good half of my observations, omitting the most baroque of adventures and losing sight along the way of so many already ephemeral figures, and this only increased my astonishment that a public so indifferent in principle should have proved so curious about the filthy, albeit evocative, underside of the court of miracles that was my subject.

What is now turning out to be even more ephemeral than my characters is the Paris that I experienced and described, which seems to change its skin by the day. When I returned to the scenes of my old exploits, I was appalled by the ravages visited upon memory by slow urban development and sudden death.

In the book I was already able to record the brutal disappearance of the Saint-Séverin district, with its pick-up-sticks players and its hordes of derelicts at Les Cloches de Notre-Dame, a bistro that I called "the most splendid caravansary in Paris." This winter the Hôtel La Belle Étoile and Rue Galande's North African cafés were still there, but the transient population continues to wither. Oudinot, the sometime "Bois de Boulogne Murderer," is plowing along the devil knows where. Robespierre is in the clink. Joséphine the hermaphrodite has vanished. But the Arabs, as patient and efficient as termites, continue their systematic investment of these lower depths of Paris.

On the other bank of the Seine, Saint-Paul, which for me was cleared terrain, quite deserted, is now suffering chaotic upheaval due to city planning supposedly intended to preserve local color. The rubble-filled lot with its frolicking kids in front of the entrance to the Charlemagne Jam factory is now occupied by a cube of yellow stone which completely blocks the view. Fortunately, the Russian bistro on the corner of Rue du Prévôt is still there, along with its great farmhouse-like main room, its movable pork-butcher's counter, its hot-pepper vodka, and its odd clientele in Cossack dress.

But even if the outward appearance of plebeian Paris is gradually altering, mysteries still await around every corner, behind the façades of its houses and the hoardings that surround its vacant lots. There are always more stories to tell, more secret places to discover, more outlandish characters to come across.

Every day—and every night—I think of ways to extend my book in tentacular fashion, so much so that those two hundred and fifty pages now seem to me ridiculously skimpy. I still unintentionally go down cul-de-sacs or happen into cafés where I have never set foot before and where the offbeat reigns supreme. Café Curieux, for instance, Alcide's place in Les Halles, which is more like an antique store than an ordinary tavern.

Or the opium dens around the Gare de Lyon where the Chinese hold fish fights, or the boat discovered in the Cour des Artistes up Boulevard Blanqui.

I have just retraced my steps, in the company of a photographer, along the paths that I once followed haggard and haunted above all by visions of cooked food. The experience disappointed me. Landscapes that hunger and cold had graven in my memory and that I had learnt to perceive not only with my eyes but also with my hands, nostrils, and backside have now lost a measure of their brutal poetry. One's perspective changes a good deal depending on whether one is a living part of the décor or simply a stroller, a flâneur—in other words whether one's belly is empty or full. So the images in this edition illustrate only one aspect of my vision of the city.

All the same, they are the most eloquent possible testimonials to the unknown Paris I explored. This Patrice Molinard, whom I did not know previously, has an eye. By which I mean that you don't need to pull him by the sleeve, because he grasps the poetry of an urban tableau instantly. His lens automatically captures the fantastic aspect of a street or a person. His photographs are exactly right. And, happily, they are devoid of the "atmosphere" that usually floods this kind of photography. These are objective, limpid documents. It is up to readers to find the poetry in them. Molinard does everything to banish the picturesque, which I loathe, and which too often exploits the poor. His photos let us see: in Éluard's words, they *donnent à voir*.

Whence the perfect understanding that attended my return Paris tour with Patrice Molinard. An understanding that, I must confess, extended to the sharing of the Beaujolais binges that are hardly avoidable when you associate with the capital's hardest drinkers and—why mince words?—its most confirmed drunkards. But photography, even more than drink, alters one's vision of a neighborhood. The camera's field of view circumscribes particular and isolated objects. The result is a proof of authenticity that literature, after all, is hard put to it to present. I am happy, therefore, that my "unknown Paris" is now to be thrust in this new form under the noses of a public that either does not know or else scorns it.

JEAN-PAUL CLÉBERT

1954

ONE

I

ONCE AGAIN I am going back into the city, and once again via Porte d'Italie.

As I was crossing the plateaus of Burgundy and the forest lands of the Aube the nights grew colder, the road workers' hutments and the cabins of the woodcutters of Sainte-Menehould proved uncomfortable, and after plodding across three, maybe four regions of France as a member of the sodality of drifters, and taking a quick look-see across international frontiers, I am returning to my cradle.

It is winter now, and with its coming, since I cannot do as the migrating birds do, and rely on thermal columns to carry me to a more temperate zone, I hibernate like an animal going to ground and falling into torpor, I winter like a boat laying over in a port sheltered from the ice, I shrink, I curl up in some corner of the city, I build walls, ramparts, around me, I wrap myself head to toe in woolens, I isolate the delicate clockwork of my brain, I huddle up, dig my hole, go into my shell, put myself on low, and move at a snail's pace.

Once again I shall be spending four or five months inside Paris, that vast gathering-place of daily calamities and miracles, searching each day for enough, substantially enough, to eat and drink, and each night for a quiet and untroubled place to lay my head, while of course leading a full and joyous life.

And I laugh to myself, because in the eyes of a cop directing the traffic I am just another tramp back in town, ruddy-faced, stoop-shouldered, filthy lumberjacket, shoes gone to hell, rumbling belly, empty haversack, and a recent prison release order in my pocket.

But this is where I am going to write a book.

*

I have choices: I could head right or left, rediscover what remains of Paris's extramural "Zone"* and look for a bed there as of tonight in the clusters of ragpickers' corrugated-iron shacks, or else circle the whole capital like the ex-cons banned from the city who have their encampment at Gennevilliers, on the fringe of the department of Hauts-de-Seine, and prowl the outer boulevards unable to pluck up enough courage to plunge into the dangerous maze of macadamized roadways within; alternatively, I could go and settle amid the hardworking folk in the quarries of Montreuil or in any number of other parts of the inner suburbs. But I simply cannot resist the urge to go immediately up the Avenue d'Italie and make my way as quickly as possible to the city's liveliest neighborhoods despite the interminable empty boulevards, for crossing Paris takes longer than crossing a whole department. I give no more than a passing glance at the *cafés-tabac*, no more than a fleeting once-over to the buses, the plane trees, the urinals, and I sniff in surprise at the smells of gasoline and of the great monster of the city. I hurry up. But it is just too bad about a place to doss tonight. Once again, I'll skip it. I am just too eager to see the face of a friend, to experience the indescribably simple pleasure of entering a familiar haunt, shaking hands, and saying in the most casual way "How goes it?," the pleasure of playing the innocent, pretending that a year or two's absence means nothing and returning to my game of belote as if it has been interrupted only the day before. An ephemeral pleasure, of course, for ten minutes later I'll be telling my life story, and within two hours everyone will know about the hazardous exploits whereby I managed to meet life's daily challenges, and beg me for more, and I will be only too happy to tell my stories over again, because the most serious listeners are entitled to details, and have the right to draw on the

---

*The Zone was a 22-mile ring of wasteland left after the demolition, completed by 1932, of Paris's military fortifications. Developed only gradually and anarchically, by 1950 the area was still occupied by many thousands of indigent squatters and transients. —*Trans.*

experiences of others, which are never useless when it comes to the vagabond life. That is what bistros are for.

Once I reach the Pont Neuf, the lateness of the hour notwithstanding, I am at home. Here, within my apartments, I sit down on a stone divan and smoke a cigarette. This is the start of a fresh voyage, just as fruitful and thrilling as ever, into the labyrinth of the capital, mysterious from time immemorial, into the lower depths and under the roofs of a Paris to which the public is forbidden entry: Paris from below.

2

THE DISCOVERY of Paris.

What an extraordinary voyage of exploration!

It always amazes me that neither the Musée de l'Homme nor any decent popular geographical magazine ever pays attention to the city populace, ever offers the public at large an ethnographical view of the poor districts, and that the big dailies would far sooner enlighten their thousands of readers on the rites and customs of the Navajo than on those of the old-timers of Nanterre; and I am likewise amazed that despite the great mass of books—and good ones—devoted to Paris ancient and modern by chroniclers of the weird and wonderful social life of the capital, Parisians themselves remain ignorant of their city, disparaging it or invariably confining their rote thoughts and observations to the poetry of the quays of the Seine and the virtues of the national art museums, finding it bizarre that an ordinary man, but one who knows how to see, hear and smell, and to use his senses like outsize antennae, might still in this day and age bother himself with new sights and sounds, or be aghast, stupefied, dumbstruck, at a complete loss for words and quite unable to sleep until he has raced over to his friends to tell them of his discoveries and drag them along to share and delight in them.

I first discovered Paris at the age of seventeen, and lost my virginity as I did so. At a boarding school in Rue de la Pompe from early childhood on, I learned to jump over the wall and head down Avenue Henri-Martin, so redolent of Provence, to the Bois de Boulogne and its lakes,

intending to sleep there beneath the weeping willows because I found slumber on the grass dreaming of adventures far preferable to the soul-destroying dormitory with its blue ceiling light and an atmosphere I already sensed to be that of a hospital or asylum, an atmosphere that was making me chronically ill. I would roll myself up in my overcoat. But I could never get any sleep, for the still unfamiliar sounds of earth and trees prevented me from dozing off, the sensation of being there all alone kept me awake, and my imagination ran wild until dawn, when, chilled to the bone, my limbs rigid, I would wander down to the water's edge, chatter with the rod-and-reel fishermen who were the place's only denizens, and perch on a chair to contemplate the pine trees and savor the only moments of real life in my existence as an imprisoned adolescent.

I used to go over that wall four or five times a week. And one fine night I stayed over for good. I landed crouched on my heels, holding my breath, with a ridiculous bundle under my arm and in my pocket funds sufficient for a few days (though I did not really know for how long, having not the least notion of what a solitary and uncertain life might require). I ran gaily down the street, then slowed to a free and easy pace, venturing forth into an unknown land, simply following my nose but too joyful not to whistle as I went, spent the rest of the night traversing half the city and then drinking my first grown-up coffee in a travelers' brasserie near the Gare de l'Est. That was now ten years ago.

Oddly enough, once I had found and elected to live at Boris's place near Porte Maillot, my discovery and experience of Paris had the Luna Park funfair as their point of departure. Boris was a lad older than me who had dropped everything to join the *maquis*, but he missed that boat because, since he had the use of an old mildewed flat, he began chasing skirts and squandering whatever money he had—he did not know what else to do with it.

So it was that every night we hastened over to Luna Park, that paradise lost, that multicolored, marvelous melting-pot since razed and replaced by asphalt. We went on every ride, our favorite being the bumper cars, and spent a small fortune wandering around in circles, wolf-whistling at servant girls, especially the less ugly ones, and at pairs of lookers on their night out, but all for naught, all our moves wasted, and settling for two ho-hum pieces of stuff. Many a time, though, there were so many, massing, swarming, that wherever you looked the landscape was crowded with legs, breasts, bright dresses, short skirts, silk stockings and crimson lips in an epic carnival where anything went and hands strayed at will; here women who on the metro would redden with fury should someone as much as brush their knee were ready to stretch out in the bottom of the boat in the Enchanted River and satisfy our tactile curiosity with the best will in the world. So much so that an hour or two later we would leave arm in arm with two great-looking chicks and make our way into the Bois de Boulogne, there to stroll about, go down into the dark but highly animated tunnels of the air-raid shelters, engage in mildly erotic games, emerge, drop into a few local bars, and repair to the aforesaid flat, with its highly austere furniture and pictures and its two adjoining bedrooms, fragrant with virtue, of the young sister and the grandmother—both now fortunately evacuated to the Non-Occ Zone. We drank a bit, tumbled the girls, and . . .

But all of this, normal enough for my age and my condition as a young city-dweller, was as nothing compared with another, exotic Paris within easy reach, as revealed to me precisely thanks to these easy loves, when one girl or another arranged a rendezvous with me in a distant neighborhood on the edge of the city, far beyond my customary horizons, for in the main my dates were daughters of the people—typists, factory and office workers, sales girls, easy lays or jailbait on the make—all of whom toiled in the city center but bunked in the Zone, so that I was obliged to trot with pounding heart and a hundred francs in my pocket, on a Saturday or Sunday afternoon or a weekday evening between seven and eight, to metro stations quite unknown to me with names at once weird and attractive to my ears: Télégraphe, Place des Fêtes, Chevaleret, Marcadet-Balagny, Philippe-Auguste. There I would wait kicking my heels under the scrutiny of men on their way home from work or would go into cafés where I felt uncomfortable, not having yet learned, even after several weeks, how to adopt the insouciant attitude or utter the key words that could unlock the human warmth

of corner-bar community—and what is more I was still wearing a tie. I let myself be led through strange and startling landscapes, down streets swarming with housewives and vegetable barrows, along lonely quays and canals, by endless factory walls punctuated by farm gates; and I made love on banks of slag, in dark deserted corners well away from disconcerting gas lamps, or in hidden courtyards far down tunnel-like passageways. Today I would be hard pressed to name (or locate) those settings, far more firmly fixed as they are in my mind's eye than the faces of even the most beautiful of the girls: gas works, apartment buildings fit for troglodytes, unlikely skyscrapers silhouetted against the void, lowlife hotels, *bals musettes*, empty lots, labyrinthine streets, city gates, suburban bus stops, overhead metro lines, traffic tunnels and, beyond it all, prospects of a desolation that I found picturesque.

And when, as often happened, I was stood up, I ventured forth hands in pockets, swallowing my pride, and before I had gone a few hundred yards began to discover the wide world.

Now that I live in such places like a fish in water, now that I have mastered all the tics, habits, obsessions, vices, attitudes, lingo and garb of an old-timer, now that I stride through the city from one end to the other knowing it like the back of my hand (though still making fresh discoveries every day), I nourish the naive hope that writing this book will bring me satisfaction; I should like it to be a sincere and exhaustive documentary account of the liveliest face of Paris and of all the marvels it harbors in their natural state, all the extraordinary characters who miraculously survive there.

A baroque inventory.

But it is impossible. There are too many things to say.

It would take years, and the bulk of such a book would repel any publisher before it could have the same effect on readers. God knows how many notes I have taken in my two or three years of a vagabond existence *intra muros*, scribbled down and piled up any old how, who knows where, nor how many more are stored in my head—so many faces, conversations, backdrops, scenes, views of poor districts where life is animal-like, rife with danger, hidden from sight, where the law of the jungle rules and hustling is the norm, where miracles happen all

the time, where days are inhaled faster than a puff on a cigarette—so many things seen, heard, things to be shouted from the rooftops or kept secret for fear of being taken for a stool-pigeon, so many, many things that I have had to confine my daily ten pages of writing to a low and spasmodic regurgitation of the first to come to mind in an unpredictable disorder corresponding to the mood of a memory that spawns others, plays tricks on me—and all this amidst the relentless, hypnotic quest for a square meal and a quiet lodging. This depresses me no end, for every face, every conversation, every narrow street, every dark corner, every bistro deserves an entire volume filled to bursting with information, tips, details, anecdotes, comments....

Too bad. There's no help for it. Just let the pen run on.

And, after all, this is not supposed to be a Baedeker or some tourist guide.

3

SO MY EXPERIENCE of Paris was acquired thanks to girls, thanks also to one of the few professions I ever took up, being prone by nature to wandering-feet fever, to incessant bouts of ants in the pants, and subject to the particular kind of cramp that hits you at the movies when you get up from your seat and your foot seems thrust suddenly into a void, causing you to fall, rather as, after a good spell of years of regular, conscientious work, you give it up, pleased with yourself, and promptly fall flat on your face, but it's not your foot this time, it's your past, the only one you have, utterly wasted. The profession I have in mind is measurer of living spaces, which I took up during that golden age for the unemployed when architects and owners of apartment buildings had to hire a veritable army of cheap hands—young and footloose Beaux-Arts students or laid-off hairdresser's apprentices—because, during the construction of their vile termite mounds or the sale of their stacked-up cages, these fat cats tended to mislay their building plans and thus develop a need for every as-yet unrated room to be measured inch by inch. I took advantage of this after running one day into Monsieur Maurice, also known as Jérôme, former City of Paris game warden, classic small-time crook, bar-tab scofflaw, fresh-faced con man, wily chiseler, ever-innocent two-timer, and my sometime companion in cell 253 at the Hôtel des Baumettes prison (Marseille-Mazargues). Now at the zenith of his social success, he would offer tips to all comers, in the strictest confidence of course, tips whose great value you were expected to appreciate—a racket off-putting on the face of it but which according to him brought in fifteen hundred francs a day—what? how much? come off it!—but wait, I'll show you!—and having nothing to do and nothing to eat I went along. You had to cop a folding meter rule (at the expense of a working man, sad to say), then go to specified units, designed for cave-dwellers and hung with decorative wallpaper, and take exact measurements of the floors, a perfectly relaxing task....

I would show up about eight in the morning and rouse Jérôme, who used to sleep in Rue Nicolas-Flamel at an old whorehouse. I would drag him out of bed and find his spectacles for him. He would hand me a list of addresses that suggested a trip around the world: Rue de la Chine, Place des États-Unis, Rue de Crimée, Porte d'Italie, etc., and I was off with the wind at my back and enough in my pocket to cover a second last one at the corner bistro and take the metro like a grown-up, often accompanied by someone unknown to me, because we always worked in pairs but never had the same partner (to prevent organizing); we would make it to the indicated point of the compass, idle a little in a new neighborhood before getting to work, enter the building slated for measurement, show the required signed papers to the janitor, who would pull a face, go upstairs, knock on doors and land directly in family settings, petty- or haut-bourgeois apartments, workers' flats, maids' quarters; we would make our apologies, although the tenants could do nothing about our abrupt intrusion except grumble and moan about the impending rent hike. I would swing my folding rule negligently in dangerous proximity to vases and figurines imported from Japan by way of a Prisunic five-and-dime or on credit from La Semeuse department store. I called out approximate measurements to my helper, who noted them down; everything was fine, and people began telling us their little life stories and retailing their big woes. But after three days we had things all figured out, our profession had no secrets for us, and we had grasped its inherent benefits. Since we were supposed to deal with two or three apartment buildings a day against a prearranged payment, we would get to the job at ten or eleven, size up the layout of the place, measure up just one floor to the nearest half-meter, assessing cornices and so-called exposed fireplaces with a practiced eye and taking into account the depth of built-in closets, then go and sit at the very top of the stairwell and reproduce our estimates on

our paperwork over and over again for each apartment, taking care to lower our numbers slightly the higher the story, because I subscribed to the comforting hypothesis that in order to remain standing a house must be wider at the bottom than at the top. Then we would enter a few of the most rectilinear rooms, miming the motions of measuring to quiet our professional conscience, and, to burnish our image with the tenants, asking if they had any complaints to lodge with the management company but ignoring any such that became too long-winded. We would try to wangle a drink, and sometimes we succeeded, taking it seated in the kitchen just like regular deliverymen, basking in our own importance and ogling the women, for the husbands off at work numbered in the dozens (I remember a seductive little brunette who greeted our unannounced arrival in a transparent slip, made no effort to cover her thighs, invited us to sit down on the edge of the couch, and offered us port, but we were two, the situation was blatant, delicate, and doomed to turn out poorly). Often we would return to the concierge's, park our asses close to the fire with our elbows on the table, and pretend to be plunged in endless calculations involving the multiplication of squared and cubed figures and the assessment of coefficients, ventilation, visibility, and age, but glancing sidelong at the old biddy until she proposed glasses of coffee and cookies (I know from experience that no kitchen cupboard is better stocked with sweet stuff than a concierge's). Noon was long gone, and we went for sandwiches at the *bougnat** across the road, following up with very slowly sipped brandy and liqueurs, especially when I was working with Drelin, who was a connoisseur and found it quite natural to spend the better part of his pay and almost the entire afternoon drinking, then finish up the last three thousands of a four-handed game of belote, with a gray winter's dusk falling, before we went to deal with two more blocks of houses. Back at Châtelet, we would find Jérôme only now getting

---

*A café-bar of the kind that once purveyed wood, wine, and coal, a formula introduced by nineteenth-century migrants from the Massif Central whom the Parisians nicknamed *Bougnats* (derived in combination from *charbonnier*, or collier, and Auvergnat, an inhabitant of Auvergne). —*Trans.*

washed and dressed, and once he had handed over our crisp folding money we would all leave to show off in the hookers' bars in Rue Quincampoix and Rue des Lombards, then go down to Les Halles to eat, usually with a not-too-ravaged girlfriend each. We were living like kings.

But meanwhile, for several months, I had been discovering a baroque Paris, the terra incognita of its most intimate crannies; like a Romantic hero, I had lifted the lid, or the roof, off its houses and taken an impromptu look inside, intruding like a burglar into bedrooms, breaking into armoires, pawing through wardrobes, surprising people at the dining table, at the window, listening to the radio, in the kitchen, reading the paper, making love, throwing crockery, mending clothes, doing their washing, in the john, or at the bidet; I poked my nose into the private moments of an old stick giving her cats milk, a respectable woman reading *Confidences* magazine, a servant girl squeezing her blackheads, or an old man mulling over his memories; and I contemplated identical décors time and again, despite slight variations of color, arrangement or disarray, placed my feet, or sometimes my house slippers, which I loved, on identical linos and identical doormats, ran my hands over identical wallpaper, jumbled the same carefully plumped-up cushions, jostled the same harridans and the same mothers with children wearing the same aprons and the same dead expression of resignation to the drudgery of housework—to the point where I could not take any more and dashed down the stairs two at a time and fled outside and realized yet again that the real show is in the street.

Overall, nonetheless, there was a good deal of originality amidst the sameness. I discovered a mushroom farm in a three-room flat. As soon as you entered you were struck by the odor of soil and dead leaves, and I would have had to clamber in damp darkness over little mounds of earth on which white spots were breaking out in order to take my measurements. I chose not to, but instead to interview the fellow who lived there, who offered me a sweet white wine in the vestibule, where he was obliged to cook, eat, sleep and wash, and who told me that as tenant of the place for more than thirty years he had every kind of

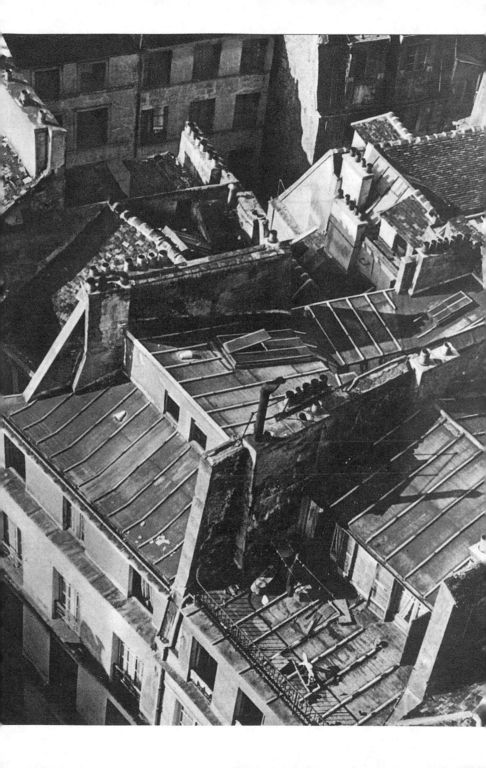

right, including the right to convert the floors and baseboards into a waterproof frame for a slug-ridden bed of earth. I made no attempt to contradict him, merely asking whether his farming efforts turned a profit; just enough to scrape by on, was his answer. As I left I wondered whether the next door would open onto an oyster bed or, who knows, a factory producing half-women for freak shows.

Two or three times a week I was able to enliven the conversation during our bistro nights in Rue des Lombards with La Toulousaine, she of the lovely thighs and the big mouth, mistress of Monsieur Maurice, by recounting my little discoveries of the day while downing quantities of Beaujolais to help dispel various clinging odors encountered here and there, as in the case of a nutty old woman who was continually burning *papier d'Arménie* in her place, most likely since her early childhood, without ever opening a window, which had caused me to stagger dangerously and almost collapse into the nearest easy chair amid a brightly colored pseudo-Tibetan décor punctuated by photographs of ectoplasm, a décor from which I was able to extract myself only thanks to an immense effort of will of which I am still proud, for although my sense of smell is acute, though welcoming to all the human and animal odors that accumulate in all kinds of communities, it is quite unable to accustom itself or to take pleasure in aberrant cultural fashions, and I only hope I never set foot in a Chinese temple or a Russian church where they burn incense sticks.

And I never tired of sharing my impressions of an aviary that I came upon somewhere near the Buttes-Chaumont, an artist's workshop filled with birds flying free and not the slightest sign of a cage, an immense glassed-in space that stunned you with cries and colors, as if that very morning every songbird, whistler and layer from the pet stores of the Quai du Louvre had been released, a true marvel, a place where I would have loved to spend the afternoon counting and identifying the birds if only the guy, a young man with a strange expression, had allowed me to do any more than poke my head through the doorway, after which he immediately pushed me back into an anteroom that served as a sort of airlock or protective screen. I detest him for depriving me of such a wonderful spectacle. I also detest, but much

more, another man who did allow me into his den. The wretched lodgings of a very minor ledger clerk, a couple of square inches on a top floor that I needed to measure up so as to be done with a building of no interest in the Saint-Pierre neighborhood. I entered, followed by the dried-up little man, who closed the door carefully behind him and rubbed his hands together. I paid no mind to his attitude, concentrating on my notes and aware only of the intense heat in the place. I had pushed a writing-desk aside in order to kneel on a couch when I noticed a bizarre heap of what looked like thin blood sausage in the folds of an old newspaper not half a meter from my hand; I froze, trying to tell myself that it was something quite harmless, and certainly not a snake, though I saw it moving slightly. This was the moment if ever to swear in the saltiest language the boulevards could teach, but I had utterly lost my vernacular and all I could do was retreat in rather poor order and look around. They were everywhere, slithering under tables and around the feet of chairs—even at a distance I dared not glance into the baskets standing beside the fireplace, and I stared anxiously at the floor as I left with my tail between my legs, ignoring the gentleman's polite and soothing explanations. I went down the stairs primly hoisting my trouser cuffs. And I must have had dreams about this visit for a good week. That lousy bastard (and I don't give a damn if he likes the term or not) is an underling in some ministry, as I learnt from the owner of the *bougnat* opposite, and he carts his vile pets around with him in his briefcase, taking them to the office, putting them in his desk drawers and playing with them in his free moments. Afterwards I studiously avoided his neighborhood and any metro stations from which he was liable to emerge. The experience made me much more sympathetic towards the good Monsieur Dassonville who, though passionately loving all the animals in creation, asked no more than to walk his tame duck Grisette peacefully around the Île Saint-Louis and take her down to the quayside for a swim. In short, it was less living quarters that sparked my voyeuristic tendencies than their inhabitants, the oddities, the peculiar, the offbeat and startling, caught in motion, captured unawares just as in all innocence they exercised their particular passion, their *violon d'Ingres*, their obsession, their dada—all the hobbyists, collectors, packrats and connoisseurs of curiosities, of whose activities you cannot say whether they are profitable or gratuitous. People with weird occupations that reward them in ways often quite obscure—do-it-yourselfers, inventors, rummagers and jugglers of brilliant ideas. I have no wish to dwell on the shiftiest characters, those who have clear minds and business acumen, the myriad astrologists, horoscope readers, alchemists of the heart, and business advisors who make crazy piles of money thanks to the naivety of poor folk and whose great number is only hinted at by a glance at the papers specializing in small ads. Legal crooks, they promise wealth, or the return of a strayed spouse, or youthful breasts for three postage stamps. One revolting specimen of their race whom I ran into had a face like a fetus from hell; let me read the flyers he sent out all over France: "For a small fee will teach infallible method for improving your standard of living; why settle for mediocrity? Riches are within your grasp. Will tell you about two hundred kinds of work from home of proven profitability. Just send five hundred francs"—in exchange for which sum the guy advised selling ballpoint pens, which he would supply at a supposedly knock-down price, or collecting mushrooms from under the grillwork at the bases of Paris's plane trees, or typing addresses on envelopes for him, or raising guinea pigs, or making cut-out paper figurines, or doing any of the other one hundred and ninety-five things of the kind. But all this is just too revolting and I would much rather get back to the gently mad or harmlessly obsessed, like the collectors—not of stamps or matchboxes or cheese labels, which is senseless, but rather of true oddities.

The Old Gaffer, for instance, who possessed the finest collection of erotica that I have ever seen, filling his attic room to the rafters and including books, manuscripts, statuettes, engravings, and notably an enormous ledger from the Department of Administrative Revenue containing meticulous pen-and-ink reproductions of graffiti copied with great skill from urinals and like places set aside for solitary tasks; some of them were in foreign languages, making it impossible for me to experience all their charm, but most were in slang. The book as a whole clearly represented dozens of years of conscientious work at an incredible number of standing or sitting facilities in what are called rest rooms. There was also a pile of large cardboard boxes filled with exotic prints, somewhat banal in content in my view, considering the surprisingly similar appearance of the genitals of men and women throughout the universe, but remarkable by virtue of their sheer quantity, and let me congratulate the owner here for his vintage photographs from the heroic age, yellow and faded but still vivid, showing gents wearing sock suspenders and curled-up mustaches performing imaginative acts in the most dignified manner upon various parts of the anatomy of nymphs with hairdos like pastry cooks' hats. The old guy poured me a glass of sweet wine (an aphrodisiac?) from a phallic carafe whose sheath-like top slid back delicately, then unpacked all his boxes, filched most likely from somewhere in the depths of his ministry, and proceeded to point his finger at all kinds of details that it would have been hypocritical of me to find uninteresting. But despite the obviously contagious heat generated by these collections, the fact was that he had no stove in his room, and in any case my partner was growing impatient outside on the stairs.

And then there was the Polyglot, whom I discovered one evening at the very top of a twisting, exhausting and dangerous staircase which reminded me of the steps up the Eiffel Tower. He was rinsing a meager lettuce at the common tap on the landing; his digs were a dull-green two-room flat smelling of something hard to define, a gas lamp casting a feeble, diffuse light on a grubby interior dominated by an immense table covered with felt like a billiard table and piled high with papers and publications, including a large Russian dictionary which served to initiate a seated conversation washed down with a liter of white wine. My hospitable host was an old man who, though decrepit, had preserved a distinct nobility and the kind of serenity of face that only long celibacy can bestow. I lost no time before asking him, naturally giving spurious reasons for my curiosity, why he had such an astonishing number of dictionaries, manuals, guidebooks, and lexicons that they were causing the floorboards of his nook to give way and politely nudging his packets of pasta and rice aside. According to him, he was a former intelligence-service man with a perfect knowledge of thirty-seven languages, European as well as American and Asian, and he claimed in addition that he was able to communicate easily with natives of variously located regions in both hemispheres. Unfortunately he could not speak the language of the Eskimos, and had not yet found a Greenlander conversation manual at a reasonable price. This was, so to speak, the great disappointment of his old age.

Apart from his unused interpretive skills, however, the man's conversation was rather mundane, and after visiting him two or three times I left him, despite his burgeoning claustrophobia, pawing through his dictionaries. In the meantime I had learnt from him of the existence in the apartments on the lower floors, which were much larger than the rooms higher up but hardly better appointed, of another fine specimen of an eccentric, an individual whose mania, or rather obsession, was a determination to conserve his vital forces (it was high time) and to use every last calorie, to which end he would not throw away the merest crumb from an already highly ascetic diet. He would put his garbage can out no more than two or three times in three months, making soup from various kinds of leftovers and peelings that he sorted carefully and kept in little cardboard containers. Similarly, he sought to maximize the efficiency and minimize the expenditure of all physical movement: outside his door there hung an antique tapestry sash that set off a tinkling bell, and the rather significant number of his visitors (for he worked out of his home as an astrologer) gave him the idea that the force produced by their pulling on this cord could be put to work, which impelled him to get up out of bed one night and attach the sash with wire to the chain of his water closet. The old fellow was very proud to confirm that with each visitor his toilet bowl was noisily and effectively emptied without his having to lift a finger. Before long, however, he began to complain within himself about his system's two main drawbacks: first, the lack of visitors on Sunday, and second, the understandable irritation of those, such as the gas man, who came to see him while he was out at the market or at his game of belote, and who would work the bell pull repeatedly in vain, but, from the gurgling sounds of the toilet flush, be convinced that Monsieur Charles was indeed at home, but either too

deeply concerned by private matters or plagued by persistent trouble of an intimate sort. . . .

Naturally, all these eccentrics, most assuredly real and with fixed abodes, shall remain nameless here, albeit to the displeasure of our friends the newspapermen and other relentless burrowers, because they are very firmly attached to their peace and quiet, shunning the spotlight and detesting unannounced visits, in which respect they are the diametrical opposite of all those who require a public and are never content without the comments of others. I had already been lucky enough not to have been torn limb from limb by either the bird man or the fungi man, both of whom took me at first for an insurance agent, the bane of their lives. As for the ophiophile, a sign on his door made things clear enough: PLEASE SEE THE CONCIERGE.

4

MY EXPERIENCE of Paris at street level was also acquired as a hawker of newspapers, when for several months I sold *L'Intransigeant* during that paper's glory days, striding at a rapid pace down the Grands Boulevards with my papers under my arm, mechanically uttering the hallowed cry: *"L'Intran*, get the latest, *L'Intran!"*—so mechanically, in fact, that sometimes in the evening, my last copy sold, I would wind up in front of La Madeleine or on Rue de Rivoli with a dazed look on my face and my pipe jammed in my mouth, still shouting, which made the heads of passers-by turn, startling me and making me laugh. I used to take delivery of *L'Intran* as each new edition came out, starting with the eleven o'clock and ending with the Special Final at eight, in the courtyard of the *Populaire* building on Rue du Faubourg Poissonnière amidst the throng of accredited sellers, toothless crones who would go and squat down at metro entrances and old gaffers, near-derelicts driven by hunger to abandon the quays of the Seine and, spry if croaky-voiced, hustle along the busiest thoroughfares following unvarying personal routes that it would have been mean to poach—all these women and men more irritating than jock itch and obsessed with their prerogatives; and amidst the irregulars (of whom I was one at first), the jobless and homeless scratching together a pittance in this way without municipal authorization, forever on the look-out for the cops, and pale students, some timid, some arrogant, whose sales figures barely allowed them to peddle their Latin Quarter rag or put on airs and graces for Pigalle whores or chat up old gents on the Champs-Élysées, while I for my part was covering myself with glory, topping four hundred papers in sales, getting bonus after bonus, earning real money, eating like a pig for practically nothing in the paper's cafeteria with the staff writers, whom I addressed on a first-name basis but did not envy, sleeping in a fine room on Rue Dupuytren, near Odéon, where I got rid of my last unsold copies on bad evenings, if it was raining for instance, or so cold that my fingers were too stiff to make change. Alternatively, I would end my day at Place de l'Opéra, on the Café de Paris corner after the tables had been stacked up outside, longing between one customer and the next to leave soon, worn out from walking since morning; or wind up in the bars and brasseries of that neighborhood, where my relatively acceptable dress kept the headwaiters at bay; or at the counter of a whores' bistro, notably the one on the corner of Rue de Sèze where all the classy hookers of Rue des Capucines would gather—I knew them all but never slept with any, yet I was more intimate with them than their customers and continually coddled in every way; or again, at the café that is now an imposing but always empty brasserie on Place du Havre, where I would set my bundle of papers down on a table and watch it dwindle all by itself as I drank a rum, watching out of the corner of my eye as the coins tumbled down in a regular cascade and waiting for the waitress from the *café-tabac* nearby, who was sharing my room for reasons of economy.

And if I ate well, I drank just as heartily in the different bistros of Rue du Croissant, a narrow street that ends in a bottleneck, where I would spend my mornings and early afternoons before the paper came out, playing belote and talking shop with the deliverymen on bicycles or motorbikes and the sales managers, or looking out of the window, glass in hand, watching the trailer trucks loading unsold papers which a black man would first spray with blue ink to make them unfit for sale and discourage illegal distribution. My best pal, though he was solitary and silent, was Grévin, so nicknamed by reference to the waxworks museum, because between two glasses of wine, his brain swimming from the one to the next as uncertainly as a bottle imp, he would pass the time asleep, motionless, leaning forward on his stool, eyes closed and arms crossed, unaffected by movement, by the din, by people calling him. Unless of course someone was offering to buy a round.

TWO

I

PARISIAN itineraries. Leisurely strolls quite obviously (and fortunately) unknown to the tourist trade, for there is nothing to see on these routes except for poetry in the rough, which paying travelers would never appreciate: the poetry of masonry, cobbles, boundary stones, carriage entrances, dormer windows, tiled roofs, patches of grass, odd trees, dead ends, byways, blind alleys, inner courtyards, storage sheds for coal or building materials, wreckers' yards; the poetry of workshops, still vacant lots, bowling alleys, bistros-cum-refreshment stands; the poetry of colors but also of smells, a different smell for every doorway. Serpentine itineraries winding on endlessly, interminable itineraries open to anyone who knows how to wander and how to look, who has the nerve to go through *portes-cochères*, into workers' housing precincts, down private streets, who has the calmness of a guy at home everywhere, who whistles as he walks past the inhabitants of the three or four streets arranged like the spokes of a cartwheel that make up a village sealed off from the city, inhabitants who are curious but wary about this stranger upsetting their kids and their pigeons and who suddenly fall silent. The women in particular don't care for this intrusion and they stop knitting on their chairs and peep out from behind their curtains, and the men in the *bougnat* also go quiet, and you expect to be thrown out not by the owner himself but by a customer outraged that anyone should come without knocking into this homely room, like a farmhouse kitchen with its comforting décor, all wood, zinc, and glass, with its cuckoo or pendulum clock punctuating the conversation, oilcloth-covered tables, stove in the middle, its chimney pipe newly replated or teetering and held up by wires, prints on the wall, photos of cycle racers and soccer teams, outdated advertisements for apéritifs and drinks now forgotten or at least favored only by old-timers—Amer Picon, Gentiane, Bonal, Claquesin; a suggestion paint-brushed in red on the back of a Post Office calendar—or written in whitewash on the mirror—for a country wine from the proprietor's home region, now adopted by the regulars: Mâcon, Sainte-Cécile, Pomerol, or Puisseguin; on the table covers, games that are simple but suggestive of leisure well earned: checkers, yellow dwarf, pick-up-sticks, dominoes; on the back wall an almost illegible menu that elicits bitter laughs and stirs memories in the old: snack, 65 centimes, a dozen oysters, bread and a glass of white—and it is less the price that sur-prises than the notion that a serving of oysters or snails or mussels might ever have been considered a snack now that a decent horse-meat salami costs a hundred and fifty francs and a pound of onions thirty or forty. . . .

Parisian itineraries: mazes, detours, shortcuts, about-faces, back-tracks, hills, descents, dead calm of abandoned streets whose charm is so great that, though exhausted from a long spell marking time in the southern Zone around Montrouge, I did not hesitate to take the long way round back to my den in Les Halles, leaving Boulevard Kellerman, climbing to Place des Peupliers and following Rue Charles-Fourier (where from five o'clock onwards dozens of fellow vagabonds park themselves in front of the basement door to the sordid building of the Mie de Pain charitable organization, queueing up in orderly fashion, not wishing to lose their place, because tickets—red for soup and a bed, white for soup and the right to lie on a bench, and no particular color for the right to doss on the concrete floor—were handed out on a first-come-first-served basis). Drinking a glass or two with one or other of them at Chez Francis, the bistro across the street whose owner was pretty fed up with the kind of clientele he had but did not let it show; then going up to Place Verlaine via Passage Vandrezanne, which seemed like a cutthroat's haunt at night but a Provençal *calle* by day, resting up for a while in Cité des Artistes, a cluster of dirt streets over-looking Boulevard Blanqui, to which you got down via a little street unfindable from below, passing through a locksmith's yard, down a

flight of flat-stone steps ending at hoardings and into an alley full of
lovebirds just out of a cinema or a dance hall and dawdling there as
long as possible, backs to the rickety fence of a little courtyard garden.
Then slipping into Rue Corvisart, so solidly middle-class now with the
disappearance of the many former day and night refuges, which I regret less, every time I go that way, than the disappearance of the winding bed of the romantic Bièvre river, transformed for civic purposes
into a collecting sewer that no longer even waters the gardens of the
Gobelins Manufactory; getting as quickly as possible past the Salvation Army's Palais du Peuple, an opulent, solid building whose modern entrance hall, devoid of the usual squalor, makes youngsters used
to sleeping rough hesitate, afraid to go in—and I understand them,
because the place has an especially sinister feeling, not sinister like
some dilapidated hovel but sinister in a more menacing way, like HBM
housing*—yes, I understand them, and every time I found myself in
Rue de Cordelières without a penny and my eyes bloodshot from lack
of sleep, I gave the place a miss and hastened to the vacant lot on Rue
Deslandres, and the *boule* pitch, and stretched out there, to dream if not
to sleep with the most beautiful cluster of houses in the whole of Paris
before me, the Château de la Reine-Blanche and the ancient windmills
along the Bièvre, whose course is now Rue Berbier-du-Mets, still over-
looked by reassuring rustic architecture just a few meters from the
hullabaloo of Avenue des Gobelins. And when a bicycle lamp alerted
me to the approach of a cop on his rounds and I was forced to decamp,
I would retreat to the Village Palmyre, a provincial haven behind La
Glacière where I had a bolthole among sacks of sawdust, a quiet spot
little known to derelicts where I could take my ease with the tacit
agreement of an understanding good lady.

Itineraries, then, that were sentimental in nature, that could be
marked out on the map of Paris for Sunday strollers eager to be amazed
and prolific with their exclamations, itineraries that could be indicated, after the fashion of those in the Blue Guides, by means of clear

---

Habitations à bon marché (HBM): low-cost housing projects introduced at the end of
the nineteenth century.—*Trans.*

typographical symbols for good views, doorways worth looking at, alleys to explore, and of course bistros, hostelries and way stations for necessary halts, with visits all carefully timed. You could show ways to cross Paris from one end to the other via exclusively picturesque streets, so long as avenues were avoided and eyes and ears closed at intersections, before, once across, getting back on the trail—and all without ever seeing a single officially certified site, without ever invoking the past to breathe life into old stones or stir Baedekerian or Joannesque* emotions in visitors by means of more or less specious historical anecdotes, as on guided tours that leave their victims footsore and exhausted—and unenlightened, for let us not forget that Parisians love but do not know their town. So much hokum, so much filler. The revelation of the life of a city is not accessible to the public but reserved for initiates, for a very few poets and very many vagabonds. Each individual's perception of that life depends on their temperament and emotional resources, on their particular vision, be it deadened, disgusted, or razor-sharp. The city is inexhaustible. And to master it one must indeed be either a vagabond poet or a poet vagabond.

---

*Adolphe Joanne was the founder of the *Guide Bleu* (1841), which was known at first as the Guide Joanne.—*Trans.*

2

IT TAKES longer to cross Paris than to cross a whole department. Just as you leave a country, a region, or a town for a change of scenery, to see fresh things, breathe different air, look at new faces and feel far removed from your usual routine, I change neighborhoods within Paris, moving from one to the next, having exhausted the first and anticipating the second. But it can take me three weeks to get from the hospitable quays of Grenelle to the Zone at Les Lilas, or a fortnight to climb from the Fort du Kremlin to the Maison de Nanterre, and with no more and no less in my threadbare haversack or in my old backpack with its broken pockets than if I was off to Cherbourg: a couple of shirts, a toothbrush (that small, ridiculous-looking object whose possession meant I was still not a true bum), a packet of tea, a box of matches and a bar of soap.

Vagabondage.

My longest journey, a good month long, was a tour of the Fourth Arrondissement, the vital center of Paris and a web of stunning diversity, ideally suited to the evocation of an exotic world close to home. From the Desmolières bistro on Île de la Cité to Rue des Blancs-Manteaux, or from the old City Morgue to Rue de Venise, there are hundreds of kilometers to cover, every street, lane, blind alley or cul-de-sac with its own personality, its own life, and every clump of buildings, tumbledown houses, shacks or tenements its own closed universe, café-bars, shopkeepers, whores, habits, rites and customs having nothing to do with those of the next block, which has its own architecture, its own states of mind, opinions, and occupations.

To cover this country there are six bridges, two branches of the river, and a major artery with heavy traffic to cross. Behind Notre-Dame life is quiet and uneventful, the little streets as crooked as tree branches are unknown to the tourists, as close by as these are, and the houses and inner courtyards are living museums of the history of the Cité. Only the hordes of cops—whose academy and place of entertainment are nearby—disturb the calm on Rue Chanoinesse. Rue des Ursins winds along lower down—lower even, it seems, than the water level of the river—and appears to be uninhabited, for I have never seen anyone at all enter or emerge from its venerable frontages frozen in mineral immobility, including that of the remarkable Hôtel du Lion d'Or standing across from a public urinal notorious among its habitués for erotic graffiti, among them a long tale to which in all decency I cannot expose my publisher—but readers cans always go there to see for themselves; there are of course political inscriptions also, but as usual these are of no interest, their messages boiling down to "Long Live Me!" and "To the Scaffold with X!" But the area eschews bistros, so to speak, which somewhat lessens its appeal. The Quai aux Fleurs is merely a parapet (nothing floral here) high above the water and accessible only via a double stairway leading down into the river, its two feet linked, God knows why, by a narrow passage set back into the base of the retaining wall, and there at the bottom of the steps, like Hindus at the edge of the Ganges, sit derelicts and dreamers dangling their feet in the stream, washing their shirts or sleeping perilously on the last slippery step. There are no regulars here, however, for even though the spot is well away from passers-by it is very inconvenient: because of the straitness of the passage everyone gets in everyone else's way as they strive to reach the sacred river, the water that is the source of life and the cause of the (relative) dearth of parasites. Those present are mainly illegals, out-of-work, or odd-looking characters you need to keep a close eye on, maybe some banned from the city risking everything for the pleasure of cleaning themselves up, certainly some just out of prison, dandifying themselves and tossing their release papers into the drink. And (as it took me weeks to notice) not one person fishing.

On the other side of an ironwork footbridge, a municipal monstrosity, lies the village of Saint-Louis, jealously guarding its complete

autonomy, doubly fortunate to find itself amid an extraordinary landscape and free of heavy traffic, the sole trucks getting in being those
delivering milk, market produce from Les Halles, or ice. I have never
yet lived on Île Saint-Louis. But I worked there once, with a merry
crew from Marseilles, converting an attic into a completely new apartment at the top of one of those magnificent houses dating from who
knows which historic century, with their magnificent stairs whose
steps are so high that you cannot take them two at a time, their cob-
bled inner courtyards boasting a well and decked with flowers as in
coaching days, houses entered through imposing vaulted archways and
endowed with immense windows that must be a godsend for the local
glaziers.

Today, however, every house on the island is classed as a tourist attraction and bears a yellow plaque giving the names, titles and dates of
birth and death of the former occupants. And there is talk of felling
the poplars along Quai d'Orléans and Quai de Béthune.

3

SAINT-PAUL, a surrealist construction site that is the very epitome of the "social fantastic"* of postwar days in the heart of the old city, is disappearing bit by bit: a few walls are still standing, but nothing is holding them up, not even the beams planted amid the rubble that are meant to buttress them. The old neighborhood of Jews and ragmen has been razed to make way for HBM housing (again!) but meanwhile the kids from Lycée Charlemagne are playing marbles on the esplanade. The majestic entrance to the Jam Factory leads nowhere except to a bizarre version of a Roman forum. Rue du Figuier, its elbow gas lamps definitively extinguished, is covered in gray dust; the Toison d'Or Hotel has its windows shuttered and its doorway filled with great ashlar blocks, a sign above still reads "De Luxe Wines and Spirits," and one is tempted to drape dust sheets over these last stone furnishings; Michel's bistro has no customers (does it even have a proprietor?); Rue de l'Hôtel de Ville has lost the whole of its right-hand side, while the other side leans dangerously over the void; and the Hôtel de Sens seems to have shrunk to the size of an architect's model. Rue des Jardins, however, is still home to junk dealers: every hole in the wall is stuffed with iron bedsteads and stacks of paper, Aux Fleurs—the Jewish butcher's shop —is piled to the ceiling with rags, and the Grand Hôtel de la Goutte d'Or is now more than ever a seething shelter for large families.

*Le fantastique social: a category promoted by Pierre Mac Orlan as early as 1926. As Jean-Paul Clébert would note in 1996, it encapsulated the "modern" shift of the fantastic "from fortified castles or wildernesses to the city, especially to the city streets, emerging in alleys, shop windows, cafés, and even flea markets." (Dictionnaire du Surréalisme [Paris: Seuil], s.v. "Fantastique")—Trans.

Only Rue du Prévôt is still whole and entire, but it is dead, an ossified corridor where the cracks work their merry work, destroying the last inscription: "Light and Lantern Repair," surrounded by graffiti in Yiddish. Across Rue de l'Hôtel de Ville, startlingly, is a new building where a construction crew puts up, and where the workers' association the Compagnons de France has its headquarters.

4

I LEAVE Saint-Paul by Rue François-Miron and make for the Jewish quarter proper. This street too, leading from the church of Saint-Gervais into Rue Saint-Antoine, has a small-town feel. Traffic is moderate and the residents are sedentary—small shopkeepers and home-based workers. As a consequence life proceeds here on the sidewalk in summertime, with wicker chairs, sewing, and gossip, and in winter in the bistros rather than in bunkers where all you do is sleep (and sleep worse most likely than under the stars). At the point where not so long ago Impasse Guépine used to plunge away down, the walls of the tumbledown houses have been cleared away and the space now serves as a *boule* pitch for the adults and a battleground for the kids. But under the fine snow the place is very sad. From the only corner bistro I contemplate the flanks of houses exposed to the sky, slashed open in the midst of their life, and across the way the Arab café whose exterior manages all at once to suggest a cheap club of the local type, Turkish baths, and a Mediterranean brothel. I was once the legal tenant of digs under roofs overlooking Rue Geoffroy l'Asnier, via which I could reach the bleak prospect of Rue du Grenier-sur-l'Eau (now a precarious fretwork of wooden supports shoring up its sides) and Rue des Barres. But it is so long ago now that I cannot recall what feelings this kind of empty warren must have sparked in me.

I have never slept in Rue des Rosiers, but I still have hopes of spending a week or two there, for the Jewish quarter is strictly speaking not in Paris at all. Between Rue Frédéric Duval and Passage des Singes (with its double courtyard where you can sleep comfortably and wash yourself at an articulated pump if you are canny enough to let yourself be locked in overnight), you are purely and simply in Israel. The posters for theater shows and shipping companies, like the names and signs of the stores and the childish graffiti chalked on the walls (very few political slogans) are all in Yiddish, Stars of David are everywhere in the shop windows, and all the retailers have cards dangling from strings announcing that parcels can be sent to Palestine. Along the sidewalk men with magnificent beards, wearing the ubiquitous bowler hat, are engaged in endless and passionate discussion. Butchers sell their meat in city suits and keep their hats on as they serve their customers. For the most part, moreover, the shops are devoid of buyers but full of schmoozers, and it is impossible to tell the owner from his clients, for everyone looks alike (to my eyes at least) in their traditional costume.

This too is a universe closed in upon itself. The cycle of trade is timeless. The area has its own synagogue on Rue Pavée, its public baths on Rue des Rosiers, its bookstore on Rue des Écouffes, its bistro on the corner of that same street, its cinema, its theater (and, before the war and no doubt shortly thereafter, its whorehouse or whorehouses).

Every time I venture into this neighborhood I regret not speaking Yiddish, because all the zest of the human and physical scene escapes me, I can apprehend it only with my eyes, which gives me a false impression, and only wish that I could sit down to table with these people, talk with them, become intimate with them, know the women by their first names, the men by their idiosyncrasies, the restaurants by their Central and Eastern European delicacies, the food shops by their specialties—unleavened bread and meatballs, matzos dunked in black coffee, paprika for Hungarian goulash, halva, *Käsekuchen*, poppyseed for Mohnstrudel Viennese pastries, pickled herring and rollmops pinned to pale gherkins with matchsticks. But it is very difficult. Despite my great ability to adapt, the facility with which I am able to ape the demeanor, tics, language and habits of others, to the point where I can pass just as easily, in the relevant environment, for a truck driver, an antique dealer, a pimp, or an intellectual—despite all this, I have never managed to penetrate the Jewish milieu, and every time I visit I feel like an outsider, almost like a tourist, and, my old clothes and all-purpose knapsack notwithstanding, I am unable to linger there longer

than the time it takes to drink a hasty cup of coffee; I get the impression that the men are scrutinizing me, questioning my presence, and I hurry away without pressing the point. If only I had a friend my own age with a solid entrée who could get me invited to family meals or religious celebrations and teach me the rudiments of Yiddish.

For consolation I repair to Place de Vosges for a glass of wine at the *café-tabac* on the corner, then stroll under the extraordinary vaulting, browse a little in the bookstore, test-squeeze sleeping bags at the discount camping-gear store, or smoke a pipe in the middle of the square. An anachronism of a square: a historic precinct where civilization has not yet penetrated, where the weather is fair even in the depths of winter.

5

THOUGH I never slept in Rue des Rosiers, I put up three or four times at hotels in the Saint-Merri district, an utterly different world, nearer to Les Halles in terms of the ambience, packed full of prostitutes' bars, in fact that is all you see, small spaces one after the other in Rue des Lombards, on every corner of all the nearby streets—Nicholas-Flamel, Brisemiche, de la Reynie, Aubry—where the ladies sit demurely, wallflowers, at tables or on barstools, patiently awaiting their next customer. There is nothing wild about them, and it is easy enough to play belote with them or share a stiff drink without business ever coming up, just pals together, along with the proprietor, Jo-les-Gros-Bras or Big Dédé; the girls are pretty wonderful, their opulent charms a pleasure to hold in the hand and good and firm—they are fresh in the main, ready to render small services, and their conversation, earthy as it is, can supply much scuttlebutt and intimate news of the neighborhood and much information about the rites and customs of the workers of Les Halles and about blacklisted police informants—although in this last area talk does not go much further than that, for even if everyone reads *Détective* magazine the prowess of sports stars is of more interest than the doings of the underworld. They wear the traditional costume of their profession: tight black skirts, gaping bodices barely able to contain abundant mammaries, short fluffy fur coats, and black fishnet stockings with fancy designs and the fine mesh that is so erotic (but why?).

Rue Quincampoix is curiously bereft of bistros, at least in its red-light portion, but it is thronged with women whose appeal is above all a matter of volume. Their motionless bloated figures are posted like gas

lamps beneath black or red umbrellas. Old Catherine weighs in at a good hundred and eighty pounds, and has to squat to fuck. Fat and bulbous as they are, these ladies may not be garden fresh, but they do not lack for customers among the butchers and tripe dealers of the area, men well accustomed to handling soft, violet flesh. For my part, as an ethereal guest at the Hôtel de Nantes, what I like is paying polite morning visits to the girls, my neighbors, and contemplating their surroundings: the sinister hallway, the greasy stairwell, the room off a half-landing, the iron bedstead, the wire mattress where the good woman plumps herself down, the ragged hand towels, the bar of soap no bigger than a fingernail that vanishes down the plughole, and the yellow light bulb needed from noon on.

6

BUT THERE is no finer journey, none richer in encounters, than a complete circuit of Paris, a slow and attentive crawl under a good wintry sun the full length of the borderlands between the city proper and its outskirts. And from time to time, when I have two or three hundred francs in my pocket and if possible a companion whose eyes are not too rheumy, I go up to Porte d'Aubervilliers via the oh-so-sad Rue de l'Évangile, where the milkman's horse-drawn cart seems like a hearse with jingle-bells, and catch the circle bus, letting myself be driven along, handing my tickets in installments, two at a time, to the conductor—who thinks I'm cracked, and a confounded nuisance— until I spot a gap in the barrier of HBM housing and, jumping off my moving balcony, proceed on foot following the line of the old fortifications, now no more than a dirty ribbon of grass and beaten earth save for the restful prospect of clay mounds where smut-faced kids play joyfully all week long and of little narrow and well-trodden paths like those made by cattle on their way to the watering trough.

A thousand times the poetry and horror of the Zone have been described, investigated, photographed, filmed, reconstructed in the movie studio, boosted abroad as part of France's national heritage of culture and good taste, bent to literary, artistic, moralistic, and political purposes and force-fed to the most indifferent by all the chroniclers of social *bizarrerie*—and this far better than I could ever do as an occasional haunter of the city's edge. While our emotions in the face of such relics of a stillborn civilization may always be the same, the landscape itself changes: the skyline alters, ruined walls crumble, garden allotments move away, workshops and cemeteries spread amoeba-like, clusters of prefabricated shacks appear and disappear according to the shifting tides, sports pitches and little parks sprout suddenly here and there, only to fade for lack of sap and soil and turn back into waste ground, host to the last wild grasses; and all this takes place from one day to the next, so that, to keep pace, you would have to track the topography of the Zone, as well as keep a necrological record of the large families settled there, and rely on direct observation, because all other sources of up-to-date information, including those of the newspapers, are ephemeral at best. Everything that I saw over six winter months is now no more than memories.

As few people realize, the Zone does not date back to medieval times, but merely to the Napoleonic age, nor was it created as a space for military fortifications, as others suppose, but instead by an Emperor who simply wanted to outwit bootleggers, smugglers of alcohol who had no qualms about tunneling under the barriers and avoiding the customs officers; their underground passageways were sometimes as long as three hundred meters, like the one from Passy to Chaillot, and they often debouched inside intramural communities of hovels where the police preferred not to stick their noses. Hundreds of little houses had to be demolished to create flat terrain open to surveillance, and all construction was forbidden within a fifty-yard belt, although this quite failed to prevent the mushrooming of a new town of dugouts and shacks.

7

THE SAINT-OUEN fleamarket is no longer a place for good deals where good folk used to go on Sunday mornings and either wander about without looking for anything in particular or poke through an incredible mass of heterogeneous objects in search of a spare part for their bike only to go home with the wherewithal to build a gramophone, or with a Chinese vase, a rug for their hallway, or baby clothes for their latest picked up for a song (thus making everybody happy, the junk man for having made a few francs and the customer for having saved a few). No, the market has now become a center of attraction for bad deals, just like the Foire de Paris or the stalls of the *bouquinistes* along the banks of the Seine, where people still browse but no longer buy, the prices having rocketed up and made the books just as expensive, even though second-hand, as those in regular shops and bookstores. As early as eight in the morning, luxurious motor coaches and American cars roll up at Saint-Ouen to offload hordes of tourists in search of local color at a fair price.

Between dawn and the arrival of these first customers, however, the action is at the other end of the market, on the otherwise little frequented Rue Lécuyer. The last rag grubbers bring their old stuff on the last pony-drawn carts or in patched-up jalopies. At this end, at any rate, things look much the same as at the Montreuil or Rue Saint-Médard markets. No sooner does a family pull up and stake out their place by means of string and a couple of cobblestones than a throng of fellow ragpickers and trash-can scavengers descends on the still unpacked crates, delves into them, unfolding and spreading the fabrics out on the ground, comparing notes on the quality, purchasing items

for resale later, demanding a friend's price, taking the cream (as Big Dédé's beautiful daughter would say) and leaving the rest for the idiots, or paying in drinks at the two bistros on this now bustling street, namely Le Chat Noir and Chez Thomas. Chez Thomas has one side truncated by the Zone and remains standing only by some inexplicable miracle; low-ceilinged, but luminous as a fish tank, it is home to the finest squad of clochards, cheap-goods dealers and small tradesmen in the vicinity of Saint-Ouen. Each of these characters deserves to be mounted and placed under glass, along with his biographical details and the full version of his tall tales. I spent hours in there sipping bad Juliénas with two or three old locals, mysterious denizens of this bizarre neighborhood, which is a maze of byways, lanes and dirt paths leading off, at right angles to the main thoroughfares, to single-story maisonettes with little flower gardens and fences made out of planks and old wire mattresses. Passage des Malassis, Impasse des Acacias, Allée du Puits—this was where I used to lurk as a sort of clandestine presence, rather frowned upon by the womenfolk, the dogs, and the gangs of kids, because as per usual I had an ugly face but seemed too young to be a real clochard. As I may have said already, you do not run into many rosy cheeks in a court of miracles, and a clochard worthy of the name, and accordingly of respect, has to be gone forty. When it comes to young ones, let them go to work in a factory, there is no shortage of jobs, otherwise they are just good-for-nothings! (No less!) Anyway, I just let them jabber on, and slept as best I could in a lean-to by some waste ground, a kind of rabbit hutch three of whose walls defied the laws of gravity and of avoirdupois while the fourth was gone, provisionally replaced by the remainder of a raincoat belonging to the Zouave, my taciturn co-tenant, as we lay under a roof of tin sheeting weighted down by half a dozen big cobblestones which the wind caused to rattle loudly in a way that was far from reassuring. The Zouave in question was a former rag merchant from Île de la Jatte who had suffered setbacks, probably marital ones, and left his home to live alone—and wash up in this place at the same time as me. But he also thoroughly detested me and lost no opportunity to let me know and feel it, pulling the entire tarpaulin that was our cover over himself and telling me what I could do if I did not like it. I didn't, and soon left that lean-to. But not before I had a chance to appreciate the area's resources.

Between one Sunday and the next, this part of the Zone, which is in a sense not so much outside Paris as underneath it, has a life all its own. A whole city of rag dealers. Little houses of reinforced concrete with vegetable patches as well as improvised dwellings put together on the spot, simply plumped down on the ground, and invaded by sparse greenery. But also sordid shacks along the old metro line, just crates stacked one upon the next and standing up only thanks to an ingenious system of beams and posts; plots half vacant; signs saying PRIVATE PROPERTY on doors open to every wind and every comer; and mean dogs sleeping the sleep of the just in barrels of which almost nothing but the hoops remain.

With the weather brightening up, I decided to leave and go camp at Porte de Montmartre, and after a few last rounds at the bistro on Rue des Buttes with the families of some secondhand-goods dealers who had settled down nearby in two sturdy houses (by which I mean houses standing without extra help), houses draped in sheltering foliage and flanked by barnyards complete with chicken coops and rabbit hutches that made you think of Alexander Selkirk's cabin, I went off down the truly countrified Rue Toulouse-Lautrec (another one who could never have imagined that a benevolent municipality, profligate when it came to posthumous recognition, would graft his name onto a factory road amid a landscape of fallow fields and greenish rubble—perhaps, though, he would find it restful) until I came to the railway cutting, now abandoned to its sad fate and overrun by weeds, a part of a meandering local line leaving the city by way of the foundations of skyscrapers and ending up in the forecourts of giant factories.

There were plenty of suitable places to sleep hereabouts, shrubbery galore, sandy burrows protected from wind, cold and rain, and I settled in easily. On the far side of the railway line a clump of dark shadows signaled a derelicts' encampment with potato sacks strung up to form roofless tents where four or five individuals of indeterminate sex slept, chewed tobacco, spat, drank wine and engaged in monologues. Their presence was reassuring. The place may have been poetic, but it

was also sinister, unquestionably dangerous. Prowlers moved silently among tufts of rye-grass. Alarming figures would appear all of a sudden at the top edge of the cutting and stand motionless there as though weighing whether to climb down and pay you a visit. But what for? You never knew. Was it to rob you despite the manifestly slim pickings offered by a solitary sleeper like me with no baggage except a tattered knapsack? Or in quest of erotic gratification—not the properly homosexual kind but rather that of men frustrated and obsessed? Or merely a wish for talk, a desire to share one's solitude? The area was full of Arabs, of Indochinese, of hopelessly out-of-work types—you felt their presence everywhere but to find them you actually had to trip over them, causing them to sit up in alarm, for all these guys sleep with half an eye open (except when they are dead drunk) for fear of the police patrols that periodically descend like hordes of predatory birds. The cops form cordons and drive the panicked suspects back against the factory walls like so many wild rabbits, and at such moments one is well advised to scram, to get out of there on the double even if your conscience is perfectly clear. Time to move on, to find digs elsewhere.

On Boulevard du Bois-le-Prêtre, alongside the wall of Batignolles Cemetery, there are people living in structures of fabric and canvas; protected from the public's curious eyes by a thick curtain of luxurious vegetation, these dwellings are legal addresses in the eyes of the French law, a status seemingly granted to any fixed abode within the reach of the cops. Across the way, at the corner of a street whose sign bears only the words "17th Arondissement," is the Café d'Alger, a pink-painted bistro where drunkenness is continual and rowdy and whither all these fine folk, including me, hasten their steps, as soon they have fifty francs to their name, in order to celebrate that fact and forget the woes of this vale of tears.

8

THE ZONE.

The Zone is gradually disappearing, like a grease spot being vigorously rubbed. At Porte de Pantin, through the mounds with chalky paths running down their sides that mark the site of the old fortifications (quite invisible today), workmen are carving out a railroad-like trench for a planned expressway. The tumultuous city advances, gnawing away at the chlorophyll-deprived vegetation. It is advancing so quickly that a mobile home up on blocks now seems like an anachronism. On the far side of Boulevard Mortier, very tall and very dull modern buildings are the bounding walls of a new prison. The bus that crosses the waste ground is aerodynamic, and its sliding doors scatter the sparrows. They are replacing the elbow gas lamps on Rue Paul-Meurice. Roadways Department men are digging channels for black pipes that gape like cannons. In Rue des Prévoyants an insurance agent is meticulously examining the façades of the houses.

But all along the sinuous Avenue du Belvédère red saucepans hang like fruit from the branches of the bushes. Between Porte des Lilas and Porte de Bagnolet you still find that archaic amalgam, a community of ragmen, scrap-metal dealers, chair bottomers, panhandlers, raisers of poultry or of white mice, ensconced in a patchwork of uncultivated plots and shacks separated by hedges of folding bedsteads (remarkable by their number), dwellings constructed more of wood than of concrete, more of boards and sheet metal than of brick, structures whose purpose is not immediately apparent: cabin, toolshed, rabbit hutch, outhouse? Amid cabbages and sunflowers, bathtubs do the job water towers do in the rich suburbs, but we are in the Twentieth Arrondissement. Two or

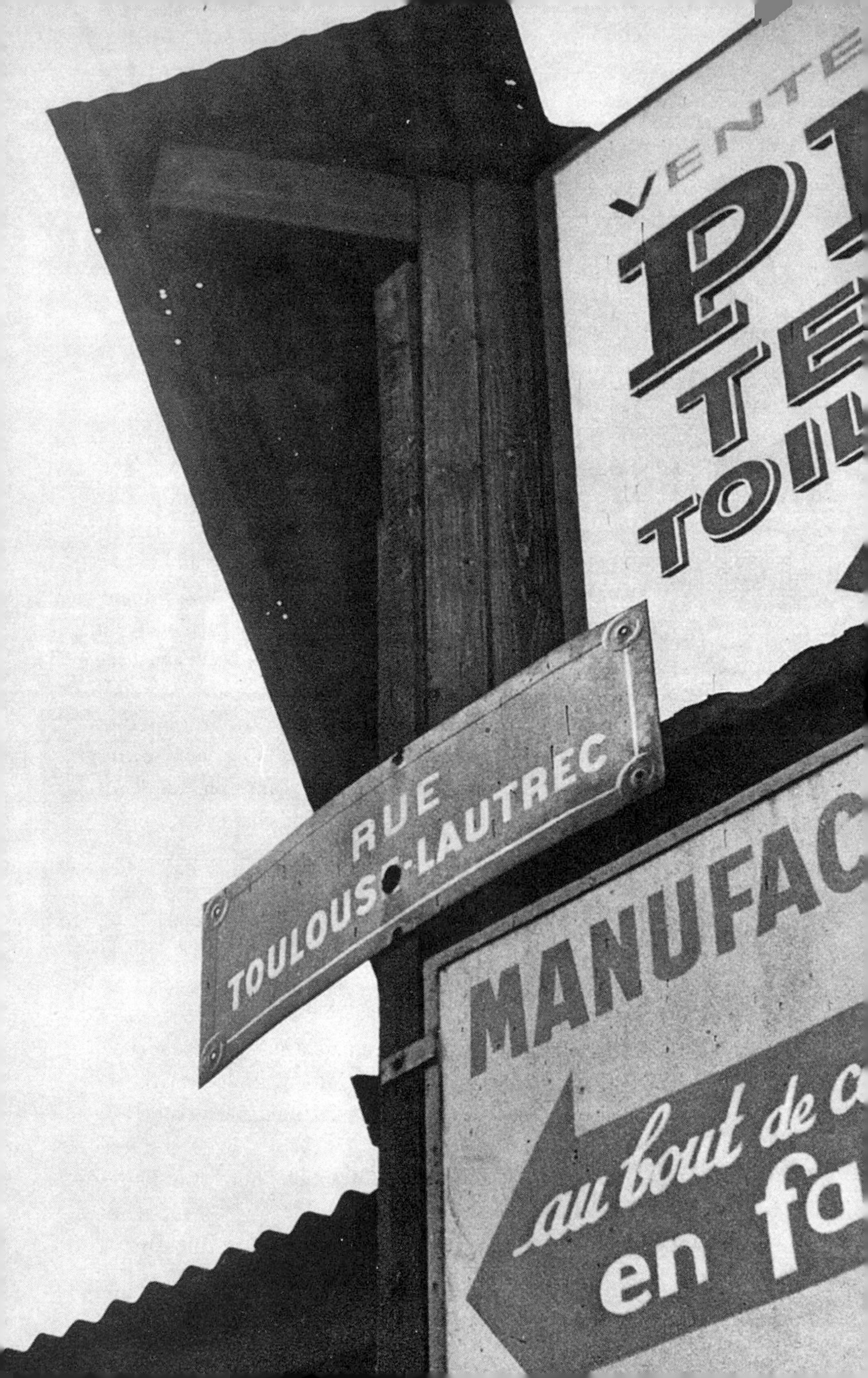
VENTE
RUE
TOULOUS -LAUTREC
MANUFAC
au bout de
en

three trailers stand on wooden piles that are beginning to vanish into the earth, having been in place since before the war or before the exodus. An old truck painted pink and brown, like fairground spicebread, has a hooked nose of a front end, white curtains at the windows, and greasy yellow smoke rising from its roof by way of a cowled chimney. It is Monday. There are no kids in Rue des Fougères, nor in Rue des Glaïeuls, only flowering yucca beneath damp garments fluttering on clothes lines. An old fellow is rinsing lettuce at a fountain whose pipe is bound up with straw. An old woman is tearing down the boards of a fence with a hatchet and chopping the wood small by the gutter. The paths are muddy and full of dandelions and the lots are dotted with unproductive Brussels sprouts.

I go over to Francis's place to buy three Gauloises at four francs fifty each. This dive, like the hovels nearby, is crammed into a hollow, crouched beneath its roof of planks and tiles (an obvious luxury), and no larger than a place to doss, most of the room taken up by the bar and a roaring Godin stove with a silver-painted chimney pipe. The low ceiling is full of holes plugged with paper. Between the boards underfoot you can see and smell a mud floor. In a recess are three little tables and a banquette where it is pleasant on Sunday evenings to eat Madame Jeanne's *pot-au-feu*, imposing platefuls of which she serves at a price commensurate with her usual clientele, a mix of ragpickers, Gypsies male and female, and the good folks who rent or own the parcels of land hereabouts. This is, as they put it, the only bistro in "the village." I am at home here. Part of the family. I listen to the boss talk. Old Francis is a former baker who has lost an arm and the use of one leg but not his smile and his ever-ready welcome; also a tramp around 1910, an honorable and fruitful period for knights of the road. We are bosom buddies, Francis and I. I listen to his stories with my legs wrapped around the stove, my belt unbuckled after a substantial meal, a glass of the proprietor's special-reserve brandy in my fist, all ears for the portraits he loves to paint of the eccentrics of every feather who haunt this patch of the Zone, or for his memories of the good old days (hardly long gone) when the café was a place of "ill repute," when shootings and knifings came as readily as insults, when Dédé-the-Baker, a notorious counterfeiter, would come and hide in the Beaujolais closet, and when police raids were an everyday occurrence. But those times are fading now, he tells me. The bistro has become cozy, and quieter than a weekend *café-dansant* on a Monday; and the customers, as I can see, are now all respectable people. No kidding. I acquiesce tongue-in-cheek. What a motley crew! Rose and Madame Noémie are two beautiful Gypsies, well-upholstered and always laughing, who flirt with the men and drink like fish. And then there is Martin, Martin most of all, maybe the only guy in Paris entitled to call himself a water-carrier, because every morning he goes to the fountain, armed with blue ceramic pitchers and battered watering cans, to meet the all-purpose H2O requirements of ten or fifteen locals, performing this service, running this errand for the tobacco seller, the baker, the grocer further away in town on the far side of the barracks, and so on, and getting himself paid for the most part in kind—in cigarettes, in cups of coffee or glasses of wine, or in bowls of soup ordered up in a peremptory tone, for he is not one to hold his tongue; he automatically checks the counter and will not go to fetch needed supplies unless his bowl is filled to the brim in advance and placed in plain view; in short he lives the life of Riley, sleeping in a more or less well-protected hut of which he is the legal owner, early to bed and late to rise, getting to Francis's place only about ten in the morning (to the despair of Madame Jeanne who has nothing to extend her soup with), greeting the company, clamping his gloved hands to the sides of the stove, approaching the boss, who is at a landlordly breakfast with a salad-sized bowl of *café au lait* and slices of bread and butter, and declaring, with a provocative glance and in a theatrical voice, "Ah! How I love your coffee!"—an envious cry that in no way prevents him from savoring his first demitasse of the day in obvious bliss. Madame Jeanne tells me that yesterday, having taken him to the weekly market so that he could carry her shopping bags, and seeing him shivering with cold, she sought to console him by promising a good hot cup of java on their return, to which he replied, all innocence, "In a bowl?" He was a card, that Martin. Drink brought out an extraordinary eloquence in him, and we were treated to disjointed reconstructions of various stages of his life. He had spent ten

years in holy orders, but one day had an "adventure" with a woman, never wished to repeat it, and thereupon cast aside his cassock for reasons known to him alone at the time—and possibly to the said woman. A real card, Martin. The Gypsy ladies teased him, offering him everything, including themselves, and saying they would work to make him rich if only he would marry them, but he would take umbrage and march out, grumbling, leaving the door open behind him, for he was extremely thin-skinned, though he never omitted, before making his exit, to take advantage of a customer's turned back to polish off the contents of any glass left perilously unattended on the bar, then he would scurry off up the bumpy path outside and the whole room would erupt in a gale of laughter.

The liquid refreshment that made him eloquent also made him sentimental. He would sing sad old songs with romantic melodies and refrains that touched everyone. And rightly so. It was there that I heard the most beautiful ballads and *chansons* rich in vernacular, perhaps not the best known but extraordinary in their candor and realism, which Martin like the others knew by heart and which never seemed to end, for each one told a true story with many episodes. Night would fall. Old Francis bought a round. People delved into their pockets in search of enough change for the last few smokes of the evening. Good humor reigned. Everyone was their neighbor's best pal, from Pablo the Gypsy acrobat to Zizi the Rapier, who one night went raving through the vegetable plots about how she wanted to find her girlfriend Mado and cut her throat, and in a dangerous state of inebriation rooted through every nook and cranny where Mado might be holed up in fear of Zizi's reprisals for an illegitimate dalliance. Mado ran among the fences until, exhausted and frightened to death, she took refuge at Francis's place, only to come face to face with the vindictive Zizi. Fortunately the boss had the presence of mind to toast the armistice, and the antagonists reconciled in a clammy embrace.

Truly a fabulous bistro, where the excellent bottled wine was cheaper than the plonk on offer elsewhere. I would happily have lodged there had there been a room for rent or even the corner of a shed. I dawdled until closing time—around ten or eleven o'clock, the regulars being earlier risers than me. Only old Francis was still there, dragging on a cigarette, a habit that gave him an incessant little cough and a sniffle that had nagged him since the last war but one, and his wife doing her sewing, that old beggarwoman sucking up her umpteenth red, bundled up in her clothes and far better there in the warm than stretched out in her bed alongside her cold bowlegged husband; she started making heavy rolls out of imposing heaps of change spread across the oilcloth, her day's takings gleaned in the passageways of the metro, where she feigned selling needles and thread so as to remain within the law but year in year out brought home two or three thousand francs a day (quite enough to raise eyebrows among all those allegedly unprejudiced and pseudo-charitable souls who live in a townhouse and run a car—and not a clunker such as the rabbit-skin sellers drive, but a solid family Peugeot). In this way she supports her man and has enough left over to go with him every Saturday night to Les Halles, where the pair enjoy a slap-up meal and empty seven or eight bottles of Alsace between them, which by break of day puts them in the jolliest mood and fills them with confidence for the future.

Which is all well and good, but now it is eleven o'clock. The winter night bars the way to any reasonably protected resting-place. All the same, I have to shake a leg. The cold hardens the ground and loosens the socks. Despite (or rather because of) the warm intimate atmosphere I am leaving, solitude makes my mind a blank. Where to go? Behind me, as he bids me goodnight, which is kind of him, old Francis closes his door and turns the light off. He is going up to his bed, in a room with no fire but out of the wind, to slip between sheets which, freezing as they may be, will nevertheless husband his animal warmth. Of course, I could always have discreetly conveyed to him that three of his bistro chairs arranged for a few hours around the still warm stove would have constituted a precious contribution to my circuit of the city. But one has one's dignity (strange to say), and Francis takes me for a "straight arrow" despite my fuzzy jowl and tangled hair, and he has never asked me how I spend my time, just a few polite enquiries about how I am getting along with my everyday problems. So here I am, nonplussed, alone in a silence that bodes nothing good. Fortunately, I have smoking materials, including matches, in my pocket, and I roll myself a cigarette. Once my eyes adjust to the darkness, I set off along Rue des Fougères. It is definitely too cold to sleep under a hedge, and I reach Porte des Lilas without solving my problem. Another moment of indecision. Should I go down beyond Ménilmontant and towards the Buttes, where there is no shortage of hidey-holes, or stick to the Zone as far as Porte de Pantin and make my way to the coppiced huts inhabited by clochards? But the cold grips me by the shoulders and forces me on down Rue Saint-Fargeau. And there it is: I'm on my way. The spring is back in my step, I gather a few butts by way of provision for the night, and fairly hop, skip and jump myself into Rue des Cascades. Another magnificent neighborhood, with street names inherited from the former high-perched village traversed by brooks—Rue des Rigoles, Rue de la Mare—streets twisting and turning this way and that, quite unlike the broad and endlessly long avenues lower down, which are the bane of bums. Up here the distances are shorter, and almost too soon for my liking I am in Rue Fessart. Climbing the railings of the Parc des Buttes-Chaumont is out of the question: the cold would chase me out quicker than any cop. The empty lot of the old Pathé film studios is likewise impractical. But I know some priceless places to flop behind some garages. I climb. I go over a couple of walls, and now I am *chez moi*, in a courtyard at the far end of which are sheds that are never locked, ragmen's storage places where I can settle in, snug as a bug in a rug, among piles of paper and sacks. I chew on my last bite of the day, spit it out, and so to bed. The trick is to wake before daybreak, before the arrival of the fleamarketers, who take a dim view of intruders.

9

ONCE AT the end of Boulevard Poniatowski I look out over the great trench carved out by the Seine and spanned by the Pont National. Starting out empty from the Ivry side, every morning and for several hours, the SITA garbage trucks come across to make their rounds on the Boulevard, great green screeching insects in slow and laborious procession. Some bear the warning DO NOT CLIMB ON TRUCK. DANGER. As though anyone would take it into their head to clamber onto one of these mechanical monsters, its fanged maw opening and closing with a clatter like a cemetery gate, ready to ingest any such daredevil raw along with its usual diet of less-than-appetizing refuse.

On the far side of the river, on rising ground, is a narrow stretch of Zone with a good view in every direction but not so much as an inhabitable shack to be seen. There is no dearth of clochards, however: temporarily lodged in nearby shelters on Rue du Château-des-Rentiers and Rue Cantagrel, they are outdoors from the crack of dawn until four in the afternoon, when they start panhandling for the seventeen francs they will need for a loaf of country bread to dunk in their free soup. Since they have a roof assured for the night these local vagabonds can happily snooze on the grass, in ditches, or beneath scrubby clumps of trees whose thin branches offer them some cover and protection, forming darkish arbors over their curled-up bodies, and provide them with fuel with which to get an all-purpose fire going nearby between two or three cobblestones.

At the very top of the ridge, lined up side by side, fully exposed to the wind, three guys are taking a shit in perfect unison. The moment they get up, their silhouettes are stark against the sky, pants about their calves, a reassuring symbol of tranquility of soul, of the serenity that comes from duty performed, and let the chips fall where they may. I run into the three, moreover, just a few minutes later, touring the closest bistros over in Ivry, sampling house plonk and buying smokes in singles, their eyes screwed up, cheeks flabby and grog-blossomed, whiskers greasy and breath lethal: meet old Tripette, the Widower, and La Bouscaille—three fellows from around Charenton come to pay the capital a visit, to get a change of air, and to let off a little steam—or, in the words of the tavernkeeper, to give everyone a big pain in the ass. They are talking shop. Everyday worries: the high quota of cops; the disappearance of paper and metal from the trash cans put out for 3 a.m. pick-up (these receptacles, which the *Almanach Vermot* calls night boxes, may now contain only kitchen and household garbage); and, as always and ever, ways of getting by.

"If you are looking for poverty," La Bouscaille tells me, "just stay where you are, you'll soon get your wish. We are heading straight for grief."

10

To the top of Avenue Eugène-Thomas, three days a week, clochards
from the Zone and Gentilly Cemetery, old-timers from the Fossés de
Bicêtre, down-and-out junk dealers and ragpickers exiled from the
Maubert, Gobelins, and Château-des-Rentiers fleamarkets, all bring
their (seemingly) unsalable merchandise, items inferior to those displayed at Saint-Ouen or at the Bastille old-iron fair, or by the fake
Gypsies or Romanies of Montreuil, or the grubbers of Saint-Médard.
An unshakable poverty is on view along the sidewalks—which a benevolent Roadways Department is at present restoring (meaning that
the old coach cobblestones are being replaced by poured-concrete
slabs): unmatched pairs of boots, ragged jackets and trousers, garments
at a hundred francs, surplus pieces of leather, printed papers much
stained but still readable (a set of *Illustration*s of Great-War vintage or
prints of wreathed period oil portraits), bundles of postcards, bits of
scrap metal, bags of bent and rusty nails, broken or defective concierge's knickknacks, and so on. Unmatched, stained, bent, rusty, broken, defective—just like these poor devils, their faces plaster masks of
no-more-hope. And past these heaps of treasures for the taking stroll
shopkeepers and petty bourgeois from the Avenue and housewives
from the brand-new housing, casting vague glances down at what lies
at their feet and passing remarks.

Down at the other end of the street, however, business is good. Respectable vendors liquidate overstock from the large stores, peddle surplus from the Occupation and offer items from estate sales, haggling
fit to wreck their vocal cords, not to mention their uvulas, and raking

in dough in thousand-franc bills that they roll up and stuff with their thumbs into the depths of their lumberjackets.

But up above, opposite Les Canons de Bicêtre* and all along by the fortifications, things are not pretty. I feel an urge to sit down and call my whole adventure off—assuming that it can ever be called off.

A woman junk dealer without a spot, having usurped that of a regular, laying out her pretty kickshaws in some kind of order on a patch of grass, a deplorable altercation has broken out. The man is flinging all her wares aside. Flying through the air goes a stream of rubbish, broken china that somehow contrives to break even more. Yelling and screaming on all sides. A babel of argot—Yiddish, Polack, Low German, Berber, Kabyle, Romany, even English slang, notably that of a tall old American standing nearby, clad like a Pyrenean shepherd in three layers of deerskin, whom nobody understands save possibly the old Jew in a corner, who winks.

Mumbling to myself, I make my way via the Poterne des Peupliers to Avenue Romain-Rolland, where I am bound to find tall grass and soft turf for a siesta amidst the usual assortment of odd characters, whole families and discreet couples spread out along a good stretch of road creating the impression of an exodus, some asleep with mouth open, others chewing on salami, putting paid to liters of wine, scratching flea bites, or rocking tots in baby carriages which are thus for once being put to their original purpose. Where do they come from, these people? Where are they going? What are they doing? Mystery. They keep their distance. Since they never ask me any questions, all I can do is follow suit, keep my mouth shut and look at them only out of the corner of my eye as I stake out my own spot, light my fire and make myself a cup of plain tea without sugar, which attracts the attention of my nearest neighbor, who comes over to see, but on realizing that the only nourishment on offer is of the liquid variety, merely grumbles about the

*A café whose name commemorates the cannons of the Fort de Bicêtre, which played a significant role in the Prussian siege of Paris in 1870.—*Trans.*

rain that is on the way—he is a strange bird, long-leggedy as a giant grasshopper, the skin of his face and hands, like a mushroom's skin, peeling off in little flakes, somewhat distingué nevertheless with a shoestring tie and a buttoned collar (rare indeed in this neck of the woods), and drawing on old butts through a cigarette holder. I motion him to sit down, but he casts me a reproachful(?) glance and goes off back to his patch of grass. Another one!

There is an alarming number of dingbats wandering about in the moonlight. Not mean or screaming lunatics, slavering and glaring murderously, but frighteningly thin human beings walking in silence, flitting past, so to speak, about two or three centimeters above the asphalt, hands in pockets, collar pulled up in the midsummer heat, forelock wild, eyes unfocused, passing down the street, by houses and people, and through the city with ectoplasmic ease, pausing only to observe a cat, or the kids at play in the squares, asking for food neither at shelter doors nor of their peers ensconced on benches, and never, ever entering a bistro.

One or two have a musical instrument under their arm.

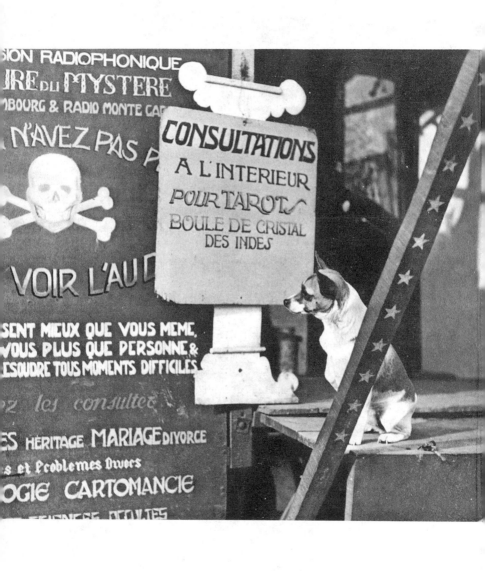

11

MY NEXT stop on the jaunt that I have been recounting for the last few pages is no longer in the Zone, which skips over it. I am talking about the Cité Universitaire, a piece of private property of unheard-of luxury as compared with the desolation of the waste ground flanking it on either side, a property where, neglectfully, clochards never set foot. God knows that if ever they did, it would seem like paradise to them, with its wide-open entrance, patches of lush grass, soft lawns, the cover of shrubs and thickets, the moonlight dancing among pleasant buildings, and the total absence of cops on the beat. But "correct attire is obligatory." (The regulation does not specify whether it means no sticky, mud-spattered clothing or no two-piece bathing suits.) I have spent fine summer nights there. Washed, shaved, with a fresh change of clothes, leaving my haversack in a nearby bistro, I would don my espadrilles and enter the precinct in high spirits, answering a post-libation call of nature on a graveled path before going from one dormitory to the next in search of whatever I might find by way of conversation, dinner, drink, and jocularity. I would ogle girls from every country—broad-assed French chicks, pretty, narrow-waisted Americans in very long skirts, Scandinavians who were too horsey, blathering Germans, and South Americans whose dark eyes saw everything, understood everything, and said it all. Then I'd go and lie down in a clearing not too far from a group of the aforesaid, playing the local ladies' man, the typical dirty-minded French male, chatting up the nearest to hand and occasionally gratifying my desire for tactile and olfactive exploration. All you fine chicks, young and fresh, who found pleasure with this city vagabond, I thank you! And farewell! Off I go to rejoin my own tribe on the banks of the Seine.

12

AT NIGHT the banks of the Seine can easily take on a fantastic feel. Everyone knows this. Every last hayseed visiting the capital has delighted in a crimson-and-gold sunset over the Grand Palais—that prostrate, rusting, horizon-blocking pile so reminiscent of a presidential junk-room. The very naivest of English lady tourists has reveled at dawn (around seven or eight o'clock, because now that you are actually in Paris, you must see absolutely everything) in the rise of that selfsame sun behind the Gare de Lyon's charming little clock. But the only way truly to honor, truly to appreciate the staggering landscape of the quays is to trek from one end to the other and back again, all the way from Rue de la Zone* to Quai du Point-du-Jour, returning along the opposite bank of the river. Staying as close as possible to the water's edge, although, stupidly, you are obliged to climb higher up to get past certain bridges beneath which one might lodge happily were it not that the quay becomes submarine (why this inexplicable aberration in the riverside architecture?).

Hands deep in your pants pockets, cig dangling from your lips, eyes scrunched up against the smoke, you get a free visual feast just to yourself. You walk alongside abandoned barges, by sandpits and cranes half-buried in the damp sand, zigzag between trees, slip under concrete colonnades where trickling water gurgles from piss-streaked walls, halt from time to time to try and descry the mug of some friend asleep face down beneath a pile of old clothes, lean for a moment against a bollard to roll tobacco, breathe in deeply to fill the lungs with

*Now Rue Escoffier.—*Trans.*

air supposedly briny but in fact indefinably fetid, rife with myriad odors emanating slowly from the spaced-out gridded gates numbered like the houses above, glance inside out of simple curiosity and grope about briefly to see whether the opening is not perchance unlocked and momentarily home to a member of our merry band, go by couples half-lying on benches and exchanging intimate caresses, sneak a glance at them hoping to get a glimpse of thigh, whistle softly, look, watch. All around, the city sleeps or pretends to sleep. Objects begin to take on a life of their own. The utilitarian décor on either bank takes on greater clarity and immense significance: factory chimneys, glassed-in workshops, suspension bridges, gasometers, processions of blinking lights, flat-roofed houses and gable-roofed houses, administrative buildings and businesses giving directly onto the quayside like private estates, customs warehouses, little watchmen's shelters entered by exterior stairs, and, every hundred meters or so, picture-postcard views of bridges only too well known and consigned to the oblivion of familiarity.

The cold slashes the roofs into sharp silhouettes. And causes vapor to rise from the drain ventilators upon which bundles of humanity are sleeping.

The only glimmer of life comes from the windows of the huts of the rescue service for the drowning—sad little cabins, each with a bedraggled and dirty flag, far more evocative of the old Morgue than of some return to the joys of life. I climb up onto an iron catwalk and knock at a door. Hope to drink a hot cup of joe and play a quick game of belote with old Pierre (or maybe I should say old Paul—discretion is apparently called for even here). The interior of his den puts you automatically in mind of a forensic investigation *à la* Simenon: a warming-table in the center, upon which he will place the swollen body of the night, and where he can prepare and consume his chow. A twenty-four-hour shift is long. Visits from buddies are more then welcome. A chance to chew the fat. Hanging on the wall is the trusty hand-mirror used to detect a victim's last exhalation. The gas lamp dangling alongside its pull-string resembles a weird limp condom. A palish green light fills the place. The latest tales concerning death on the river are imparted

confidentially. There are spicy details, as for instance the fact that in winter the drowned remain underwater for a week or two, whereas in the summer they pop back up to the surface the next night. And no one laughs, for even though their profession so closely resembles that of the mortician, reputed to be the jolliest of fellows, these suicide watchers are a grim, morose lot. And no wonder. Their sole distraction is a crossword and the edifying *Petit Larousse Illustré* dictionary.

Nothing is as horrifying as fishing corpses from the Seine as they drift with the current on the way to better days in another universe. Mistreated and misunderstood kids, girls knocked up and abandoned, the unemployed and maladapted, the nutcases and the obsessed—all those beloved character-types of popular novels whose contemplation attracts rubbernecking readers like so many scatophagic insects battening on fresh shit. Firemen belted and helmeted as if prepared for an urban cataclysm rake the water gently, test the bottom with poles, dip and drag grapnels and heft four-clawed anchors—ghastly instruments of torture at the mere sight of which your skin crawls and you just hope that their hooks will not puncture the swollen flesh of a corpse and pop it like a balloon. For hours riverbank locals have been awaiting the moment when the flabby white mass comes up into the light, is lashed with ropes alongside the boat and borne along like that, floating with head high, bloated belly bursting the last shreds of underwear, an asexual and terrifying sea-monster whose stench must be nauseating....

There are only five lifesaver's huts along the river, as compared with seven along Paris's Grand Canal.* This is understandable, for the toll of suicides occurring between Quai de la Rapée and the Moulins de Pantin is far higher than that along the touristic portion of the Seine. The canal system offers the city's most horrible prospect. In the countryside the setting is made magnificent by flanking rows of poplars and by locks as decked with flowers as rail crossings, and you feel an urge to take a trip on a barge, with damp laundry clacking, the guy swabbing the deck, the kids racing along the perilous gunwale, the pretty girl

---

*The early name of Paris's canal system, now composed of Canal Saint-Martin, Canal Saint-Denis and Canal de l'Ourcq.—*Trans.*

shaking her salad dry, and the captain sitting on a crate, grasping the wheel and drawing on his pipe. But on the outskirts of the big cities canals attract mist, dust, rain, wind, and filthy air, concentrate the smells of clinker, coal dust, gasoline, and diesel fuel; pick up animal carcasses, trash, rotting hulks, and tree limbs; strew their banks with loose rocks, coal, bricks, rubble, sacks of plaster, and girders; and find themselves imprisoned in a world of scrap iron, workshops, shacks, old trucks with slatted sides, junked freight cars, board fences, construction sites closed to the public, dead-end hotels, and soot-blackened apartment buildings. City canals are a great rubbish dump. Here more than anywhere else the poverty is glaring and the nights endless and frigid. Lone nocturnal or twilight walkers are all morose, sad drunks, living a dog's life or suffering from cancer of the face. Instead of necking, couples jerk each other off brutally, wild-eyed, as though striving for one last climax, never speaking of the future, or of your beautiful breasts, of saying I love your nipples, how big they are, I want you to caress me gently and afterwards take me dancing; instead, they hurl back and forth the age-old stories of getting laid off at the factory, of a period still not come, of that's it, this time I'm in the family way, and of well, my girl, you can see your regular about that, I don't want some whining brat from God knows who, sort it out yourself, I'm going for a drink. And she cans it. He goes off to the bleak bars of Quai de la Loire, she to a corner by the tunnel into which the Canal Saint-Martin disappears on its way to Rue du Faubourg du Temple, a place appropriately named the Bief des Trépassés, Dead Man's Reach (although this may refer merely to the Gibbet of Montfaucon, which used to stand not far away). The luminous face of the clock on the vertiginous footbridge surveys the scene with indifference.

In summer, all the same, the banks of the Canal Saint-Denis are imbued with a quiet poetry. The landscape changes once you get past the lifesaver's hut on Quai de l'Oise (and this one is surrounded by flowers and greenery, along with a rustic bench, and the occupant may be seen there in the evening in a tangerine-orange shirt with the sleeves rolled up, contemplating the water overflowing onto the sidewalk).

Just after the Pont de Flandre, to the left, is a side channel whose

name or purpose I have never known, a motionless stretch of water flanked by two immense, seemingly vacant and abandoned buildings with ground-floor colonnades that remind you of Rue de Rivoli. Seen from above, from Quai de la Gironde, they give the odd impression of a fragment of Venice captured and fixed in time. Beneath the crumbling architectured vault stands an old pre-1914 locomotive, rusting and ridiculous.

Just before the locks, houses appear on a level with the water, which offers clear reflections of a bike, a baby carriage, windows, a laundry line. Potbellied and as tall as buses, or else so low in the water that one would be loath to jump aboard for fear of scuttling them, the barges wait in line. We are at the height of summer, and young boys and girls with budding breasts dive in and splash about. The little old guy who operates the footbridge, the last drawbridge in Paris, at the Bassin d'Aubervilliers—another dock installation inaccessible to the public, cut off here by a body of water and at the far end by the iron railing that runs along Rue de la Haie-Coq—doffs his jacket and hawks onto his ancient contraption. Some Arabs, one of whom looks like Salvador Dalí, are taking the air at the bottom of the wall, their dirty feet bare in the sunshine.

But after the locks comes the Zone, which has intruded itself here, all along the water, in the shape of a succession of garden plots, narrow like those of the crossing keepers. Once in a long while a wooden shack appears, home to a large rag-dealer family eating their lunch outside on their doorstep for all the world like respectable suburban householders. The menfolk already have the look of the rag grubbers and junk dealers of Île de la Jatte and Île Saint-Denis, while the women could easily pass for *pétroleuses*. One fellow whose acquaintance I was never able to make has contrived a den for himself out of string and rags where he must be able to get to his feet only in a crouch.

On the side of one of these huts, written in large white letters, is the word DÉSODEUR, which sounds like "bad smells," but which, since these folk are hardly given to witticisms and word play, can only be the surname of the residents.

A curious feature of this area is the little green tractor that still tows the barges, accompanying them until they are past Pont de Stains. At the corner of Rue de la Gare (which runs back down to Porte de la Chapelle) is a large sign that says "Café-Bar," with an arrow, but despite patient exploration of a warren of walls, courtyards, outhouses, potted plants, and rabbit hutches, I have never managed to find the public establishment in question. You have to wonder where the locals go to tipple.

Between the two bridges, mainly on the left bank, one's sense of smell is over-stimulated by a succession of odors, as follows (read slowly): cheese, very violent, then, by turns, gas welding, fresh periwinkles, and new rust.

13

THOUGH not vital or urgent like the taking in or elimination of food, the job of keeping clean (meaning something more than three moistened fingers drawn quickly over the eyes) is a serious enough business from the point of view of someone quite unable to find the price of a shower at one of the city's "public" baths or to pay an exorbitant sum demanded for a few items of his personal wardrobe to be washed and dried. The sole easily accessible body of water is of course the Seine, and it attracts the unwashed like flies—everyone whose filthiness is beginning to torment them and who experience the odd but voluptuous need to scrub their epidermis despite the chill air, the glacial current, and the hair-raising effect of cold water. In winter the task is brutal. Of course, a fair number of good citizens claim to get indescribable pleasure from thrusting their head under freezing-cold water from a faucet and clapping wet cloths onto their torso like soldiers at the front. What they forget is that before this wake-up exposure they have been luxuriating in a warm bed in a heated room, and that once washed they can restore their body temperature by means of a substantial and calorific breakfast. I should dearly love to see their faces, their reactions were they to find themselves at first light down by the Seine, or by the Marne just beyond Porte de Charenton, having spent the night in a ditch or on a patch of grass near the riverbank, traveling alongside yours truly, stomach beset by nausea, gaze unfocused, calves in spasm, face twisted by an aggravating crick in the neck, a strong aftertaste of cheap wine on the roof of the mouth, and palms moist; following the river towards the center of the city in the vague hope of treating their feet to something other than hard-caked dust and of slaking their thirst, both internal and external, with free-flowing clear water, so ridding their skin of the woolly, itchy overlay that has been serving as a winter coat; but managing only to get a quick glimpse of a glistening surface streaked by distinctly unattractive gauzy tendrils of white mist; advancing at press of sail over long stretches of smooth pavement which seems to be splintering from the frost (it is actually the cracks in the flagstones that give this impression, but at six or seven on a January morning one tends to wax lyrical); deciding to do no more than go and sit at the bottom of a flight of stairs almost as narrow as a stepladder, there to gauge the odds of catching cold just after gauging, the day before, the risk of sciatica setting in; but eventually, taking their courage in both hands, rolling their sleeves up the elbows, and plunging said hands into the bitterly cold fluid before sprinkling a few drops on the tips of their schnozzles, between their eyebrows, on their frozen ears, and on their oh-so-intelligent foreheads. But this hardly meets the requirements of a healthy body, and how I should love to see their faces drawn back like a turtle's into the warm and cozy hollow of their shoulders as they proceed falteringly in search of a sloping point of access to the stream that obviates recourse to acrobatic maneuvers scarcely recommended at such a matutinal hour, and find themselves obliged to go up as far as the civilized river's edges of Quai de la Rapée or Quai Henri-IV to find a gentler slip in the form of one of the watering places thoughtfully designed for dogs and cattle and to facilitate the launching of boats brought on trailers, or else one of those Parisian beaches, thronged in summer by bathers and mosquitoes but especially deserted at this time of year, which have been set up at intervals over the ten kilometers of quayside of the city proper and are spots of illusory tranquility where tourists can dumbly contemplate men and beasts delousing themselves and splashing about. I should like to see their slow and feeble motions as, having found such a place, they remove their sweaters and kick off their one-and-twos with their teeth chattering; to observe their antics with indifference as they lie prone a few inches from the water, staring at their image before resolving to get out a rusty razor and the everlasting blade that they rub daily on the broken base of a bottle to sharpen it and make it less likely to break the skin, as they try to see clearly in the murky stream, which reflects nothing but unintelligible clouds, and as, the movements of their fingers stiff from the cold, they strive to smooth out their wrinkles. Ah! for the paradise lost of a real bathroom. After ten minutes and only half his face scraped, a man gives up, straightens his aching back, dabs at himself with a rag, puts back on his upper clothing, damp now from spray, as fast as he can, and rushes off along the quayside to get his sluggish circulation going again, ready to start the procedure all over again half an hour later, at the next slip—the one, perhaps, at the Pont des Arts, the pleasantest in terms of its surroundings and its accessibility with its two stone ramps leading down into the river, who knows how far, and its overhanging parapet that facilitates a practical combination of washing and cooking. One might as well take one's breakfast here, and after completing one's toilet—shaving the other half of one's face and giving one's toes a good soak—the genuine vagrant camper can make himself a cup of hot-and-wet to which a pinch of tea would be a welcome addition, his all-purpose pan balanced on a makeshift stove in the shape of an enormous tin can with a hole in the bottom and charcoal for fuel. A moment of bliss. As for the fellow a few yards away with no such equipment, for it is a great rarity on the banks of the Seine, he must make do with a fire built of old crates and green wood at the foot of a wall blackening by the minute, and the remains of a bottle of wine.

Washing one's balls is something else again. Despite the very relative modesty of your clochard, when it comes to displaying such portions of his person it is challenging and dangerous for him to expose his hindquarters or manly accoutrements to the gaze of curious passers-by bent double over a parapet above. And worse even than the risk of shocking such gawkers is the need to avoid attracting the attention of cops on the prowl quite liable to haul you in on a double charge of affronting public decency and exhibitionism. Sheer prudo-religiosity! So just how is one to clean those parts deserving of a good scrubbing and close inspection? Wait until summer and go about daybreak, when the street cleaners (on non-rainy days) send water streaming through the gutters? Hardly. There are toilets in the bistros, of course, but you

have to get in and, once in, you are very cramped. So! The best thing is to say fuck it and go for broke: set yourself up comfortably and let trouble do its worst; choose a discreet spot along a stretch of riverbank peopled solely by cranes and sand plants, and just too bad (or too good) for the old crone across the way who comes wandering along at the crack of dawn with her bottle of milk and her darling little poodle.

Upstream and downstream of the dead city the prospects are better. In the three seasons of the year when your skin doesn't freeze and crack like a pedunculate morel the banks of the Seine are invaded by a great host of natives whose main common trait is their anonymity, human bodies dragging along on two thin twisted stalks, fantastic animals that a Martian could never imagine covered by layered skins which are shed and flutter to the ground, exposing a white assemblage of bones with no sensory system apart from long hands groping the surrounding air, feet as curly as young ferns for feeling the little undulating ribs on the muddy black sand, unmoving and half-closed eyes as empty as glass marbles, and a bushy topknot that in the water might be taken for a clump of seaweed. Standing motionless on the bank, dozens of Arabs, vagabonds, laid-off workers and mental cases stare at the horizon, at thirty meters of slow-moving river, and at a row of scraggy plane trees beyond which trucks, another set of strange beings, slide along their track trumpeting in a preternatural way. They can see the Suresnes, Longchamp, and Charenton locks. And most notably the ghastly Île des Ravageurs, just before you get to Pont d'Asnières, a formless conglomeration of factories under demolition, barren plant life, tumbledown shacks, and a thick carpet of human waste and toilet tissue; alongside, the Seine blooms poetically with rainbows of petroleum, fuel oil, and gasoline, but the surface filth, with its brown patches like the eyes of grease that rise to the top of a broth, is relentless and all-enveloping, being subject to the laws of capillary motion, and resembles gray stockings covering up hairy legs—distinctly unfeminine. But the strand here is no less appealing to the eye than a chic Deauville-style beach, never mind the dross and the sticky mud that stand in for warm sand, never mind the grass with its efflorescent turds wrapped up in paper like bonbons and the naked bodies of men sleeping under

a pale sun with a damp handkerchief draped casually over their cock—
their Bobo doll—and becoming less transparent as it dries.

During the good weather all the bridges of Paris, all the quays, riv-
ersides and canals are places where much washing goes on. Flapping in
the wind like the bedsheets of the bargemen's wives, shirts, under-
shorts, rags, canvas pants and odd socks dangle from the nearest wire,
or from low-hanging branches; or else they are pinned to the ground
with dirty cobblestones, or even allowed to dry on a person's own
body, next to the skin, should their lucky owner have no change of
clothing and have to present one damp side and then the other to the
morning sun. Where the two branches of Paris's Grand Canal come
together, crouched or kneeling like true washerwomen, men are scrubbing, twisting, spreading out, wringing and rinsing pieces of fabric,
then scrubbing them again, usually without soap, in clear water that
can never dislodge the soil. A civilized man is blowing bubbles like a
kid. A masculine woman is gesticulating like a crazy person on the
quay as she tries to retrieve a piece of laundry that is just out of her
reach and floating off downstream, and shouting and screaming in a
manner quite out of proportion to the garment's intrinsic worth. A
man fishing offers her his net, and the good woman slips and very
nearly stumbles right in, but catches herself just in time and rounds on
her helper. Stripped to the waist, a sailor, who has washed up here god
knows how, after who knows what stints as a galley oarsman, is tortur-
ing his forearms as he strives to reach the small of his back. The back in
question bears a magnificent tattoo of a Chinese junk whose sail seems
to roll like the sea with each of his motions. He leans forward, tauten-
ing his pants, which split silently and expose white flesh. A dog races
up and throws itself into the drink, re-emerges and shakes itself, spray-
ing water around like a sprinkler's nozzle, goes back into the river,
swims through a sea of corks crowding up against the prow of a barge,
and returns filthy as an old comb, its eyes gleaming with delight.

Sitting comfortably, buttressed by three cobblestones, I am tending
a fire of burning boards. Sheltered from the wind by a stone wall are
four or five of us spread out in different poses behind the plane trees,
each brotherly couple of bums vaguely busy cooking up spuds. All are

unknown to the others, names serving no good purpose save for nick-names assigned according to mood or whim and save for the fact that waking next to a fellow clochard in the lee of a pile of stones is reason enough for exchanges of the culinary and verbal kinds. By my side, Rabout, a Kabyle as curly-haired as a goat from his home village, is stirring a clear broth and dunking crusts of bread in it. Life is good. The sun is rising. I have slept well, awoken not too stiff. The cops have left us alone. On the bridge the worker ants are hastening towards their jobs and their end-of-the month wage packets. Self-propelling barges putt-putt along in front of us. Paid vacationers play catfish at the sewer outflows.

To wake up in the morning on the banks of the Seine as the cock crows—and all the cocks crow along Quai de la Mégisserie on the Right Bank and Quai Montebello on the Left—is a blessing, and the privilege of the vagabond. Before long the sun joins the celebration. But to stroll along those same sidewalks and see those same poor fowls caged, turning round and round in their confinement, desperately attacking the netting with beaks and wings under the gaze of Paris's peasants, is a dismal experience. The spectacle becomes truly outrageous on Quai du Louvre, where chicks on view in the windows, pecking, grooming, nibbling, are dyed different colors like fondant candies, blue, pink, green, yellow, violet, so many little puffballs, the poor downy creatures having been injected even before birth by a long needle plunged into the egg. What possible purpose can this serve? Surely this does not turn them into household pets?

How long will it be before the trees along the avenues, stray cats, lawn grass, and lions in the zoo are likewise many-hued? And why not the down between girls' legs—why shouldn't that too be blue, pink, green, yellow, or violet? (Already, every Saturday evening, you see suburban housewives emerging after an afternoon at the hairdresser's sporting mops of hair and wigs with streaks of gray but also dyed in all those same colors, either pastel or bright.)

14

CHRISTMAS Eve being by definition a sad moment for the penniless, they try to get over this hump in the most cheerful mood possible,
generally by going on a three-day drunk, something that is fairly easy
in view of the long-drawn-out public festivities, and their best bet is to
go up to the Foire de Pigalle, a vast and almost free attraction where
the unexpected invariably occurs—and far more appealing for this
reason than the Foire du Trône, which gets going only when spring
arrives, a better time to be on the road than in the city.

Alone and freshly shaved, clean from tip to toe, I go up there with
the intention, first of all, of wetting my whistle, a necessary prelude to
the honorable pursuit of possible romance. I am trying my luck, with
limited but adequate means, for, while lotteries are as a rule nothing
but a mug's game, stalls with multicolored wheels of fortune almost
always offer easy pickings. Just ten francs can win you a full hamper—
two bottles of wine, spicebread, a kilo of sugar and the like. The where-
withal for a respectable snack on the nearest park bench. How often,
with my devil's own luck, have I staked my entire fortune, small change
of course, on the first number I see, at random but with confidence,
since I am not superstitious, then watched it circle—too far, or too
slow and weak ever to make it to the top—but no! there it is, right on
the ace of spades, the winner! The kilo is mine! Up your ass! I think to
myself, grabbing the precious packet and decamping without further
ado, snatching a hundred francs for good measure as I go, smiling at
my good fortune and off to do sweet fuck-all, relaxed now, my hunger
diminished by the mere thought of the sugar in my pocket, and looking forward to forty-eight hours of relaxation thanks to Wallace's

fountains (if any are still in working order, seeing how few of us still use them).

There is a trick to this, of course, as I explain a little farther on to Fernand, the weightlifter of Place Blanche, who is strolling around after his dinner in an expensive jacket. There is actually an almost sure-fire way to win, but you have to find a stall where the guy is running the show by himself, then watch what numbers keep coming up, because after two or three hours his arms will be pretty tired and the strength of the mechanical gesture with which he sets the thing spinning will have become standardized, so that the same winners recur, generally no more than three or four of them in all, bunched together of course, which increases your chances to one in three. But the trick is known to the operator, and if the guy spots you the bastard will alter his throw, change hands, or slow down the wheel with the foot brake. All the same, the wheel of fortune qualifies as an "institution of social value." Just think, I tell Fernand, suppose I win four or five liters of wine, I could treat you to a superb night of drinking. Fernand laughs, but couldn't care less. He makes more money than I could ever make just telling his life story, pitching his act, bantering with the gawkers, gathering up coins and folded banknotes, and occasionally pinch-lifting a twenty-kilo weight using only his thumb and index finger. Fernand has a fine trade, and he has a fine troupe of strongmen showing off their Roman biceps on the streets of Paris. I first met him years ago when I was working at the Foire de Pigalle myself as an attendant at the Auto-Skooter bumper cars, when all I could see of the other attractions was a flimsy white-painted wooden fence and, in front and on the far side of it, rows of standing figures, their moving faces lit from above and tinged with the blue, white, and red of bulbs barely discernible in the half-darkness. I fancied myself in a circus ring, playing the clown as I capered in front of a darkened audience, leaping from one dodgem to another, using an expert eye to spot my yellow pennants fluttering sporadically atop the cars' masts against the wire net of a ceiling, just below the flying sparks, and clamping my soles to the narrow bumpers, grabbing tickets vaguely proffered, whistling along with the old tune coming from the loudspeaker, happy with my job as a

kind of monkey swinging from one branch to the next before bounding onto the wooden walkway and delivering the tickets I had collected to the cashier. I wore overalls like a camp monitor and espadrilles, and a cap perched on the back of my head. I looked out for girls on their own, and there was no lack of them, continually being hailed by solitary males trying to catch their eye between turns and pile-ups, the smarter guys preferring to ogle those still standing on the platform and pull up in front of them and signal to them with finger or head to get in—and the girls went for it, getting themselves treated to ten or even twenty rides with the guy's arm around their shoulders or his hand on their thigh, because he would let them do the driving the better to grope them a bit until the girl decided to get off, with or without him, and the two of them prepared to play the game all over again. As for me, I had to wait for the slow times, with only three or four crates cruising and the rest parked crowded together, and no one much around, then I could go for it, sitting on the seat back with one leg on the fake door, hurrying up these stragglers and picking up a fare as I did so, and maybe even a chick into the bargain, but that was another story, the boss didn't want any of that, he ranted and pissed the shit out of us, and all we could manage to get away with, when we caught a live one, was to let her ride for free—in off hours, of course—and the kid would throw herself into it heart and soul, and you can bet we did too, slapping her ass, and she would shriek, or feeling her up gently behind, at a slight angle, and she would whirl round giggling, as we feasted our eyes on her bare knees and thighs, most of them couldn't care less, not even bothering to pull their skirts down, and we left them, aroused but obliged to go and take care of the money. Later, after midnight, as the fair was closing down, there were always two or three still wandering about as we parked the kiddy-cars in the middle of the ride's floor, and we would join them and take them drinking at a nearby bistro, where they let us lark about with them, if not more. They were housemaids, office workers, girls living alone in their room who, after a hasty meal, got the blues in front of their one-ring burner and came here to forget; among them too were babes from distant neighborhoods, rich kids who reckoned they were seeking adventure, and *demi-vierges* deeply perturbed when they were groped down some dead-end alley, in the former Rue de l'Élysée-des-Beaux-Arts or on the Escalier des Trois-Frères, pushed into a corner or up against a doorway, bemoaning their disarrayed skirts and petticoats with racing, thumping hearts as hands burrowed beneath their clothes. There were whores too, of course, sick and tired, by midnight or one in the morning, of touting their services and shifting from one foot to the other on a street corner without turning the slightest trick, who likewise came to watch us turning out our lights and throwing tarpaulins over our contraptions, to have us buy them a *fine,* a brandy, and to laugh with us—their pals, their little brothers—and when they were down in the mouth, and hadn't the courage to go back on the job, and if someone took their fancy and nostalgia for a shared embrace took hold of them, they would say to hell with it, and we would go off and paint the town red, spending our week's pay and they their takings from the day before, sharing like good friends, until four or five and daybreak. We toured all the bistros, tippling on after closing time with the drapes drawn and the boss duly paying his round, chewing the fat with would-be hard men, pimps, guys with fake tattoos, small-time burglars, and gaudily dressed queens who deigned to raise a glass with us but never got too friendly, the idiots, because for them we were not emancipated—not "that way," but just exploited, and then we would go and bed the girls, make them really happy, they put heart and cunt into it and the excitement lasted until long past dawn, we could hear one another and we called back and forth between one room and the next. And the next day, a bit green about the gills, it was back to work, to the shittiest part of the job, checking the motors, about which I knew precious little, and cleaning up the ride, which I did holding my nose.

The liveliest bistro in that neighborhood now is old François's place, which some nights seems like a genuine seamen's dive, a distinctly odd thing despite Paris's obvious(?) resemblance to an ocean port. It is a *musette,* a dance bar where, since the war, sailors on the ran-tan end up along with soldiers on leave and the last tough guys from the Butte Montmartre and nearby areas. You reach the dance floor through swinging doors and the atmosphere is truly that of a western, with

fights breaking out regularly between Legionnaires and United States Navy types, nor are the fisticuffs artificial: glassware shatters, girls scream, bodies fall and spring back up, the spectators do not retreat an inch, the boss calls the cops, and the occasional firecracker goes off—a free show in which you participate fully, heart thumping and reflexes in an uproar, but no harm done, just everyday mayhem. Most evenings are calm, though, just so long as everyone obeys the unwritten rules: keep to your own spot, be minimally polite, do not step on your neighbor's toes or blow smoke in the face of the person opposite or send your fellow-drinker's glass flying. The whores are quiet and favor a seated posture, advertising their charms by purely vocal means, challenging the general apathy of the male customers with strictly respectable gestures, and confining themselves to the traditional wake-up call: "So, nobody fucks here any more?"—though this tends to be uttered startlingly during lulls in the conversation. In short, a great little place. Across the street, an accordionist stirs dreams of escape, while brief inspection fails to distinguish whores from housemaids and girls out on the town, which can be confusing.

THREE

I

FIRST, eat.

But how? How to come by substantial nourishment if all one has to offer in exchange is a tenacious albeit quite normal hunger? How, when you find yourself at the curbside trying to decide where to go? How?

2

I'M HUNGRY.

Around me the world turns, the landscape is the wheel, the streets are the spokes, and I am bound to the hub, a pathetic puppet in all likelihood being broken on that wheel, pilloried.

Hunger makes you seasick.

As night falls, I navigate the city. There is no storm, but a swell that is much worse. A soft, regular undulation that makes me nauseous. Ahead of me the roadway rises slowly, interminably, seems to hesitate for a moment, then descends just as gently, indefinitely. To negotiate the downslope, I must alternately lift my foot and thrust it forward, and I bungle this every time. I am looking for a safe place, a port to lay up in, some little *impasse* whose end would bring me up short and offer refuge. But in the city a cul-de-sac is a rarity, almost a miracle. At night Paris is a warren, the streets are infinite, endless, they proliferate, grow longer, merge and interpenetrate, shrink and widen as if viewed through opera glasses, or meet at sharp angles, even right angles, constituting a vast trelliswork, a tangled scaffolding of iron tubes laid flat on the ground. Paris by night is a labyrinth where every street opens onto another or onto one of the boulevards so aptly described as arteries—a labyrinth through which I make my way in fits and starts, like a blood clot, jolting down the steepest inclines, emerging from bottlenecks into empty space. And so I go, walking, plunging, flowing—a river hoping somehow to debouch into the sea, haven of peace and freedom from care. But that is impossible, for there are only junctions, intersections, forks, everywhere tributaries, right and left, upstream or down, everywhere identical borders clearly marked and impassive, unaffected by the nagging progression of the streets. I sink into the night like a child's paper boat on a stream, I am tossed this way and that, my ankles are stuck, my legs weaken, give way, hollow out, I lose my footing, all I have left are my arms to move me forward, I am drowning silently, descending in my dream into the parallel watery maze of the sewers that wend their way beneath my own route.

Just me—and the hunger that gnaws at me tonight.

How do you eat in Paris—at least one hot meal a day? How do you manage it when you are broke, homeless or dossing in an attic without gas and electricity, and if you want to avoid the hellish round of shelters, soup kitchens, infirmaries, charitable organizations dispensing more pious words than good bread and demanding their due in advance in the shape of hymn singing and sweeping up? How, when you clearly cannot afford the metro and hitchhiking is impossible in the city except at those rare times, at night, when the trucks and carts are headed for or leaving Les Halles? How to get to the farthest reaches of outer neighborhoods to knock at the door of some pal for whom hospitality is still a sacred principle? Just how? Rack your brains as you might, open your eyes and stare at the ground, nurture pipe dreams or swear under your breath to your heart's content, nothing will be of any use, you might as well give up and let fate provide.

It is at night that hunger catches you off guard. The daytime offers distractions, encourages social encounters, stirs curiosity, whereas solitude, silence, relative inaction, and exhaustion from walking fast bring to mind the inappropriate (or is it?) fantasy of sitting peacefully on an imitation-leather banquette with a glass of red or a sandwich, a hard-boiled egg, a basket of croissants—comfort and nourishment that is extremely expensive considering how few calories it provides—and other appetizers (another outrageous word!) suggestively placed in the middle of the table by the waiter. As he plies the sidewalks in search of cigarette butts, the vagabond not yet fully prepared for a state of affairs

that he may or may not have chosen is continually plagued by such imaginings.

In Paris hunger takes on monstrous proportions because victuals (an atrocious term—it sounds so much like vitals) may be sensed behind every wall, seen through every window, piled up, arranged, labeled, or else scattered, abandoned, spoilt. A main pole of attraction for someone beset by hunger are the menus posted in restaurant windows; they catch your eye from far away, from the other side of the street, wielding a magnetic power that rivets you to their perusal, to a deliberately slow reading of these veritable poems—pure, living, visceral poetry whose words and expressions speak not to the soul but to the stomach, whose rhythms stimulate not so much the gray matter as the marrow of the bones and the gastric juices, and whose reading aloud, so far from striking chords of illusion, precipitates mouthwatering activity by the salivary glands.

You are surprised to hear yourself say the words "I'm hungry" aloud, because they become an expression, a trio of syllables, an onomatopoeia whose meaning is ephemeral, unintelligible—a foreign vocable whose meaning can be found only in the dictionary of memory (this is the facticity of ordinary language).

But, once you have deliberately chosen this kind of existence, this modus vivendi, once you have said screw it once and for all to the future and pooh-poohed your old-age pension (along with work at the conveyor belt, a forty-eight-hour work week, plus the dishes, the do-it-yourself projects about the house, weekend family leisure activities, premature wrinkles and nothing seen of the world, or of girls aside from the concierge's daughter, and, at retirement, a two-room rental flat with your own furniture, and tremulous and halitotic games of belote, until they bury you, along with the life you might have led, like a stillborn calf), then, obviously, you have no right to whine about being hungry, for the rules are the rules, so whenever I am tempted to complain I keep my trap shut, withhold comment, shun the company of the well-nourished, and fall into step with pals who know the score but who likewise talk only of other things. Which said, in the vast bordello of the capital there are those who die of hunger who have never been consulted, who could not care less about the joys of freedom and tramping, who have for their part wagered on work well done rewarded by a life of ease (the ease of the grave, more like!), those whose demise we learn of from a quick scan of winter newspaper filler—old men and old women dying all alone in indescribable squalor or eaten alive by rats on a rusty bed (and I am not even thinking of the derelicts, Arabs, and old folks in homes paying five or six hundred francs a day for the right to chow and bed), all those who are doomed from the start—from the day of their birth!—and who know it, and can count the days left to them, having no chance at all of escaping, or even of playing for time, of wangling so much as an extra week. Nor are they always old. And then there are those who prefer to end it all, hidden away somewhere, or else on the metro tracks, driven by a surge of naïve rebellion, hoping at least to hold up the trains. They hold up zilch. Normal service is resumed right away, and the trains are up and running.

3

I'M DYING of hunger, he was screaming.

The theaters were emptying. The man was shouting in the middle of the street, bearded and wearing a short jacket, in the pouring rain. I am starving. Oh! Give me something so I can eat. The "Oh!" cut me to the quick. He was not addressing anybody in particular as he wobbled back and forth. I'm hungry! He moaned, wept, begged, sniffled, coughed, then shouted again, screamed again. People scurried for the metro, for a taxi. They had no idea whether he was drunk or sincere. They simply avoided him. I'm hungry! He did not take his hands out of his pockets. At the end of the street, all the same, they turned to look at him before they disappeared. The man continued to stagger, a phantom-like figure albeit so close, a siren of distress piercing the fog. No sooner did he brush against a group or a couple than his appeal scattered them, tore them apart, the women hastening their step, the men turning their backs. From an entire theater audience piling into the street not a single twenty-franc piece was forthcoming: the bourgeois loves to show charity, but it has to be asked for politely, and discreetly—you must sit up on your hind legs and beg, not create an abominable scene like this on a public thoroughfare and ruin such an otherwise delightful evening. How perfectly dreadful, my dear! Why don't they put a stop to this sort of thing, darling? Give me something so I can eat! Oh, I'm so hungry! He could barely stand. His litany was ever more monotonous. I was stricken. I had heard that same voice in a German prison from a man, stark naked like me, running up and down in front of me with a chalkboard eraser jammed in his mouth yet still able to scream: "Kill me. Oh, kill me!"

That "Oh!" stays with me in the depths of the night. I have never reached that hunger-induced delusional state in which the stomach climbs into the brain and devours it. The crowd was clearing out now. There I was, stuck center-stage, unable, being broke myself, to do anything, incapable of coming up with some kind of scheme, wanting to flee, to abandon him, but rooted to the spot. He did not see me, indeed saw nobody, and went on bawling his malediction to the heavens, a malediction that had my flesh crawling for days, and kept me from feeling my own hunger. Where is he now?

But that man must surely have ended up mad. Driven mad by his own long exposure to an asocial form of life: the daily, desperate quest for bad food—too much drink offered and too much nourishment withheld—and a carefully nurtured hate for the wealth on display so close by, coupled with the masochism of indigence. Because...

4

...BECAUSE, in Paris, if you are not going to starve, you need a number of assets: an open mind, an ever-curious eye, a sharp ear, a hound's nose, a fleet foot, and a certain contempt for private property—in short, the vagabond's usual baggage. One does not immediately appreciate just how little food is required to sustain a life on the edge. The whole trick is, in winter, to have a bowl of hot soup and a piece of bread every day, the rest of one's nourishment being made up of a relatively meager amount of various and unpredictable items whose very heterogeneity usually ensures that the vitamin requirements defined by science are met. A great many armchair adventurers keep the sluggish rhythms of their carcasses active by consuming nothing more than steaming hot Maggi bouillon, four or five times a day, and dunking crusts of bread into it. I am thinking especially of all the youngsters in their little intellectual's digs—brothels of ratiocination where they hole up to jerk off and get stupid together in the contemplation of the basic truths. None of which prevents life from flourishing among them—far from it! They may be found sprinkled all along the Seine, overlooking three kilometers of quays. Or buried in the old districts of the Left Bank, nesting like swallows beneath thousands of roofs in identical maids' rooms with no running water save that in the WC on the half-landing, no ventilation save that from a prison-like skylight, no space other than that, precisely, of a cell, all with the same bookshelves built of crates, the same camp bed with a ragged coverlet tossed over it, the same bric-à-brac of old metal utensils, the makeshift camping gear, and the same décor of photos cut out from *Life* or postcard reproductions of modern paintings. I have slept in countless dumps of

this kind, legally or illegally, moving in and moving out, bouncing from one to another with no recollection of what made one different from the next. And I learned to appreciate the irreplaceable value of tea, drunk in such places by the liter (whereas ordering such a libation in an ordinary bistro would be sure to raise any waiter's eyebrow), accompanied or not by baguettes, and I found that you ended up none the worse for wear, meaning that you were ushered into a kind of embryonic life perfectly suited to the working out and discussion of metaphysical problems at the cost of only relative inconveniences, such as an aesthetic leanness or, alternatively, a corpulence caused by fatty anemia. All it takes is the luck to have found, bought or borrowed some kind of little stove, made the inevitable sacrifices needed to supply it with fuel, and formed a few smart ideas about gastronomy.

Among these youngsters, however, and I tip my hat to them, were some whose "means of support" were quite special. One such was Élie, who lived in a flat as ancient and austere as the old spinster it belonged to. I would go there to kip from time to time, sneaking in, because the old dear would never have understood that at my age I might have no money or work, being certain that I procured both just like Élie, who she believed worked in some company or other and who naturally had no desire to disillusion her, so I was supposed to creep in after eleven, when she had gone to bed, and leave before six in the morning, when she got up, with the inevitable result—given my indolent nature and my great appreciation for the real bed that I was sharing with Élie— being that I did not always awake in time, nor was I loath to spend the day there and remain until the next morning, taking the opportunity to wash from head to toe, shave, and browse in the books, living my life in slow motion for that day as I took several minutes to cross the room, turned pages with infinite caution as though reading incunabula made of lace, and glided about like a fish in a tank until Élie's return vouchsafed me greater freedom of movement, though I still had to communicate with him by means of grimaces or scribbled notes. Happily Élie had some records, which broke the irritating silence. At the time he was approaching thirty, but he could not remember ever having lived on anything but random foods notable far more for their low commercial

rather than high calorific value, especially the canned apple sauce that
had seen him through a good part of the war years and "Maltymel," a
sort of thick brown syrup with a dubious and quickly cloying taste
that had the economically advantageous effect of limiting his consumption; now he too was on bouillon cubes, whose multifarious in-
gredients kept the motor turning over comfortably enough—and all
washed down with plain sugarless tea, that universal beverage whose
taste you forget by drinking so much of it. Not so, though, at Blagatoff's place. Another likeable lunatic, but much older, who lived in a
smelly hutch in the leatherworkers' district, Blagatoff taught me how
to brew Tibetan-style tea, which he had been drinking exclusively
since the previous postwar period, and he was in the pink of health.
This tea, bitter and black, was boiled for the longest time and enriched
with a pinch of coarse salt and a pat of margarine, the prime purpose
of this being to impress visitors, though in the long run it turned out
to be highly nutritious. Blagatoff himself had the curious habit of
haunting food stores, which according to him (and he was a lettered
man) were the antechambers of paradise, and he took a perverse pleasure in entering such shops on the pretext (which seemed obvious to
the shopkeeper but which was in fact secondary to him) of begging for
scraps of food or spare change: he would use every ruse in the book to
loiter as long as possible, wandering up and down, looking, examining,
inhaling, sniffing, and reveling in all kinds of smells—rollmops, sauer-
kraut, smoked hams hung up by the trotter, giant loaves of rye bread,
herrings in oil, various trans-Alpine cold cuts, and prepared dishes—
with no particular concern about being tossed out without anything
to show for it under his arm or in his pocket, leaving with a blissful
smile on his face, delighted to have thus rehearsed a meal. At first I
strongly suspected him of pinching small food items, but not at all. He
told me that looking in windows did not satisfy him, because, more
than mere contemplation, his olfactory sense—he called it "nasal"—
was what nourished and gratified him. Life led him, you might say, by
the nose.

But the most highly prized foodstuff among those who eat almost
nothing is unquestionably rolled oats—"Quaker Oats" to those in the

THE MERITS OF TEA · 141

know—whose cost, no more than small change, and ability to expand and become very filling when cooked, makes it truly precious, and it has the added advantage that it can be prepared in a host of ways, for example with salt, with sugar, with nothing, with garlic, with onions, with clear broth, with meat broth, with tea, with plain water, with rice water, with noodle water, with crusts of bread, with vermicelli (luxury), with red pepper (ditto), with margarine, or with ground meat (slap-up feast).

5

IT IS A cliché to say that Les Halles is the belly of Paris, but it is not fully understood that the place really does fill the guts of a whole horde of people, that it is a magnet for all the diurnal and nocturnal bums who come there to glean fragments of nourishment—scraps, trimmings and discards quite invisible to the eye of the wholesale or retail grocer stepping on them or of the city worker sweeping them up, yet source of life and bodily warmth for so many old men and women clinging in bunches from the municipal street cleaners' carts and picking through piles of refuse where only the odd poignant orange retains any luster....

Like all fellows of my calling, which is that of having no trade, that of the good-for-nothing and the ready-for-anything, I once worked in Les Halles: hands freezing cold and eyes stinging, at an hour when ordinary cafés were closing and turfing out their customers, I used to cross the Pont des Arts footbridge or the Pont Neuf (I was living at the time in Rue des Canettes, in a tiny room with a cot for a bed, no window except for a murky transom above the door and not so much as a pitcher for water to wash with), reach the toiling Right Bank, go and drink endless black coffees at the counter of the Pied de Cochon and watch the well-heeled coming in, after parking their cars outside, and climbing the stairs to the second floor with good-time girls in tow to eat steaming crusty onion soup that cost three times as much as it did at sidewalk level where I was, playing the night's first game of 421 with head washers in stained smocks and aprons who came in to clean off coagulated blood and savor dry white wine before going back to turn powerful jets of water on the bones, still covered with flesh, of animals whose fate it was to become delectable charcuterie.

After they left, I in my turn would walk through those great railroad-station-like hangars as giant trucks unloaded vegetables—almost two in the morning by now—till I reached the stall of Mustapha the Turkish banana merchant who employed me as a weigher and checker, and there till morning I wrestled crates and display tables and bunches of bananas from the stores where they had been ripening and weighed great tottering mounds of them on a scale that when I climbed on it myself barely moved. Sometimes, instead of making a two-hourly visit to Fauveau's, once it was finally open, there to drink one *café-crème* after another, laced or not depending on the boss's humor, I would go to Rue Berger and make a sign to the cashier at the chicken-and-egg seller's, who always managed to find a replacement for a quarter of an hour, time enough to meet me in the stairwell of the house next door where I fucked her standing up without so much as loosening my belt and she with her skirt hiked around her waist, which she liked, and she would slip me a cheese or a few eggs to build my strength back up and stave off the pangs till my next official mealtime, which was ten o'clock, when I got off work and was free and easy till the next night and would go to Place des Deux-Écus and treat myself to an enormous steak with all the trimmings that cost the better part of my day's pay and smoked a de luxe cigarette before setting off to beg door to door at all the friendly café-bars thereabouts, especially those in the vicinity of Rue Saint-Denis, in the company of fellow down-and-outs from the derelict throngs around the Square des Innocents—a name that so aptly describes these denizens of the place, wandering among the sacks of potatoes and piled-up boxes much as their historical predecessors wandered centuries ago under the arcades, between the columns and beneath the wooden balconies of the Cemetery of the Holy Innocents, oblivious to the fearsomely vile stink of prodigious piles of human remains, dirty-gray entanglements eroded by rain and rodents, like conglomerations of crisscrossed pirate weaponry, or like dry firewood—and indeed they gathered the bones up and tied them into faggots of tibias and femurs to make comforting, warming, blistering flames—joyful fires that they built upon nice round skulls (so leading Rabelais to remark that Paris was a good town to live in but not to die in, for "the starvelings of Sainct-Innocent warm their asses with the bones of the dead"); those transient yet ever-proliferating folk still found ways to hold out their begging-bowls and cry poverty to the gentlemen, merchants and fancy women who came by in the evening to take the air, for the Square was much frequented then, and the living must have smelled barely more fragrant than the dead, with the ladies' frippery, rumpled and plundered in the shadows, exuding warm, aphrodisiac animal odors that excited male escorts quite unaffected by the sweet rot enriching the earth around them, or by the naive and cruel fresco of the Dance of the Dead so close by. (It was here some time later that a tender-hearted soul named Fradin, most likely a retired shit-sniffer living off his rents, set up a sort of "hotel," according to the old books, where guests slept all in a row with their backsides on old sacks and their feet sticking out onto the cobblestones and the napes of their necks resting on a cord stretched taut a few inches above the ground, which at the crack of dawn the wily hostel-keeper undid, thus causing a general collapse of heads and putting an abrupt if not too painful end to the dreams of his guests. . . .)

Later on, no longer employed in Les Halles but living nearby, I holed up like so many others in an abandoned back room, a choice, cheap hideaway I found in the bowels of a wholesaler's shop in Rue Saint-Honoré, for the neighborhood as a whole had no solid base, and resembled a great perforated basket, each building secreting within its walls a mysterious labyrinth leading to God-knew-what cellars, sewers or catacombs, and every shop on the street being more of an antechamber than the usual cube with no back exit, so that by pulling aside a rough curtain or moving a pile of empty boxes one found one or more passages leading off into obscurity, descending and narrowing, getting darker and darker, dirtier and dirtier, and more and more cluttered by piles of loose masonry, fallen earth and stray objects that had survived the passage of time and now jostled one another and accumulated like silt; the walls of these tunnels, as beams and architectural features

diminished, tended to retreat abruptly from the groping hand or eye, and extreme caution was advisable when making one's way through such mazes, which owners preferred not to know about, where strange mineral and vegetable odors of humus, fungi, verdigris, saltpeter, rotting flowers and damp earth flared the nostrils and invaded the throat, while candles provided but a feeble, vaguely worrisome and usually unwavering glow, and it was best to stop in good time and give up any hope of discovering the causes of such speleological wonders, for, lacking chalk, string or wire ladder, you were liable to get lost, go round in circles, batter at the walls, panic, split your lips or bang your head on stalactites, fall with your heart in your mouth into pits, snares and booby-traps, you would scratch yourself, sweat, try to keep calm, piss, call out, laugh hysterically, wring your hands and rack your brains, pummel your memory, call upon your primal sense of direction, only to end up sitting, waiting, fighting hunger and thirst, gently fading, long after striking your last match, huddling, rolling up into a ball, shrinking, crumbling, letting flesh and bone rejoin the mineral, the geological realm.

As for me, I was living, eating, sleeping and dreaming on a heap of sacks of potatoes, having spent my entire fortune on illumination, venturing out only to scavenge and take the air, each time passing the employees and proprietor of the shop, who gave me vegetables or oranges but clapped palm to forehead behind me as I left. It was here too that my friends, who had digs just like mine or were the proud owners of shadowy corners of this providential quarter, came to visit me, slithering like worms through the gaping holes and cracks that rent all the façades of the block.

One autumn evening we indulged in an orgy that was quite fabulous, albeit peaceful and indeed devoid of the sensuous pleasures of fornication, for we were all men, with only rats and bats for company. I had won a little dough in the lottery, a tenth prize paying out ten francs on a ticket bought at a stand at the Foire du Trône, and for fear of seeming ungenerous my fellow bums had come up with a host of inspired ideas, contrived the most artful dodges, saved up for days on end, and striven to outdo one another in stratagems designed to provide for

this now famous blowout, and if possible buy out an entire butcher's shop, or at least send two of the more presentable members of our company off, armed with capacious shopping baskets, to requisition (*sic*) meat, poultry, cold cuts, and drink, the results being more impressive in terms of quantity than of quality: a ton of food of every variety which we consumed in about twenty-four hours by virtue of rapid, eclectic, and joyful ingestion followed by slow, massive, and dolorous digestion. All this took place by the smoky and eclipse-prone light of glowing embers, with us reclining on our sides Roman style, stuffing ourselves likewise Roman style, and likewise ready to withdraw to the fringes of the darkness to empty our stomachs one way or another. Eventually, one by one, we sank down replete, swollen, hiccupping, hands crossed over rumbling bellies, seeing stars above them, imagining a breath of fresh air, and listening to oaths, and to the burps and farts of bestial satisfaction, to the accompaniment of a young fellow playing the harmonica.

Those were the days.

But memories butter no parsnips, and now that I was a citified tramp in quest of the two things essential to the welfare of any honest man, namely food and lodging, it was time to bestir myself.

6

NATURALLY, Les Halles affords endless opportunities for the semi-systematic application of the hustler's art. Pilfering is known to go on if not seen to go on by one and all, the theft of fish being the prime example. It is simplicity itself to slip a crate off a hand-truck being whisked along through the general hustle and bustle and vanish with it at top speed but as cool as a cucumber. Around eight o'clock, just outside the market's pavilions, hefty women round up savvy housewives, bargain hunters, fanatical pennypinchers, and clever clogs, drawing them into a corner, opening a large shopping basket for the rapidly formed knot of buyers and displaying a mass of denizens of the deep, mostly unidentifiable at first sight, then offloading against hundred-franc notes two or three plaice or a couple of sea bream glittering with ice and scales. It has to be done quickly. An old biddy stands ready to signal with a nudge or a shout any sudden appearance of a suspicious trenchcoat or less-than-friendly uniform. Time to hop it. The shopping basket is closed and the rogue fishwife scuttles away, much to the distress of a lady customer who has paid up but received no fish, and the whole group takes off like flocking pigeons, navigating between endless counters before recongregating further away, the circle closing once more and the woman making up her day's take. Sometimes, though, the seller is a Kabyle or a youthful market porter stationed in a passageway, who, lacking the women's chutzpah and patter, is reduced to gesturing, whistling and showing his fishy wares at a distance after pulling them from his pocket. Habitués of the market floor and hangars are no longer surprised by this, and they close their eyes to it. Many a time the fish comes from a crate unfortunately (or fortunately) set down far away from a stack, or dropped and burst open, its contents slithering silently all around before being grabbed by the swiftest fingers. None of this proceeds without its perils, without shouting matches or the exchange of blows, but everyone has to eat and it is the work of an instant to escape into the throng, or even from the grip of a policeman, leaving him holding the corpus delicti, which will still never be returned to its true owner.

7

BUT YOU always come back to the same old question: how are you going to eat? At those times of day when Les Halles is abandoned, deserted, deathly sad, all the houses seem to have been abandoned too, and the great flat sidewalks become too long to go up and down once the road traffic from a different world reasserts its rights of way and forces you to take special precautions. But how are you going to eat once you find yourself at the other end of Paris and the cold makes you acutely aware of your need of a hot meal before you can steel yourself for a night under the bridges?

The hungry man's steps lead him unconsciously to places where food is distributed, and if not to Les Halles he is drawn to the markets that are dotted in sufficient number around the city, some open even in the afternoon. Here there is always something to be scavenged by anyone who keeps their eyes open and knows how to bend discreetly and snatch up whatever has fallen or overflowed onto the ground, and I say discreetly because one is well advised not to attract too much attention from the shopping housewives, and even less from the fruit-and-vegetable ladies, with their quite unpredictable reactions—perhaps waspish, perhaps sympathetic—but more likely to call you "Filthy beggar!" than say "Go ahead, kid, it's yours." But in the words of Le Berger, the Shepherd, who used to go with me to the souks of "La Mouffe"—the vicinity of Rue Mouffetard—what the hell did we care? The only thing that mattered was getting a bite to eat. Here we are, the two of us, as, at five or six o'clock in the evening, the stalls exploding with light, their canopies almost converging above the heads of the barely moving mass of shoppers in the street. This is the finest market in Paris. The

liveliest, the most intimate, the highest in color, and the cheapest—
not least for those who come hands in pockets and eyes trained on the
ground. The Shepherd is stuffing his finds into his beggar's bag. I walk
behind him chuckling contentedly, for I have just come by the best
tramping companion I could ever wish for. I have no idea what he
thinks of me, but for the last eight days and nights I have been lost in
admiration for his extraordinary vagabond's talents. With a guy like
this, I could just go with the flow, but his exploits spur me to hurry and
display my own alimentary survival skills. What's more, his appearance charms me. Tall, lean, lithe, clad in a superb goatskin as hairy and
smelly as could be desired, and sporting a soft felt hat—very soft, in
fact, its shape altering with every change in the weather. I could not
help calling him the Shepherd when I first met him in one of the last
remaining Arab bistros of Rue des Charrettes in Rouen, and, since the
nickname gave him a simple pleasure by burnishing his image of himself as a maverick intellectual, it stuck. We are a pair. But since neither
of us has neglected our other relationships on that account, we are also
part of a solid team, none of whose members could ever die of starvation or freeze to death, a crew of young crocks, and this has allowed us
all to kip for a time in that aforementioned maid's room in Les Gobelins, rented and paid for, God knows how, at eight hundred francs a
month, a room sadly big enough to sleep only three at a time, obliging
two or three of us to find shelter elsewhere unless we are ready to take
turns.

So here we are, doing our shopping. Truth to tell, and it is hardly
surprising, there are few luxury food items to be found along the sidewalks and under the display stands, but then quantity interests us
more than quality; at the end of the day, meaning after two or three
return trips up and down Rue Mouffetard and a rather fruitless visit to
winding sidestreets worthy of Nice, when we go down to take stock of
our haul on a bench on Square Saint-Médard, we are able to confirm
once again that vegetables are far more abundant than fruit. As for
meat, it is of course conspicuous by its absence. But thanks to the Shepherd's wholesome demeanor, his winning, dignified smile, Albert the

FOOD! YOU CAN'T BEAT IT!" · 153

butcher can be counted on for our daily ration of beef bones, where-withal for a passable *pot-au-feu*.

But biting into and chewing endless pink escapees from bunches of radishes, like gleaning stray cherries, new carrots, green apricots, peas in the pod, overripe tomatoes, and so on, can only serve as a tasty com-plement to one's ordinary fare, which for its part is best obtained by begging directly from wholesale and retail grocers. Most of these, of course, are just plain chiselers (to put it politely) sitting on their fat asses behind a cash register like croaking toads, their throats wide open and ready to gobble up enough fodder and shekels to burst their belts, their faces split by great predatory grins; and they are liable to turn suddenly into royal assholes and expel and rough up any brazen intruder driven to enter by the irresistible magnetism of foodstuff. These are the self-same individuals who swell with self-importance when you run into them in Les Halles, having long forgotten their dic-ing days as menials and renounced all unnecessary expenditures (such as standing a pal a drink) and making sure to breakfast on nothing more than a single dunked croissant in the early morning. But fortu-nately there are others too, the big-hearted fat ones, the gin-blossomed, the jocular, the alive, the young couples, the I've-been-there types— those who, despite the endless parade of credentialed spongers and charity collectors armed with counterfoiled receipt books, always manage, a quarter of an hour before closing up, to find something a poor devil can get his teeth into: ends and fat parts of hams and pâtés, furry *petits suisses*, bulging cans, refreshing handfuls of lettuce, with some merchants going so far as to clamber up a wobbly pile of crates to get old packets of crumbling crackers and cookies, outdated bottles of fruit juice or pre-war sample boxes of noodles, rice, breakfast cereal, or varieties of semolina (all obviously unsalable, but after all it's the ges-ture that counts). So little as a touch of *savoir-vivre* or genuine polite-ness can at times elicit the words "Come back now and again, my boy, there'll always be a bit of something for you." You might even be treated to a specific appointment for your next visit.

Of course, such big-hearted grocers tend to be a good way away, few and far between, and are usually located near the city's gates. And the competition is fierce: beginners from Nanterre in the west, bums and beggars in the center, out-of-work in the north, provincial tramps in the south. And nuns everywhere. Nuns seeking alms, at once austere and sickly sweet, demanding their due, shamelessly toting enormous wicker baskets as they extract charity for their old people, their indigent, their orphans, their flock, their communities, and never satisfied no matter how great the giver's good will.

I carry no torch for nuns, particularly those, the majority, who have succumbed not to faith but instead to their neuroses, whether physical, mental or hereditary in origin, or who have been driven into the convent by a flat face, a squint, a pointy nose, a hare-lip, a short stature, or a mustache, and cling to this latent, embryonic form of life, and eventually get to like it, experiencing the dubious delights of masochism and savoring other rare and allegedly more subtle pleasures. But I have to admit that some of them, having reached their change of life and kept their minds clear despite all the flimflam, have a good head on their shoulders, much influence, earthy diction, expressive gestures, their heart on their sleeve, one hell of a supply of generosity and, excuse my French, a serious pair of balls on them. You should see them careening through Les Halles well before first light, juggling with their seaman's bags and shamelessly grabbing anything more or less edible that comes to hand. Or at the meat market of La Villette, which they enter as if they owned the place and, ignoring the cries of the animals, make their way through the gore, calmly paddling in it, the three layers of their habits hitched up above their knees, their calves sticky with clotted blood, bent over, solid as peasant women as they plunge hands and wrists into the revolting mire, raking through it with fingers widespread to grasp hold of floating fragments of meat, stray organs, guts, offal, collecting the kind of fleshy refuse that would turn the stomach of the most hardened, popping their haul briskly into the bag slung over their shoulders, leaving murky furrows behind them and retorting tit-for-tat to the gross comments of the livestock dealers and slaughterers while seemingly oblivious to the terrible gong-like clang from just a few meters away that signals the end of a bovine life of contemplative

cud-chewing, oblivious too to the flashing of the knives used to slash the throats of the sheep on the conveyor belts; once their work is done, they wade back again before leaving the place and getting into a sort of small paddy wagon with a male driver awaiting them at the entrance. You have to wonder—forget about psychoanalysis—just what their dreams must be like (a domain God surely has little to do with—less, if possible, than any other): who knows whether they are ghastly or poetic, bloodthirsty or mystical?

Aside from soup kitchens and bread lines, charity hospitals and shelters, the patronizing of which is a vicious cycle, a hellish round, a practice fit strictly for those on the run, and one bound by timetables, which I really don't like, my stomach making demands incompatible with regular mealtimes (even if, during bad-luck weeks, I have no choice but to conform); and hidden away somewhere in every Paris neighborhood, if you know how to find them, are various adequate holes-in-the-wall where (in 1952) you can stuff your face for under a hundred francs (which is their chief merit, otherwise you would be better off buying scraps from the pork butcher or prepared food from the cheap places that sell it), including a soup—the foundation, whatever the stuffed shirts may think, of human nutrition. Every time the Shepherd dipped his spoon into a bowl of soup he would smile beatifically and cry, "Food! You can't beat it!"

(I normally pay no mind to what they call heredity, but there is no denying that my mother and father were of peasant stock, which must have given me the passionate love and great respect I have for soup, the deprivation of which to me is a catastrophe, as likewise for bread cut up into little cubes, while my favorite lunch is a chunk of rye bread and a piece of fatback in one hand and a knife in the other, generally dubbed a vulgar way of eating.)

Among cheap eating places I do not include student joints, where you get rubbish and pay a pretty high price for it, and from which the hirsute and those carrying knapsacks are excluded. Not so at the little poor people's lunchrooms or *bouillons* that pepper the area north of Les Halles, a mysterious section crisscrossed by streets named Greneta, Dussoubs, Marie-Stuart (paradoxically, a nest of bums!), and above all

Rue Tiquetonne, site of the Boeuf Gros Sel and the Bon Bouillon, dark, low-ceilinged communal dining rooms (the like of which I have never come across elsewhere save in a dead end behind the Place du Marché in Rouen), where poor men chew and swallow in complete silence amidst the metallic clinking of knives and forks and the general muffled hubbub, for each is there for himself and taken up by his own deadly serious business. The only chatter consists in the exchange of grumbles and formulas of politeness, but every time I go to eat there I wish I had a recording device to capture and save this soup-kitchen clatter with its scraps of conversation, as for instance this exchange between two sometime table companions of mine, one a dignified gent with a wing collar and a pince-nez on a black string, grease-stained sleeves but signet rings on his fingers, who when addressing his neighbor said words to the effect of "Pardon me, my good friend, but would you be so good as to pass me the pepper and salt?" only to hear the reply, "Get them yourself, you cunt, and salt and pepper your asshole!"

I have observed a couple of cases of gourmandism in these places: guys who have somehow earned, begged, borrowed or stolen the princely sum of one or two thousand-franc notes and come in there to blow the money, eating for two hours at table, taking every dish four or five times, putting the food away at great speed, leaving their fellow diners stunned, and not the least envious, downing liter after liter of red without batting an eye, and eventually falling asleep replete, bloated, content of soul, dead to the world, thighs spread wide, head on hands, burping and snoring, and the body, far more active than the brain, digesting voluptuously. A body that has in the end to be dragged outside and laid on a hand-truck so that the room can be swept.

I used to take it easy on Rue Tiquetonne every morning (lunch is served early, at ten or eleven o'clock) after spending the night at the Hôtel des Vosges, Gallopain's place nearby on the corner of Rue Dussoubs, and later sip wine for short spells in the surrounding bistros—the Diable Vert, frequented by North African market porters, the Vélocipède on Rue Turbigo, and especially an empty establishment where for the longest time I was the sole customer. And when I didn't have the eighty francs needed for a decent meal, I could always deploy a host of money-raising tricks on the sidewalk outside the door, and in any case my pantry, Les Halles, was just a stone's throw away. A clochard's paradise.

FOUR

I

A CLOCHARD'S paradise. It is impossible to die from lack of sleep here, for places to doss and hideaways are legion. Every nook or cranny can do duty as shelter, refuge, home, and legal abode, freely accessible to those who, precisely, live a sewer rat's solitary life in the labyrinth of jammed-in, cramped, curtailed, crooked spaces lying "under the roofs of Paris." (Such a cliché, of course. But who really knows what marvels are there? Certainly not those who talk with such authority, or write, make and see the classic films, who propagate the worn-out myth and go into raptures over the lyricism of wretched shopgirls, the *vie de bohème*, and the romantic literature of Fantômas or Arsène Lupin lifting off roof tiles as easily as saucepan lids.) All these hidey-holes are quite impossible for the stroller below to detect by simply walking down the street and looking up in the air. First of all you must have a vital need, you must be obsessed with four walls and a ceiling, with securing shelter from the weather while at the same time refusing barracks-style cohabitation. You have to sneak like a burglar past a concierge's lodge, climb a staircase ever so quietly to the top of the building, try the doors of storage rooms and glory holes until one of them opens, which one always does eventually because these places are rarely locked with a key. Who knows, however, how many attempts you must make, how many "insalubrious pockets"* you must reconnoiter, how many branching staircases and intersecting hallways you must survey, how many wearisome or dangerous climbs undertake and how many explanations concoct for the tenants you encounter? But, also, how many extraordinary discoveries you will make.

---

* "*Îlots insalubres*": so described by officialdom.—*Trans.*

2

CONSIDER the Grenier de Maléfices, the "Attic of Evil Spells," renowned throughout the neighborhood of Rue de la Huchette.

Across the way from Hôtel La Belle-Étoile on Rue Xavier-Privas are two or three old houses whose attics are deemed unfit for habitation under the law, this to the great distress of the landlord, who can extract no profit from them. Once on the third floor, you leave behind the grand tile and plaster stairwell with its magnificent wooden handrail and mount a second staircase leading up below the rafters—six narrow steps, lethal for a drunk—then go down a passageway less than a meter wide, whose ceiling forces your head and shoulders down towards your belly and almost obliges you to crawl, which brings you to a closed door with no apparent lock or handles that you must open with your shoulder. And there you are in the attic: three square meters of country floor tiles, once red, and ten cubic meters of crowded space with four, five or six long-term residents of every kind, two army camp beds miraculously hauled up there one happy day, three piles of bedding on top of which the orange of a sleeping bag suggests some sumptuous fabric. The campers are local Turks, Arabs, Armenians and Hungarians. As in a prison cell, the names of successive residents are inscribed on the walls, along with dates and would-be obscene drawings. If you push up while trying not to trample the person next to you, there is still room. For the right to this quiet coop, all you need to do is get a tip from someone in the corner bistro or from a sympathetic confrere, then climb upstairs with your kit under your arm, push the door open, greet the company, locate a still empty slot against the wall and set yourself down for an indeterminate time—until, for instance, the

pervasive stench routs one of the less hardy denizens, or for that matter drives out even one of the best forewarned. Now you are in the company of ethereal, anonymous, ageless beings whom you soon ignore, each being there just to sleep in a silence that all respect. In the company, too, of the rats whose dwelling place it is also, rats as long as your forearm. And in the company of dozens of bottles, lined up below the sloping ceiling at the edge of the room, not empty but filled with piss—nobody wanting to go down three flights of stairs in darkness to relieve themselves—and carefully recorked after use. These bottles have been there for three years, and a wag has labeled each with its vintage, giving them the dusty and reassuring look of *grands crus*. All the same, whiffs of uric acid escape and float through the room in search of a way up and out.

I have never slept in the Attic of Evil Spells—not out of fastidiousness, for I am armored against such relative discomforts, but just because, as things fell out, I only went there either to visit a friend or else to have the few educated individuals who chose to live there tell me the legend which gave this attic its name, a tall tale, well known to all the bookwormish booksellers along the banks of the Seine, which claims that long ago this street and its vicinity were hexed after a poor wretch, dragging himself around exhausted and near death on account of various and sundry ailments, ran into the Devil (still living at that time—the fourteenth century, I believe), who made him a good offer: your sight for your health—you may live to a ripe old age in perfect health, but blind. An odd proposal to be sure, which the fellow joyfully accepted, leaping to his feet and rushing forthwith to quaff a beer on tick, suddenly sprightly once more despite a few lingering awkward movements, after which he disappeared, going off perhaps to savor the pleasures of the wide world, and was in any case never heard of again. But two or three centuries later a royal edict banned the blind from the neighborhood in order to put an end to all the fake miracles and abuses of the mass crackpottery to which the old man's adventure had given rise by attracting the whole city's halt, lame and blind. Even very recently, the painter Antonio Bandeira lived by himself in this attic after arriving from his native Brazil, and knowing nothing of this diabolical story, had to leave after a time because, he said, of nightmares in which every night he dreamt that a blind man was climbing up the stairs, knocking at the door and coming into the room, approaching him and running his fingers over his horrified face, as though to identify him or perform an exorcism on him. So poor Bandeira, whose inner being, despite his great culture, had remained unconsciously prey to ancestral terrors, had to flee and find lodging elsewhere, preferring even the chill of the night outside to the touch of the blind man's spidery fingers. I'll say no more. Plenty of other guys have dossed in that room, folks for whom the legend is grotesque and risible, yet the name hangs on: this is still the Attic of Evil Spells, even if this winter its sole occupants are clochards, along with the occasional young poet from the Left Bank come in search of peace and quiet.*

*For more on these legends, see Jacques Yonnet's *Rue des Maléfices* (1954), translated by Christine Donougher as *Paris Noir* (Sawtry, UK: Dedalus, 2006).—*Trans.*

3

AS FATE would have it, the function of that welcoming place was met for me by another, known as Les Gobelins because it was situated at the bottom of the solid citizens' boulevard of the same name, a place where I was in the habit of going at five or six in the morning, with an empty stomach, to drink tea after a night of knocking about the streets: it was a maid's room, narrow as a bathtub, contemporary with Sue's *Mysteries of Paris*, occupied higgledy-piggledy by a clutch of the oddest people. To this end, I had first to obtain a few lumps of sugar, which I gleaned from the friendly local butcher, whose shop is the only one open at this late time of night; then go up six flights under the nose of an insomniac concierge given to prowling the stairs at all hours and invariably taking any visitor to task; compensate at times for the lack of hallway lighting by relying on eyes getting used to the dark; walk with a muffled tread; pull on the piece of string that lifted the inside latch—naturally there was no lock; push the door open firmly but slowly, for behind it there was always some obstacle, usually someone sleeping up against the wall who grumbled and asked to be left in peace; strike a match and look for a candle stub in a jumble of strange objects or, failing that, in someone's pocket nearby; burn my fingers; recognize the occupants of the place, greet them politely, for by now their touchiness would be at its peak for the day; trip over legs nonetheless, exposing feet shivering from the cold and quickly pulled back under a blanket; and finally, a flickering light in hand, find space enough to squat, let the insults die down, look now for the camping stove, choose a clean receptacle (which is impossible) in which to brew the divine beverage—certainly not last summer's teakettle, with a delicate crust

of proliferating bacteria poking out from under its lid; wait patiently for the water to decide to boil, almost half an hour, water that the guys had meticulously stored the day before in whatever vessels were to hand—ashtrays, vases, beer mugs, a coffee pot, tin cans, clear liter wine bottles; smoke in silence, holding the tobacco smell, which offset the odor of bodies, deep in my nasal passages; then bring out the sugar cubes and pour myself a consoling cup of burning-hot tea, at which the others would suddenly awake, experience a violent desire for some of it and clamor in a general hubbub, the heaps of clothes rising up, tousled heads of hair emerging, hands held out, while the legal tenant, our pal Jérôme, lying at the far end of the room, sat up straight, felt around for his eyeglasses, called for matches, scratched his ear, and took it upon himself to light the Tito Landi, a masterpiece of a lamp that I would cordially advise cardiac cases to avoid, because its quaint operation and its fuel—petrol pure and simple—place inexpert fingers in the greatest peril (it was customary, moreover, whenever someone pulled the wick up and brought the double-torch lighter towards it, to get as far away from bedclothes as possible and huddle in a corner for fear of the fairly frequent explosions that ensued, the shattering of the last remaining crockery, and the sizzling of the variously distributed mops of hair). Thus it was that, having wanted no more than a selfish drink of tea, I found myself cast in the role of a café waiter, handing out the hot beverage, sharing the sugar lumps, giving good stirs with a pencil, with the clean end of a greasy knife or fork, or with an eyeglass temple, spilling precious drops on someone's face or hair, getting insulted, and ending up with no more for myself than lukewarm dregs—more to eat, as the old adage has it, than drink. But, as Jérôme used to say, "What are you complaining about?"

4

Luc had loaned me his digs in Rue du Dragon, and the first time I went there the street was plunged in a thick fog from which I emerged at the *porte-cochère* of the building as steamed up as a stewpot lid. Naturally the stairwell-light timer was out of order, which obliged me to grope along in the dark, counting the floors up to the fifth, by my reckoning, before thrusting my numb fingers into my innermost pocket in search of the keys.

I carefully drew back the strip of curtain covering the door behind me and went and sat on the bed to light a cigarette and take a moment to contemplate my new temporary abode, which was stuffy and smelled of old tobacco smoke and paper. The bedroom seemed longer than it was high, with a ceiling so low that you could place the flat of your hand on it. Opening (or rather closing) onto the street were two small wormeaten casement windows with tiny Dutch panes over which varicolored paper had been pasted, creating a fine effect but also a need for continual electric light. The walls were shelved with simple boards stained walnut and perilously overburdened with books from the floor right up to the ceiling. In front of the lower shelves stood piles of magazines and journals and brochures, some as high as the table, which was itself covered, around a dusty coffee pot, by a chaos of papers, bundles of large sheets upon which a giant disorderly hand had managed to write no more than a few lines. At the other end of the room, where I was sitting, a recess created an alcove with a vast bed not so much unmade as discomposed (like a face), and bounded from its head to its foot by shelves miraculously spared the invasive mass of books but bearing all manner of objects, among them pipes, little lead

Indians, masks, bundles of postcards, and a set of baroque wrought-iron candlesticks with colored candles whose wax had melted into petrified grayish stalactites. And on the ceiling were antique maps—you had to crane your neck back to make out the contours of oddly depicted countries edged with dull strips of color. Seated on a divan or in an armchair, however, you could easily discern the curves of the oceans, the tiny painted caravels, and, on land, the weird animals born of the frenzied imaginings (fueled by the wild tales of travelers and eyewitnesses) of the Cartographers Royal. The overall effect was grayish, a hue not much different from the natural state of the walls but made extraordinarily rich by the variety of formats and paper stocks.

I stubbed out my cigarette and began clearing the table. These were the surroundings in which Luc did his stupendous work, and the outside world knew nothing of it, and gave not a hoot, having no time for the sort of free labor that did not supply it with so much as historical grist and too full of its own monstrous and all-consuming vitality to notice the little anachronistic character who, under this roof, was chewing on his pipe, dreaming with eyes half-closed and working, among other things, on a history of exoticism in France, on two or three biographies of figures completely unknown and of strictly relative interest, and on an anthology of the proletarian literatures of countries at the back of beyond. One day, however, that world would remember his existence, his name, his number, and would come looking for him, demanding that he account for himself, questioning him at length—What do you live on? What is your occupation in civilian life? Are you shitting me?—disbelieving him, packing him off to don a uniform and take the air somewhere or other in a vast vaudevillian brawl, meanwhile taking possession of his room, where he had stored up so many riches with so much love, breaking the little window panes to let in the air, the daylight, the noise, and soon the outside world in its benevolence would offer a perfect place to live, in the shape of a two-room flat with kitchen, to some retired civil servant with a pension and a fondness for the game of belote.

For my part, after stowing all the scattered books and papers as best I could, I quickly transformed the place into a refuge, a chaotic way

station, by inviting, at the risk of acute claustrophobia, all the clochards, beggars, panhandlers, trash-can divers, spongers and professional idlers that I ran into as I knocked about in every street and every neighborhood of the city: bums from Les Halles, the quays, Maubert, Les Gobelins, La Nationale, Mouffetard, Bicêtre, Clichy Saint-Ouen, even some, more refined, who opted to reside in posh areas, the Champs-Élysées or Opéra, working the outdoor terraces of the grand cafés and the lobbies of the grand hotels, and most of all the more interesting of the foreign wanderers of whom I speak elsewhere—smuggling all these rather outlandish types (though hardly more outlandish than me) past the lodge of the concierge, whom I scandalized—but to hell with that old bag, who stank even worse than my poor devils and slept on a palliasse they would likely have refused in a space invaded by half a dozen odoriferous tomcats. My two rooms were soon filled with bodies in rags, unshaven, filthy, parked alongside narrow windows that were now open and struggling vainly to evacuate the stench; and with assorted pans, ladles, mess tins, liter bottles, canned food, along with my cracked stewpot, its contents going cold—an indescribable hodgepodge of vegetables bulked up by kilos of bread crusts, or else the hallowed potato stew swimming in age-old and somewhat rancid grease; and in the fireplace a pleasant wood fire the fuel for which was collected by the beneficiaries—lengths of fence board, wicker flower baskets, layers of posters, thickened and rendered ligneous by the quantity of dried glue between the sheets, whose colors melted visibly in the flames of a fire before which we played endless games of belote, chattering, swearing, spitting (in the ashtrays if you please, thank you), smoking, taking snuff, toping....

I remember how one affluent night I brought in a disoriented young girl, a pale epitome of Saint-Germain-des-Prés who said she did not know where to sleep, in all likelihood a daddy's girl in flight from bourgeois life, and excited (or half-faking it) by the unpredictable, whom I installed in the place of honor in the big bed. With a measure of stupefaction and vague anxiety, the foolish girl with her well-developed breasts took in the oriental tableau before her and the surreal atmosphere of the place, reminiscent of an abandoned bookstore, and

became reluctant to stay, almost preferring the emptiness of the boulevards to the overcrowdednesss of this room, but I eventually managed
to settle her down by drawing the alcove's curtain and sacrificing her
appropriately in relative privacy despite the auditory and olfactory
proximity of my cohorts. Among these were Mandibule, who was forever grinding his teeth, Bidet who hailed from the Pont de Flandre
area, and Clément, my favorite, a strange violinist sans violin whom I
had met in the entrance hall of the Lido while admiring (discreetly, in
view of my somewhat casual attire) the pretty window-shoppers and
trying to excite the curiosity of respectable gents to whom I wanted to
sell supposedly pornographic pictures of nudes that would pop up in
their blue oval settings from the hollow of my hand (the most amusing
of con games with tourists, and the old geezers whose interest in such
items is—naturally!—based solely on the artistic and plastic aspects of
the models might like to know that they are indeed perfectly legal reproductions of pictures in the Louvre, odalisques, women bathing or
at their toilet, Giocondas, startled nymphs, Dianas far more often
hunting than sinning, all of them in poses tending away from rather
than toward the voluptuous, and thus likely to leave the buyer fuming
and dancing with rage—connoisseurs, you have been warned! As for
me, this was my bread and butter). Anyway, that was where I ran into
Clément the violinist, and broke the ice—and in the event bread—
with him on a bench in Avenue Montaigne, after which he held me in
thrall until daybreak with his musicological knowledge, especially historical and biographical in nature, telling me in detail, voice low and
gaze distant, about the travels on foot of the German musicians of the
great years, whose routes he had studied assiduously (when? where?
how?) and followed as an itinerant fiddler working catch-as-catch-can
at village fairs, standing in here or there for a cantor or organist, sleeping in presbyteries and occasionally in magnificent monasteries, and
visiting every single church in Swabia and Bavaria with his stomach
empty and his love life suspended. He thought it a hundred times better to starve to death than to become a washed-up musician cranking
out rigadoons and worn-out medleys in slum dance halls. It was in his
honor and at his request that I sacrificed a ton of candles, for like me

he loved their flickering flame, so much more alive than that of an electric lamp with its anonymous piped-in source, alive in the swaying of its hips, in the very variability of its liveliness, a world of flashes and eclipses, alive in its evanescence, its soothing light not ruffling the eyelids of sleepers but keeping vigil over them, animated by their breath. I had candles poked into three bottles. Often, at night, when my chronic cerebral ruminations kept me awake, I would sit cross-legged on the floor at the foot of the bed, smoking and contemplating my tenants, interrogating their countenances, their hands, intruding upon their dreams, their paradises, listening to their groans, wheezing, sighing, snoring, coughing, and scraps of sleeptalking. From where I was, antipodean to the ceiling, whose cartographic decoration seemed immensely far away, the bedroom gradually changed into an opium den. I watched the contortions of the little flames as they kept trying to achieve verticality but never managed it, as they toppled over, flattened out, and broke the spell with an almost inaudible crackle before straightening up again; I surveyed the heaps of clothing in the form of human figures, as though left behind by an escape artist, poignant combinations of linen wool fabric cloth leather flesh hair all held together with string—suits of clothes never taken off, never washed, to which their owners were attached as to their own skin—and they were indeed a second skin placed directly over the first, albeit more malleable, more donnable, the second slipping over the first like the judiciously placed inner partitions of the scrotal sac; and I observed the hands, which made me think of the red and blue feet of the platypus.

And I would think about Luc. Where was he? His absence was incomprehensible. Only some extraordinary event that he had never mentioned could have caused this unfathomable, astonishing man, this mysterious intellectual, this lunatic to abandon his berth and refuge. The wildest of tales surrounded Luc: the notion that he was queer, or an exhibitionist, not to mention his bouts of mysticism which were never taken seriously but which might have driven him to seek a cure in some provincial monastery—elastic legends nourished by rumor but based on facts, on behavior far from run-of-the-mill which still made me laugh. He had claimed to have a once-a-week lover, a mistress, one

Widow Schmidt, of whom we all knew nothing but whose existence we accepted out of courtesy until the day he decided to take us to her place; there were four or five of us with him, guys and girls, all pooh-poohing his erotic stories, as he led us somewhere behind Place de la Bastille and ushered us into a dark apartment, stuffed with frilly cushions and Chinese vases, that felt like a concierge's lodge though it was halfway up the stairway of an old building. There we were greeted by a slattern of imposing proportions with a brioche-like tiered chignon. She rose from an armchair with dust ruffles where she had been engaged in some kind of women's work, as we stood hesitantly, to say the least, in her doorway. She must have been close to the modest age of fifty and she moved with the queenliness of a Ranavalona, but with the most graceful smile she had us sit around a barely warm Mirus wood stove, discreetly slipped a thousand-franc bill to Luc, who was falling over himself making formal introductions, and instructed him *sotto voce* to go and get port and tea biscuits while she brewed the tea. Conversation soon began to lag, but when our supposed fancy man came back with the remedy for our awkwardness, he drew open the wine-purple drapes of a Breton box bed and invited Widow Schmidt to come and sit beside him on the edge, then grasped her by the arm and without further ado pushed her over onto her back, threw her skirts up with a nimble hand and, to our most genuine astonishment, pulled off her vast violet knickers and after unfastening his own belt proceeded to engage in faun-like antics, his pants slipping further down his skinny calves with each thrust, uncovering wispy shirttails, while we could hear the good woman protesting weakly: "But Monsieur Lortoir, what are you thinking? Behave yourself! We have company— whatever are your friends going to think?" All we could see of her now, at intervals, were bulging bare thighs between which the alleged homosexual was laboring in the most manly way, and this in due and proper form. We quite forgot to finish our cups of tea and nibble our *petits beurres*. Panting with scant regard for decorum, the woman craned her neck towards us and made us nearly choke or at least swallow hard with the words "Do help yourselves to more tea. Please don't be shy."

And when our friend arose triumphant and recharged, Widow Schmidt came back to earth and, wiping her crotch with a napkin she produced from under the bolster, turned coy: "Can you believe it?" she said. "What a naughty boy that Monsieur Lortoir is!"

From that instant Luc's reputation was unassailable.

5

ALL THE same, despite the abundance of hideaways conducive to
brief but restorative sleep, even the craftiest of vagrants ends up sleeping rough from time to time, either because he finds himself too far
away from the nearest such refuge, or because he is halted by painful
feet, or shoes that hurt, or the cold, or the rain, or simply the wish to
spend the night under the stars in a little-known neighborhood; or
else—indeed most often—because he is confused and disoriented by
the kind of glorious bender that leaves your gray cells paralyzed and
your movements weak. All reasons, good or bad, for fending off even
the most pressing matters and settling for a safe corner to crawl into,
curl up in, and wait and see what the day brings.

Paris nights.

Nights spent in Roadways Department shelters on public thoroughfares, alongside factory walls or by trenches half dug: solid
wooden shanties providing a distinct measure of comfort (appreciable
for me if only relative for the road workers) or else a simple green canvas tarp thrown over a plank framework. Despite the penetrating odor
of methane that invariably seeps from such work sites, I spent happy
hours there sleeping quickly (to use the eloquent expression of a cohort
of mine who claimed that he slept more than me during the same period of time).

One night when the cold had driven me from the banks of the
Seine and I had found there was no more room on the barge at the
Pont d'Austerlitz, it was so late already that I made up my mind to go
on up the boulevard and walk until first light, but just beyond the foul-
smelling Customs buildings I spotted a fire burning in Rue Sauvage

between the railroad tracks that turn away from the quayside there to enter the freight-station yards, and as I approached I saw a work-site watchman's tent, lifted a corner of it and found nobody inside. I sat for a while on a rail with my legs apart and my hands held out over the fire, blessing this new miracle, feeding the flames with wood already prepared and stacked close by, taking this opportunity to dry my handkerchief, which needed it, rolling a series of cigarettes, and snoozing on and off. After almost an hour, the guy showed up with a full liter of wine, inspected me for a moment, then invited me in.

Under the canvas, besides a camp bed, there was a long toolbox on which I sprawled. The fellow, an old redhead who drooled a little, handed me the wine and we began to tipple without touching the bottle to our lips. To get into the spirit of things, I recounted a few episodes from my life, after which he produced some leftover cheese and a hunk of bread from his knapsack and heated coffee for me. Then he spoke to me of his unfulfilled dreams. He had wanted to be a railroad crossing guard or stationmaster of a local stop in his native province, which was Rouergue or Quercy, I forget which, but did not have "enough education" and expected to die in the capital. In the morning, because I had a few sous left, I invited him for a rum at Café de la Marine, on the corner of Rue Bellièvre, a bistro painted gaily in blue that attracts men from the barges permanently moored below and from the maritime repair shops, along with crane operators and the workers who sort glass with pitchforks. (What could you call their strange job, which consists in picking all day long, like hens on a pile of manure, at heaps of broken glass fragments and bottle bottoms, sorting them by color—clear, green, blue, brown, and so on?)

In this tiny neighborhood, happily protected from any civilizing influence because it is forgotten, jammed between the Seine, Boulevard de la Gare where the only traffic is ten-ton trucks, and the SNCF national railroad lines, is a narrow vacant lot, amid a cluster of houses with little yards and chicken coops, that is rife with wild grass which you can plunge into and make yourself completely at home, and this is where a whole family, a couple with four kids, was living in a hutch four meters square. The father, a certified mason by the name of Bara,

had previously lived in a hotel in Rue Galande, in "La Maube"—the Maubert district—and he was a hard worker, but the kids bothered the neighbors, and the manager had flatly thrown him out, and he found himself in the most literal sense in the street, along with his small fry, other hotels naturally wanting nothing to do with him (he made the exorbitant claim that he should be able to do his cooking and laundry in the room, something perfectly out of the question for any respectable manager) and after mature(?) reflection he bought a prefabricated chicken hutch of the aforesaid dimensions and set it up on a vacant lot on Rue Mouffetard, but he barely had the time to begin a little gardening before an owner turned up from some far province (as one always does in such cases) and forcibly evicted him along with his better half, his offspring and his camping paraphernalia, all of which the undaunted and obstinate fellow promptly reinstalled in that patch of green in Rue Sauvage. And they live there to this day, in those same cramped quarters, stacked on top of one another like bottles of fine wine, and obliged to go down to the Seine to wash themselves and their dishes.

The Paris night so transforms the Jardin du Carrousel that nothing whatever remains of its sumptuous daytime aspect and it becomes a bizarre world with a mysterious atmosphere only accentuated by the silence. The long gravel paths take on a lunar glow and the flower beds and bushes form alarming shapes. Bizarre, mysterious, alarming— most of all because almost motionless shadowy figures haunt the place. They deploy the usual tactics of voyeurs, obsessives, pederasts, and loners of every stripe, slinking from one bench to the next, attracted like moths by the flare of a cigarette, circling the rare loving couples, gradually approaching any solitary guy, stopping a few steps away, silent, just waiting, their gaze interrogative, then going away only to return after a brief meander. It is impossible to sleep there despite the inviting abundance of shrubbery. The oddest characters, however, are not men but women. You have to wonder where they come from, these old floozies ugly enough to make a hanged man lose his hard-on, smelly and generally soused, who, so far from respecting the relative tranquility of the surroundings, croak out their sodden demand for hundred-franc bills to go and drink with, against which they are willing to satisfy the vilest requests. One comes up to me, an innocent ordinary guy, on his own, dragging on a thin cigarette and wrestling with various problems, and asks me crudely if I would like her to *show me a good time*; as I reply, I size her up from head to foot and try to imagine what sort of a good time could be had from this shameless hag and what orgiastic acrobatics her "clients" might possibly perform—here was the Hundred and Twenty Days of Sodom ready to hand at a price to suit every budget—but I shoo her off, at which she rebukes me, gives me a real dressing-down, then, softening, pulls up her dress and shows me her ass, her enormously prominent, even callipygian buttocks—not, however, to add insult to injury but simply to give me a clear idea of the repayment in kind that she could offer, and when I laugh it seems to vex her, her honor being more vulnerable here than elsewhere; I get to my feet in order to get rid of her, get lost I tell her, but just as I am decamping a second one arrives, her girlfriend, and the two of them start in on me, no longer proposing a "lousy deal" for themselves, but frankly something for nothing, just between us, just for fun, come on, behind these bushes, you'll see what the two of us can show you, you'll be so happy (for propriety's sake I omit the precise slang idioms adorning their propositions, but I have managed to record a few of the more original and colorful ones in my pocket notebook, and these I am saving for a connoisseur and cannot reveal here). At this point, tearing myself away from the pair's enticements, I weigh anchor.

6

PARIS nights spent in the featureless and tired world of station waiting rooms. At the Gare Saint-Lazare, for instance, amidst academic paintings and pitiful official notices—GET A SEASON TICKET (don't we always, darling?)—TRAVEL FOR HALF-FARE (fat chance!) WITH A GROUP TICKET (but of course!)—sit rows of people facing one another, and contemplating one another in a vague way, on narrow benches in the four corners of the room or in the two large leather armchairs grabbed and jealously occupied for hours at a time, citadels of comfort for travelers to the inner or outer suburbs; pallid procrastinators under the firmament of pinkish-blue neon lighting; the eternal general-issue homeless people who have been and will be here for days, sleeping in fits and starts, elbows and faces on their knees, straining their backs but forgetting about the pain to follow or snapping their heads back regularly as they nod off and jerk themselves awake across the frontier between unconscious and conscious, their eyelids slowly half-opening like a crocodile's third lid, but vertically; a pair of old casualties of war, together but unspeaking, having long had nothing to say to each other, nothing to discuss, nothing to remark upon, nothing to hope for; and the stinking old woman who does her business beneath her skirts, here every night, using an open shopping basket for this purpose because her attire keeps her out of the nearby public conveniences, which are in any case not free for such wretched old ladies, who can very rarely go and squat as the men do in street urinals while keeping a weather eye out for cops. (In high summer there are those that go to wash their feet in the river, offering a spectacle that delights the tourists in search of the picturesque who on Sundays lean over the stone guardrail above the quay to watch the exotic animals on display below, males and females, scurrying about, delousing themselves, sleeping and feeding—it's a wonder the children don't toss them pieces of brioche as the dads tell their little lads, "See that? If you don't behave at school, you'll end up like them." Horrible! And in the depths of winter, in the café lavatories, there are those who plunge their legs one after the other into the toilet bowl, rinse them by flushing, then sit and wait for them to dry.)

7

I HUMBLY confess (may expectant readers forgive me) that I have never slept in a Paris cemetery. And further that I have very few sources on the modus operandi for doing so or on the sensations it procures. Only one person among my acquaintances, a transient Latvian, was able to tell me how he spent several nights in a row at Père-Lachaise in the tomb of Princess Bibesco, which had the merit, according to my informant, of being vast, comfortable, not damp, free of draughts, and above all multistoried. This same drifter, a native of Riga, had once been invited by a benefactor (small-time) to a performance at the Paris Opera. After he had wisely shaken off this demanding companion, he returned at the fall of the final curtain to the bathroom that they had used and took up residence there in comfort for the rest of the night, slept marvelously, and at first light performed cursory ablutions at a washbowl unimportuned by any toilet attendant, any *dame pipi*, before slipping past service workers and making his exit unscathed through an inconspicuous side door. As you will have gathered, he was a resourceful man.

Jérôme for his part was the world's expert on the topography and benefits of Paris's cemeteries, which have virtues and uses largely unsuspected by the majority of visitors, starting with the mass of cut flowers so easy to resell on the sidewalks outside. Jérôme had engaged in the somewhat shady business of "headhunting," a fantastical traffic that nevertheless put food on the table so long as one had the stomach for it. The dodge consisted, around 1946, when cigarettes were still rationed and hence highly prized, in taking a sack of some kind—potato sack or haversack—and calling, preferably in the evening, on the Père-

Lachaise guard assigned to the common boneyard, slipping him four or five packs of Gauloises in exchange for which the old guy would delightedly lead you down a stair into the pit and along a passageway as nondescript, save for the odors, as a metro connecting tunnel, use ancient keys to open up some of the oldest chambers, urge you to be quick and careful about it, then go back up to enjoy one of his precious smokes down the footpath as he waited for the end of your visit. Equipped with powerful flashlights, Jérôme and his follower first shooed away the giant rats that dwelt near the doorways, then played their beams on rather ill-defined masses, pressed forward into the obscurity, striving to inhale as little as possible, wading through a mire of crusted slime until they could feel the corpses, grasp hold of a head by thrusting a finger and thumb into the eye sockets, twist sharply so as to snap the uppermost vertebra, and toss each skull into their sack. In this way they harvested five or six just quickly enough to avoid passing out or getting their hands slick with soapy ooze. Then they fled as fast as they could, leaving the guard to put everything back in order and lock up. Not daring, though, to take the metro, they would walk down to Boulevard Saint-Jacques, avoiding groups, causing passers-by to steer clear of them or turn to stare, to do the first cleaning, the main one, in one of the flophouses from which, even if they paid promptly and affably, they would invariably be thrown out by their third day. Twenty-four hours later they would be selling their curios to the sort of dealers you can imagine. In those days this enterprise left them (not counting the cost of all the drinks needed to keep their stomachs from turning) with a five-hundred-franc bill per (death's) head.

8

BY DINT of sleeping here and there, you end up familiar with all kinds of tricks, pointers and wheezes and all kinds of places to kip and hole up. And you soon become acclimatized to a life of bouncing around that is tranquil in its way; you get used to drifting and not giving a damn, not bothering your head about it, being quite sure that come evening you will find a pal who can treat you to a *café-crème* and a croissant, and that the next morning, after a good healthy night of walking and musing, the room of some intellectual dabbler or of some home-based whore will be available for you to snooze cozily from nine o'clock to one o'clock lying on a couch or curled up on the floor in the fetal position with tea in a tin cup and an ashtray brimming with butt ends close to hand. Life is wonderful. What more could you wish for? As for me, I would seize the chance, on waking, to scribble a few pages of a private log at the corner of a table and slip them discreetly into my pocket before leaving with a grateful handshake or a friendly kiss. By wandering the city without your pals you pick up plenty of tips that are still fresh. So now and again you show up in the very early morning at the door of someone unknown to you, whom you have never seen, who scrutinizes you on the threshold as he is taking his breakfast before going to work, you introduce yourself with a big smile on your lips, Jules or Anatole sent me, he told me you might perhaps offer me half a day's hospitality, but why of course, come on in, make yourself at home, unfortunately I have to leave, I am already late, could you heat up some coffee for yourself, please don't touch this or that, help yourself to reading matter, but try not to get ash on the carpet, see you later. A rather startling number of folk—enough to fill a calendar—still believe in

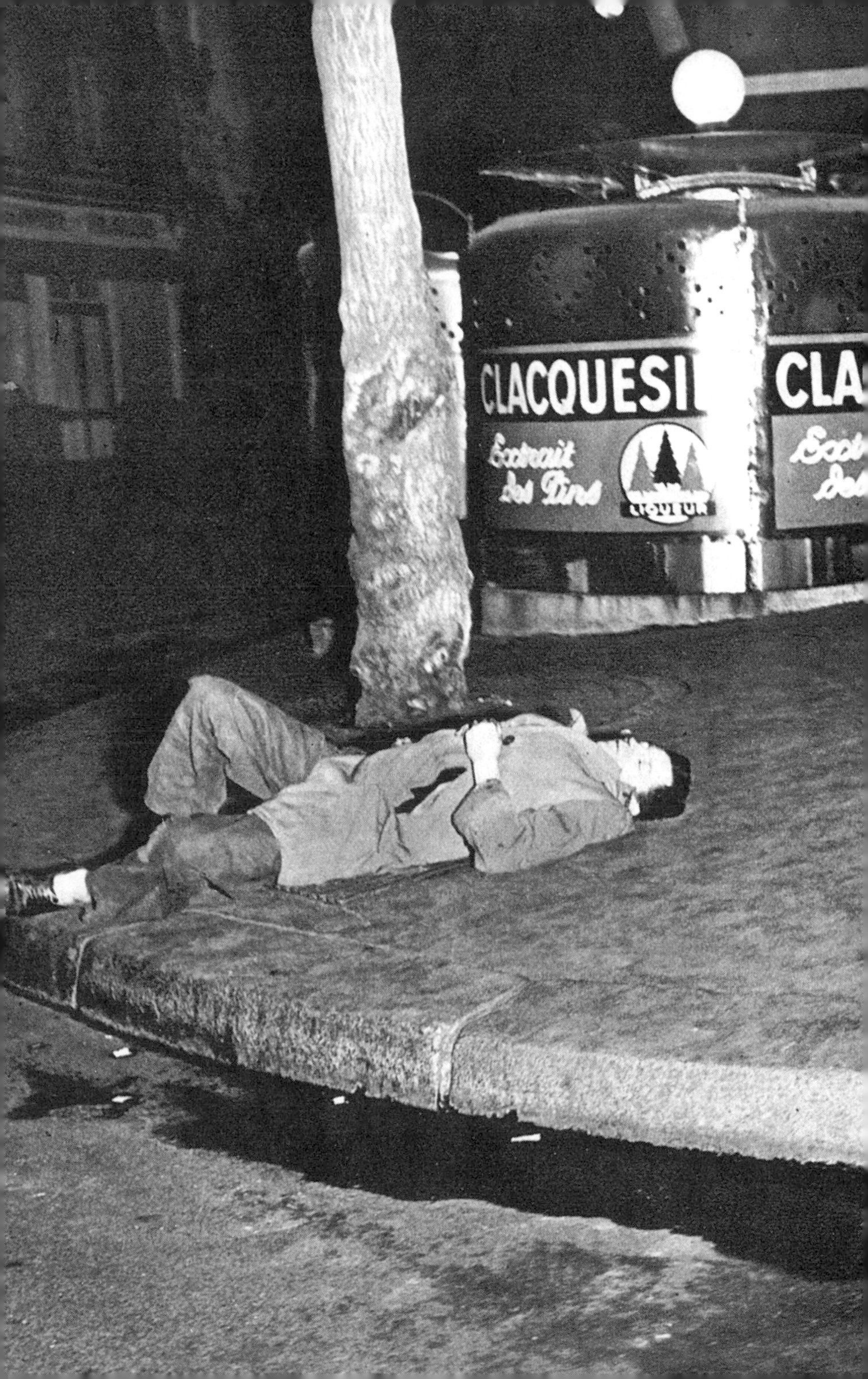
CLACQUESIN
Extrait des Pins
LIQUEUR
CLA

hospitality and helping you out for nothing. With a bit of luck and a bit of practice it is not hard in this way to get your average five hours of sleep in one place or another, sometimes with one- or two-hour interruptions, or to manage to eat by a kitchen sink. Hosts are not always spiritual brothers happy to help a pal out of instant empathy, but rather individuals who might be suspected at first glance of having reservations (like certain confirmed bachelors, professors of this or that, or civil servants in some office or other), but who on the contrary are simply honest fellows who know what it's like, who have been there themselves, been reduced to eating tainted meat even if they haven't slept under bridges, and who open their kitchen cabinets and even their sack to you without a second thought. Even guys who, as you feel right away, are not remotely tempted to adopt your kind of life, but who act instinctively out of a pure sense of solidarity: workers, barkeeps, people with no visible means of support, truckers—a whole human crew capable of making you forget for a moment the disdain, scorn, incomprehension and hate manifested by all the others—folk who ask for no explanations, no justifications, no polite palaver, but simply that you close the door properly behind you and check that the gas and electricity are turned off as you leave. A wonder that as they head out they do not recommend their own wife to you, or their chick from the night before who is still asleep. Or furtively slip a hundred-franc note into your pocket. Discretion is the golden rule, however, and it is better not to seek any account of such bewildering gestures and attitudes, which would generally be embarrassed and certainly evasive, unless of course successive rounds at night in the bistro downstairs accelerate the sharing of confidences and it emerges clearly that *he* is the one who is miserable and you are the lucky one: you see, I would so much rather lead *your* life, be free of all ties, far from all worries except the most basic ones, able to loaf and think about any number of things that obsess me or worry me or thrill me and could give me a shred of dignity, instead of which here I am tied down tied up mummified in my world of end-of-the-month bills, paid vacations, Saturday nights at the movies, Sundays with the kids at the mother-in-law's and no distraction, no escape except for the morning rag and a dirty book now and again in secret or a whore in Rue Saint-Denis, you see I slept with this girl just like that because the opportunity presented itself, she's not much to look at, and rather limited, but it was a free deal, and then the kid came along and I didn't want to dump her, we got married, and I went looking for work. *You*, you have everything going for you, you can do whatever you fancy, wander at random and cogitate at your leisure, and your eyes are bright. Listen, my house is your house, and pay no mind to the wife, let her yap, it makes me happy to see you, to listen to you, hey, tell me what you've been doing what you've seen since last time. . . .

How could you not wash the dishes, help out, do odd jobs about the house, nail down a floorboard, replace a tile in the toilet, or flick a duster over the furniture to make a housewife's life easier? How could you not tell wonderful stories, describe outlandish human scenes with bistros and odd characters, chunter on about the formation of the planets or the existence of extraterrestrials in flying saucers, recount in great detail the latest crime in the Zone—in short, serve as a flesh-and-blood anecdotal almanac, a supplier of warmth. In exchange for what? For a sourish soup with croutons and leftover vegetables from the day before, a bowl of stewed coffee, and a metal camp bed. How could I ask for anything more? Is this not true human community, where simple primitive barter is rediscovered with all its extra-pecuniary virtue?

9

FOR CAMPING out in Paris—in the official sense, as used in the regulation of itinerant performers and other nomads—during the fine seasons of spring and fall, before and after the great wanderings of summer, the only top-notch sites are so-called *terrains vagues,* meaning merely open spaces, the connotation of vagueness, no matter how apposite, having lost its initial force, and notable among these are the embankments of the *fortifs,* the city's old fortifications, the Champ des Curés at Porte d'Italie, grassy sports grounds, the Buttes-Chaumont park, demolition and building sites, and the Montreuil motocross track. Beyond railings, dilapidated walls or painted board fences you are bound to find a rock shelter, a shady corner, a patch of soft earth, a manhole, planks and cobbles adequate for even a winter stay, or a wind-breaking thicket—places into which the cops are too scared to stick their noses, and, truth to tell, don't really give a damn about.

After something of a binge, accompanied by the Shepherd got up as ever in the deerskin and the stoved-in round hat that made him look so much like a drover sans herd peddling goat cheese, I leave behind the bistro-rich environs of La Petite-Roquette and head slowly for the Père-Lachaise Cemetery. We have decided to go and sleep under the stars on the heights of Ménilmontant. We slip into Rue des Amandiers, curved like a bow, plebeian and populous, filled with gaiety, jostling and cackling housewives with their shopping-bags, smells wafting from the food stalls, sideways glances and glimpses of deep cleavages and pretty faces, even an unheard-of bonhomie from pairs of cops. Turning right, we climb Passage des Mûriers, a precipitous byway reminiscent of Toulon whose main attraction is La Guinguette, a bistro surrounded by evergreen shrubbery where we stop off to drink a half liter of sweet white. Then, a little farther on, we halt for more drinking at La Campagne, on the corner of Rue des Cendriers, a green-painted *bougnat* whose exterior is rather extraordinary but hard to describe. (Every time I mention a curious shop or dive, it always seems to have the same wooden shutters, the same walls apparently constructed of wattle and daub, the same wonky dormers, the same threshold with steps leading either down or up, often with natural vegetation, so that, since I always employ the same words, expressions, epithets and exclamations, I give the impression that I am repeating myself and suggest similarity where in reality not one of these tumbledown places resembles the next in the slightest.)

Across the way from this bistro is a twin alleyway, Impasse Finet—two clefts less than a meter wide, parallel and uninhabitable save perhaps by drunks prey to raging stomach and gut problems. The whole neighborhood, in fact, is honeycombed with short cuts, cul-de-sacs, and sidestreets, like Cité Touret, chaotic with swarming brats and laundry hung out Milan-fashion. Once across Place de Ménilmontant, we climb into the precinct of the church of Notre Dame de la Croix and take a pathway leading from it, almost invisible to strangers and exceedingly long, which takes us up between sweating and greasy walls before petering out in crisscrossing lanes that serve little suburban dwellings and bring us to a wasteland, a mound strewn with fragments of asphalt, dirty papers and yellowing nettles that overlooks an endless cavalcade of rooftops and a great dome of sky over the city. Here and there are solitary vagrants or lovelorn ragmen, drunk and musing blissfully about the sweetness of life—and perhaps more intensely about how to get their next liter.

Behind this blessed haven of peace there is a photograph to be taken that I would love to present to all connoisseurs of the Paris landscape: the view, from the Rue des Couronnes bridge, of a station for slow local trains, overrun by ivy and proudly displaying its name, MÉNILMONTANT. From this standpoint, no part of the picture betrays the impression of open countryside or of a little village deep in the provinces.

As we continue our ascent of the Butte de Ménilmontant, a flight of steps takes us up through a miniature forest punctuated by vegetable gardens and a veritable barnyard where free-roaming chicks cheep, rabbits in wicker baskets nibble, cocks crow vituperatively, and a fat tomcat snoozes with one eye half-open. Our step somewhat less lively, we reach Rue Piat, odd in that it divides into two as it wends its way on either side of a house with an exterior wooden staircase and balustrade, and ends up at the top of the hill, under the wide Paris sky, on a triangle of bare terrain, which at first seems like a fairground and which the municipality has dubbed a square, bordered by Rue du Transvaal, by elbow gas lamps long out of order, by rustic houses, and by walls with dwellings built into them. Another narrow way leads down: Passage Vilin—the spelling of whose name I would so much love to change to *Vilain* (ugly)! On the square itself a tribe of human beings lives hand-to-mouth, flat-footed, rheumy-eyed, haversacks clinking with bottles, ballooning coats and pants, fuzz-faced for the most part or sporting haircuts modeled on the cassowary's casque. Depositing our portable belongings and dusty backsides on the edge of an incline, and greeting our companions, who are busy irrigating their tonsils, with rather crude humor (albeit quite respectable in these parts), the Shepherd and I embark on the preparation of a cold meal to which various unlikely little creatures invite themselves—spiders, ants, crickets that I cannot contemplate and examine in this corner of the capital without a measure of joy, for their presence is reinvigorating, proving as it does that all is not lost, that primitive life has not yet been utterly eradicated from civilization's universe of stone.

Puffing on your pipe, your belly full and your eye beginning to wander, you can easily plunge into contemplation of the very finest vista of the city (how odd, though, that the tourists frequent only the neighborhood of the Sacré-Coeur and never think, say, of climbing up the Buttes de Montreuil). And thus, comfortably wedged in a gulley, with our packs for pillows, bundled up in our lumberjackets, we drift off gently into a refreshing sleep. At daybreak, naturally, the local roosters awaken us despite our protracted efforts to turn a deaf ear, and we gather our gear, comb our hair with practiced fingers, swill out

our mouths with two or three great mouthfuls of water, go round past the last group of houses at the top of Rue des Envierges and survey Rue Vilin wending its tortuous way via a jumble of stairways and platforms down the side of the hill. But near the top is Le Repos de la Montagne, a pink, windswept watering-hole that welcomes drifters and trash-can divers, and there we halt to break our fast on java washed down with *marc* from the owner's village. Below us lies the City of Light, rather gray at this early hour, and I am once again confirmed in my belief that it is not at night that a city dies, but rather in the summertime, around five in the morning, when it becomes a desert of stone—tinged with pink, it is true, for poetry's sake, but for the most part petrified and lifeless, the only movement supplied by passerines and swallows flocking high above.

Below our feet the old houses are waking up, cracked and creaking, rustling with secret life like tree trunks infested by termites (sounds so much more pleasing to my ear than the great din of radios, shrieking women, knock-down fighting, feats of vocal belligerence, and groans of brutal love behind the corrugated cardboard partitions of the HBM housing). Here, on Rue Vilin, only slum dwellings and seedy hotels tumble down a hillside so steep that you pass the fourth floor of the houses before you get to the front door.

Ambling through the "colonial" district, down streets with names like Pali-Kao, Sénégal, Pékin, and Gênes, we get to Rue de Belleville, of which there is nothing more to say, because this living serpent has been described from every possible angle, the sole omission perhaps being the alley, narrow as a knife blade, where you can barely raise your arm to the side, which runs behind the first café, on the corner of the Boulevard de Belleville. We propose to spend what promises to be a wet morning at the Taverne de Belleville, unarguably the headquarters and private club of the belote players of the four arrondissements which come together here. By evening, having lost and won enough to drink our fill with Monsieur Félix and the tailor Djermadjian, known to his cardplaying companions as Moïscher, we go off to chase skirts, for, whether you have dough or not, the intersection at the Belleville metro station is a happy hunting ground, rife with broads and easy pick-ups. On the fringes of this area, just before or just after the dinner hour, you are liable to encounter pairs of mature or even younger women who seem to be carefully studying and commenting excitedly on the cockeyed and overwrought architecture along the street but who wiggle their backsides and keep looking out of the corner of their eyes for some imagined beau. According to Godut, with whom I sip my dozen or so *blanc-cassis* at the Taverne, just across from the Théâtre de Belleville, they are in search of a Man. And for these women, be they married, pregnant, Jewish, or slow, the man in question is bound to be a good-looking, strutting male reeking of underarm sweat and caporal tobacco, rolling his cigarettes one-handed, whistling crudely between puckered lips, wearing espadrilles, playing cards, having no acknowledged means of support, slapping girls across the ass, shooting black looks at old bags, dancing like a prince, sporting loud ties and net undershirts, brawling for the sheer pleasure of it, a dab hand at the slot machines, and above all capable of reducing them to silence by unsheathing his weapon and going into action as they fall into a faint. A rather simple combination of qualities and defects, but one highly effective if the goal is simply to *possess*.

And the Shepherd would be on board whenever I proposed that we exploit some of those natural endowments of ours that might open the door to a good dinner in a private room followed by certain exercises which, though scarcely spiritual, are needful for a balanced body.

FIVE

NOVOCRIN
SOIGNE & FAIT RENAÎTRE
LE CHEVEU

ACHE QUI RIT

AFFICHAGE PARISIEN

B

I

JUST LIKE the Sunday of the worker who slaves away all week, and in stark contrast to that of rich kids of all ages who greet that day's coming with sighs of boredom and love to moan about how much they hate it, the vagabond's Sunday is a real festival. For then the crowds fill the streets, the sidewalks come to life, cigarette ends rain down, stray coins make their ephemeral reappearance, the café terraces offer a free spectacle, faces light up in smiles, the *bougnats* bulge with confirmed belote players and there is always a call for a partner somewhere, and a free round somewhere. The bum's life is also governed all week long, like that of old-clothes merchants, second-hand booksellers, small-bore tourists and bargain hunters, by the rotation of market days: Monday, Wednesday and Friday for Rue des Morillons, Thursday Kremlin, Saturday Saint-Ouen, Sunday Mouffetard.

Today is such a feast-day, and with Jérôme I leave our Maubert doss and walk up the hill to Place de la Contrescarpe, the most beautiful little plaza in Paris with its houses bellying out at their base as if they were overfed (an irony if ever there was), and its denizens sleeping on the sidewalk of Rue Lacépède. We go for a rum at René's, a colorless café whose neon lighting illuminates only the front room. René's is the first place to open. It is five or six in the morning. The streetcleaners gather here for their white-wine eye-openers, their brooms leaning sheaf-like against the window; they draw the backs of their hands across brows glistening from fatigue before going off to sluice the gutters or hold their noses as they pick up trash and clear away nameless rubbish, human waste, accompanied by the screeching of rusty metal emanating from the SITA garbage trucks.

Using the corner of a gray, stiff handkerchief, Bébert of the glass eye is polishing his opaline marble, which he has just popped out from behind a red-rimmed eyelid, now shut. It hurts when I am tired, he explains, my eye tears up and I have to clean it from time to time. Then he thumbs it back into place, twisting it so that it faces a world whose contours he cannot apprehend because his perspective is distorted, something which bothers him not at all, for manifestly he always looks on the bright side of life. We drink our rum while inspecting our usual early-morning visages in the mirror—pretty ragged, pretty demolished—and keeping an eye on the pale blue sky above the Rue Monge neighborhood.

As we leave we turn up our coat collars against the cold that accompanies exhaustion and makes you shiver. We go by the railings where the same man always sleeps curled up, his head oddly raised, his ear not touching the ground, and go down to pay a visit to our pals, the lads and lasses of the Saint-Médard market—junk dealers there from the crack of dawn, at three or four or five in the morning, so as to grab the best places, which they stake out with string, cobblestones or newspapers before going off to drink a lousy coffee; they come to sell multifarious wares whose exchange value is far from obvious at first glance: stray pieces of material or clothing, odd pairs of shoes, chipped saucers, alarm clocks with no hands and very likely no works, bunches of keys, handfuls of nails, old postcards, stained newspapers, even bits of scrap lumber sawed up and tied in bundles. It would take too long to list all the items that at the official Saint-Ouen fleamarket would be considered dross, but the fact is that this stuff allows the regulars to rake in their thousand francs by noon, God only knows how, at the rate of ten or twenty francs per sale. And where do these things come from? From raids on the same garbage cans that the bona fide rag dealers know how to make a healthy profit from, cans which some of these grubbers visit surreptitiously every weekday morning, hiding so as not to be chased off as undesirables by regulars brandishing identification cards and incorporation papers. Aside from the garbage cans, myriad other sources contribute items, among them a bent metal park chair painted green, let go for eighty francs, and the seller's own seat, straw-bottomed or

traditional Norman-style leather, which fetches three hundred for a poor devil thus obliged to sit on his own patch on a crate until that too finds a buyer. The indigence of the old vendors is a crying shame. Beyond Rue Gracieuse the sky is clearing up, too slowly for the three old biddies who sell books (and what books!) down by the quayside and who are at present sitting huddled together on camp stools, engaged not in tittle-tattle but in mordant discussion of how to survive, their elbows folded like crickets' legs and pressed hard against their hollow chests and their shoulders hunched in the tight clasp of their arms. Across the street another is asleep alongside the curb. Men lug their goods from the other end of Paris in wooden boxes on wheels or baby carriages with large former potato sacks bumping against their calves; others, the better-off ones, drag their wares out from the inner courtyards of nearby buildings where they have hiding places.

In the middle of the street Marceau is playing the greeter. A scarecrow chewing on his mustache, eyes barely visible beneath his cap, he has nothing to sell, so he assigns places according to order of arrival, or according to his appraisal of the applicant, having acquired the dignity of market director thanks to a tacit agreement that brings him in a good many fifty- and hundred-franc notes and a good many more glasses of red. A sweet racket, but one that pays off only one day out of seven, and Marceau has to eat for the other six, in aid of which he has two wives, which would suggest a startlingly comfortable life were not the benefits rendered quite relative by the fact that the charms of both these members of the fair sex are imperceptible to the naked eye. A recent adventure of this Marceau has turned him into a local celebrity. Having left one evening to tie one on somewhere near the distant Charenton quays, he had vanished for a rather long period when the police discovered a corpse under a plane tree and paid a visit to his wife (the official and only one at the time), who identified the body as undoubtedly that of her husband, allowed everyone on Rue Mouffetard, genuinely upset and sympathetic, to buy her liters of wine by way of condolence, accepted a princely sum from a collection spontaneously taken up by a commiserating confrere, and drank it—at which juncture, *per mirabile*, old Marceau reappeared one morning on the corner

of Rue Tournefort, as spry and proud of bearing as ever (albeit somewhat lit), with a girl in tow whom he presented to his stunned pals as
his esteemed wife, this to the outrage of the other one, who bombarded
him with curses. But everything settled down, and after the inevitable
celebratory binge the trio began to live harmoniously in private as in
public. As for the police, they struck Marceau off the roster of the living and registered his death as accidental. End of story.

By eight o'clock, Olivier is at last opening his bistro, Les Quatre
Sergents de La Rochelle, with its homely dining room, rust-colored
from a hundred years' worth of first pipe and then cigarette smoke,
bedecked with color covers from *Le Petit Journal*, and equipped with a
horsehair banquette as narrow as the seat in a 1911 Brasier and a plank
serving as a bench that makes it pleasanter to sit drinking at the bar
with your back comfortable and in great company, for the warm and
congenial atmosphere brings in more than the usual muster of old-
clothes merchants, who go in and out of the door regularly every couple of minutes, because, when they are kicking their heels by their
wares on display outside, they have but one thought, which is to nip in
for a quick one, but once they are inside their one thought is that they
might miss a customer, the possible sale that can pay for their next
round—an economic cycle, in short, that is also a vicious circle—and
never have fishing trips and houses in the country served more often as
castles in the air. Hey, the times are bad.

As for Jérôme and I, who have nothing to do except watch, listen,
offer the odd pithy comment and greet new arrivals, we sit in the corner like two bumps on a log, nice and warm and waiting for the morning to be over before we bestir ourselves and go in search of a substantial
hot meal. Things are good. All these folks are our buddies. We need
only be on the look-out for the out-of-the-ordinary. Before long we are
joined by Duval, the painter-ragpicker from Rue Visconti, who comes
in with a broken pickaxe under his arm, settles down, and after the
customary half-hour of meditation required for gathering one's
thoughts, starts telling us how he has been redesigning his raincoat, a
task begun a week ago, and asking us for advice concerning the right
positioning of the buttons, especially the one that is supposed to pro-

tect his shirt collar, and he chuckles, as always, for he is another one who never worries, who does not give a damn, as he swims blithely between one stage of life and the next—or between one meal and the next—with the nonchalance of a fish in the water.

By this time La Mouffe is bustling with clochards, vendors, housewives, wanderers, Sunday strollers, and *petits rentiers* from down by Les Gobelins who climb the hill slowly, then turn right and go back down into the anonymous city. A dense and elastic crowd. A human landscape where elbows collide and by which tourists are repelled. The time has come for us to get moving, to make our rounds of bistros where there is always a glass to be had, or a ten-franc note, for naturally our connections extend to every social stratum of the local populace. A stop at Raymond's place, which is like a narrow country kitchen, is *de rigueur*. Every one of these cafés has its own character, as does the collective face of each's habitués.

And our feast day, begun in the chill of dawn, ends in the warmth of twelve hours spent in twelve bistros spread over a couple of hundred meters. The time taken is inevitable in view of the manifest familiarity that bonds all these people, who are as thick as thieves and never act independently, and for whom a drink with a pal means ordering (if not necessarily paying for) a round for the house on you never know exactly whom—the same ones always take care of it, say some; we'll cover it next time, say others—and it's seven, eight, nine glasses downed in quick succession, wobbly legs and eyes in a state of rapture. Very rare indeed are those who never tipple, one of them being Mademoiselle Léontine, the little old woman I mentioned earlier, now arranging her folding chair and laying out her wares: a handsome pipe, a newly boned pink corset, a box of safety pins, piles of rags, shoe soles, carefully bundled and tied papers. . . . She is the only woman around here to whom everyone feels duty-bound to be polite, friendly, helpful, affable, and they never fail to greet her and wish her good sales though fully aware that she will never glean more than a couple of hundred francs for her entire stock. Lucky for her she eats so little: a salad and a hard-boiled egg suffice for her evening meal, while her breakfast consists of coffee and bread and margarine—and a small packet of margarine lasts her five days. She lives out her life in a room on Rue Princesse, halfway up a perilous building whose stairways remind you of the Crazy Cottage at an amusement park, a place where anyone can lose their way, stumble, resort to striking a match or even find themselves standing on a window ledge (and quite unable to find the concierge, who lives on the fourth floor). That room is a wretched garret that she has adorned with pine branches, possibly an obsessive reminder of some visit in her youth, maybe even a tragic one, to the forests of the Vosges. Across the window a makeshift contraption of wires and bits of the mattress from a folding metal cot supports a row of miniature Christmas trees, stiff and green but still allowing light through from a courtyard no wider than a well. Mademoiselle Léontine, by the way, is one of the most passionate readers on the banks of the Seine: I have never seen her without reading matter to hand, and she devours serialized novels and illustrated classics with equal voraciousness.

But inside the bistros it's a three-ring circus. Everybody is there. The great family of scavengers and topers. La Bretonne is there, teary-eyed, with her mountainous rolling bosom, narrow waist, wanton locks and pestilential breath, cranking out her schmaltzy songs and pouring scorn on what she calls *bourgeoiserie*. Big Dédé the truck driver is there, threatening to punch his neighbor out. And the American, red-faced, with his drawl and his Marine slang. And Claude, the inevitable, the great, the superb Claude complete with crumpled cap, hairy nostrils, rolled-up sleeves, and broad knife-thin smile, proudly showing off photos that our friend Robert Doisneau has taken of him and his legal wife. Well worth the price of a glass of red. The pictures include one of old Claude, whose official occupation is dockworker and who bears the obligatory tattoos, reclining like a pasha on his bed beneath the astonishing collection of barely clad, titillating pin-ups that he has thumb-tacked all over his room, as he blows his cigarette smoke toward their asses, and complacently displays the tattoos that have made his name: the two wind roses on his shoulders, the bunch of grapes, the naked girl who wiggles as his arms move, the prophetic handcuffs, the many blue dots that, according to custom, represent months spent inside, and others that he shows only to his intimates,

among them Robert Giraud, who has himself taken pictures of him from every angle and published them in his book (I say this not to boost the works of my pals, but because this digression requires it, and I want it mentioned*). The man's renown and revenue do not depend solely on this, however, for Monsieur Claude is also Mr. Numb, Mr. Feel-No-Pain, the Man with the Armored Skin, who sticks needles, pins or nails into a part of his anatomy chosen by any enthusiast who pays for a round: he will gather the skin of his neck and pierce it or the flesh of a forearm and run steel right through it, and for anyone who can pay the price he will adorn the knob of his penis with a tight sheaf of tiny needles, a spectacle prone to make young tourists blanch and choke. In general, though, all this goes on among friends, at Mother Marie's place on the corner of Rue Pot-de-Fer, where red is twelve francs and the basement is open to anyone in need of a quick wash and brush up.

Time now to look in at Au Vieux Chêne, that historic dive from a *belle époque* that was far more hospitable to folk of our kind—the Jardin Mabille,† as it were, of rag-and-bone men and a diurnal and nocturnal haunt of pickpockets and plainclothes cops: Au Vieux Chêne with its impressive sign, one of the finest in a neighborhood already rich in this kind of popular art, a superb tree carved from solid wood now toppling over gently and sliding down the bulbous façade. Today the place is faithfully patronized by grubbers and crippled beggars released from detention in the Maison de Nanterre and arrived here, at a snail's pace but with their mental compass intact despite the long string of bistros along Avenue de la Défense, to spend the remainder of their hard-earned change, all that is left of the pittance the Administration accords them for mindless work (whose nature I'll get to in a moment). Along the bar at present, or already slumped at the corner of one or other of the tables, are the regulars known to each other

*The Doisneau photograph described is "Créatures de Rêves" (1952). The book referred to is Jacques Delarue and Robert Giraud's *Les tatouages du "milieu"* (Paris: La Roulotte, 1950; reprint, Paris: L'Oiseau de Minerve, 1999).—*Trans.*
†A nineteenth-century open-air dancing and leisure garden (1831–1875).—*Trans.*

from that Nanterre detention center, all of them from the section known as "the Legion," which houses only released beggars, meaning those who have just completed one- or two-month prison terms at Fresnes or La Santé but must still serve forty-five days of "extra time" (how nice it sounds!) in prison-like surroundings: the tiers of long walkways along ranks of cells duly adorned with giant padlocks the mere sight of which reminds those who are familiar with it of a particularly painful sound at wake-up time; the cop stationed in a central mirador watching all comings and goings; the college-like quadrangle with its sharp-edged rubblestone underfoot, scraggy plane trees, and inmates walking round in circles; and the loudly resonant workshops—a whole blissful universe blocked off behind a stout door so that the Sunday visitor sees nothing but a flower garden most pleasant to contemplate, as if the Maison de Nanterre were simply a vast oasis of peace, a profusion of green trees, sparrows, park benches, nursing sisters, men in blue overalls strolling without a care in the world beneath the arches, by the brick buildings, and through the cemetery, where the dead are named individually even though this very labeling has a hint of deprecation. All the same, a relative freedom reigns in the Legion, where prisoners are locked up at night only, two to a cell, and are free the rest of the time to engage in such insignificant activity as the podding of beans, making piles of them on a workshop bench, meticulously stripped of all their superfluous animal, vegetable or mineral matter and carefully weighed, the lavish reward for each kilo thus sorted being two francs fifty, meaning that if you apply a bit of elbow grease and don't let yourself be distracted by the general silence, a day's work can earn you twenty or thirty francs. Mercifully, supper is collective, served in a temporary refectory set up in the hallways. The guards wear white coats. Which says it all.

All beggars, real or bogus, genuinely penniless or secretly rich, find themselves in Nanterre at regular intervals, among them the panhandlers who sit with stump leg extended in the corridors of the metro and specialists of the tendered hat or Basque beret picked up in "no-loitering" areas. Some are professionals, but no matter: all anyone freed from the prisons of the Seine Department ever has in their pocket is enough to rush to the nearest bar, pour drink down their gullet, then see what comes up, try to get a job—any job ("so long as I am out and stay out"), or, more likely after half a day or so, find a still openhanded passer-by or an indulgent fellow drinker. (The poor no longer congregate at church doors for the good reason that charitable people no longer pass that way, only selfish individuals who hasten into churches in a fearful search for refuge in these halls of silence, where they can commune with their peers amid the reassuring anonymous drone of prayer and psalmodizing, so different from an outside world that scares the bejeezus out of them and threatens to drown them in the national shit. Nor are the poor to be found in cathedral porches, because the cops prowl there, ready to roust them before they can so much as cast a glance at the motor coaches full of tourists in whose eyes beggary is a repellent curse, albeit an essential picturesque feature in their guidebooks.)

At the Vieux Chêne today is Oudinot, the sometime "murderer of the Bois de Boulogne," a persistent resident of Boulevard Suchet—not, as he makes clear, of the bourgeois residences, but of the bushes on the opposite side—who made headlines and was featured in all the trashy magazines, replete with photos and spicy details, when a corpse, still fresh, was discovered alongside his abode. This turned him into a hero and became his chief claim to fame.

Most importantly, Joséphine the hermaphrodite is here—and I do mean hermaphrodite! This man-woman (or woman-man, as you prefer) has never consented to unbutton in front of me, much to my regret, for I should have loved to contemplate this marvel and see how the two sexes can actually overlap. Officially Joséphine is a woman, and for many years the civil authorities have imposed this empress's name on him and obliged him to wear patched-up dresses. But in the penitentiary view she is a man, which breaks the monotony for a good many of her cellmates. But wait a minute, he protests, I'm not queer, I'm not against the odd little dalliance, but I like women better, especially lesbos, they're easier to seduce on account of my equipment and once in a position to get a load of it don't complain too much because I know how to satisfy them in their way and they can do the same for me. This is probably the reason why the prison authorities, who normally turn a blind eye to goings-on in the cells, but wishing to avoid too great an uproar of the Sapphic variety in the women's quarters, chose to stick him with the men. In civilian life, the priceless Joséphine sports flounces, old-fashioned shoes and a blonde wig, professes to sing tenor, or, excuse me, to be a cantatrice (and even to have performed onstage under the name of Mademoiselle de Werther de l'Empire), whereas in the fateful passageways where I used to see him he went about with shaven head and twisted mouth, dribbling and slack-jawed, clad in the convict's customary gray jacket, striped body shirt and clunky workboots.

2

BEFORE the war in the Saint-Paul district—I think it was in Rue de Fourcy—there used to be the most amazing public establishment, a brothel for down-and-outs. Now vanished save in the memory of its patrons, this house of joy, whose atmosphere one can only imagine, and regret, consisted of two rooms, namely the Senate, where the price was invariably ten francs, and the Chamber of Deputies, where the price hovered, according to whim and the nature of the service, around fifteen. An old girl who expected to end her days as a resident there entertained me by recalling the extraordinary tragicomic theatrics that the place produced, as for example the spectacle of an old clochard with impressive facial hair complaining and shaking his fist in the face of a low-cost whore, yelling in more than slightly drunken tones: "'Ten francs! You bitch, you'll be lucky if you get twenty sous!"

But the question arises of just how, where, and with whom the big city's vagrants and derelicts, those you see every day passed out in the metro, waiting rooms, hospitable bistros, public squares, at the bottom of stairways, in *portes-cochères*, in church porches, on the grass in parks, under the bridges of the Seine, along the quays of the canals, anywhere where there is a secluded dark corner—just how do these people, who almost always contrive to get hold of a crust of bread, a can of soup, or a liter of red wine, manage in this regard? I am not talking about the old, who couldn't care less, or who are content from time to time, when the opportunity arises, to lie down with old streetwalkers whose thighs are still white beneath their stinking black rags, the skin of their bellies still sweet despite the gray hairs, and who, amidst the odors of stale wine and filth and cigarette-fouled breath, quickly

rediscover the motions of the flanks and the slow caresses of love, and soon replace volleys of oaths with the sighing words that keep time with love's rhythms. But what about the young? If they are not sent packing like the swaggering sailors who wreak havoc on the fringes of traveling fairs, and if they are not more or less clean and presentable despite their haven't-eaten-for-three-days look and thus able to make it with young maidservants coming out of the movies or homely office workers getting off work, how do they manage? The mystery is hard to solve, for nobody is primmer than a pauper, and many vagabonds find satisfaction amongst themselves and many are content with waking dreams, with the contemplation of posters, pin-ups, film stars, women clad in bras or panties, or pairs of legs up in the air displaying flesh-tone stockings, because the requirements of advertising surpass those of their imagination. How many times have I myself wandered through the city, utterly penniless, gazing into the windows not of the pork butchers but instead into those of lingerie stores, scrutinizing with a detached air but most attentively the splendid photos of splendid girls with provocative breasts molded by soft fabrics, and then, from a bench, gazing hungrily at the women passing by and keeping a naive tally, laughable after the fact, of all those with whom etc.

On Quai de la Tournelle I observe a depraved man who has just ac-costed a homeless woman. The man looks the part: indeterminate age, coat collar turned up, hands in pockets. He must have offered her money to have his way with her, and she is yelling at him. She is neither young nor old, a streetwalker, dirty, her legs swathed in dark varicose veins and red plaques. "Bastard!" she cries, "I'm no whore, I don't want your money. Get away from me, you filthy pig, get lost! Hands off!" But the guy persists, follows her. She shakes her fist at him, threatens him with a bottle. "I don't give a shit for your dough, you're filth, my ass belongs to me, and it's a lot cleaner than yours too. I don't fuck maniacs, and I tell you I'm not a slut, I'm not for sale, so just piss off, you shameless louse."

I approach and the guy backs into the shadows, among the trees. He has taken out his tool and points it at the woman, who spits on it dis-gustedly. "Get away!" she shouts, "or I'll crack your skull." The man adjusts his clothing and goes off. She comes towards me. I recognize Mimi, from the Magasins Généraux.* Inevitably, she launches into an endless commentary on this revolting episode. "There are any number like that, crazy perverts, they should all be thrown in the hole, I'm telling you, I daren't even go to sleep when those sons of bitches are prowling around here. I'd have killed that one if only I'd had my man with me." And with a knowing smile she adds: "A Yank, I wouldn't wonder."

*Large warehouse complex in Pantin (Seine) on the Canal de l'Ourcq, serving (1931–2000) as a customs house and transit point for grain, coal and other goods destined for Paris.—*Trans.*

3

LIKE SO many Paris neighborhoods, such as Saint-Paul, those of La Huchette and Maubert are being transformed—and here too the changes come not year by year but from one month to the next. This precinct is still a vagrant's paradise (or chicken coop), but the ease with which it was once possible to lead an idle and quiet life there is now nothing but a fading memory in the minds of the old-timers, and reaching that goal demands painstaking research if not resort to non-traditional methods. Among the many spots that have disappeared in less than a year is the Armenian bistro in Rue Saint-Séverin: an empty, expensive restaurant now occupies the space where there used to be no one to speak of except foreigners from Asia Minor, tranquil players of pick-up-sticks, drinkers of raki, choosy nibblers at little dishes of pickled vegetables on offer at each table (like bags of pretzels or potato chips in other places, though in this case complimentary), salad plates laden with cauliflower, leeks, gherkins, pearl onions, olives macerated in vinegar, all with a fiery hot-sauce accompaniment, or large jars of sweet-and-sour oriental fruits arranged with meticulous artistry in a decorative mosaic (a fine appetizer that may still be found in Rue Bergère at two bistros of the Arabic persuasion, namely L'Algérie and Chez Prosper, where it goes by the rather pretentious name of *la kernia*). Then there was the restaurant in Rue Fred-Sauton, a bums' mess kept by a disreputable but broadminded couple, a smoke-filled room with a massive farmhouse table bought at a sale, two benches, no cutlery—each guest brought their own, wrapped in newspaper—and a menu invariably comprising soup, potato purée, blood sausage and *frites* and priced so competitively that you could eat two meals in quick succession for a hundred francs.

As for Les Cloches de Notre-Dame, the most splendid caravansary in Paris, a true court of miracles on the corner of Rue Lagrange, it is now a nondescript store, but this was where generations of beggars, clochards, drifters, jobless, whores, ragpickers, junk sellers and poor street booksellers used to wet their whistles, snack, nap, bill and coo, tie one on, gorge themselves, swap blows, hoodwink one another, hurl insults as lethal as gobs of spit, and play every imaginable game—belote, 421, loaded dice, *petits paquets*, plain dice, three-card monte, *touche-pipi*, eat my pussy, tough guy, smart guy, beggar my neighbor, tattooed man, forbidden, relegated, back from Cayenne, landlord, millionaire—with everyone puffing themselves up to convince their audience that they were endowed with all the qualities required to be a Real Man. A wretched audience it was, though, ravaged by increasing grime and advancing age. None of the folk standing or sitting or laid out alongside the bar had more to their name than their effects in a string bag and memories awash in light Beaujolais. A bewildering tribe that excluded strangers, curiosity seekers, wage-earners, and young people who had not yet proved themselves. A daily meeting-place for the entire male and female population of the ten or so nearest streets. As soon as you entered you saw the Levantine sitting by the barrel that he used as an all-purpose table and cooking up food for the community, which he did independently of the owner, who confined his responsibilities to decanting his daily hectoliter of wine into hundreds of barely rinsed glasses, leaving the other fellow free to run his catering operation, which, as small-scale as it was, turned a goodly profit. From a collection of cans of food of various sizes he would measure out soup, chickpeas, beans, various other odd feculents, and scraps of meat, and for thirty or forty francs sell two ladlefuls of this concoction, enough to fill your belly and let you drink to your heart's content without fear of your stomach bloating. From time to time the Levantine withdrew an oblong package from beneath his chair and discreetly pulled back the corner of its wrapping paper to reveal half a dozen smoked herrings, which he offloaded at cost price (said he), about fifteen francs apiece, to his best pals-cum-customers. He faced the window, and whenever he saw some guy stop outside and hesitate, he would signal to him and with his moist finger write the price of his offerings on the inside of the glass. I wonder where he is hanging around now. Only once did I catch a glimpse of his cap with its turned-back peak as he lay in deep slumber between two plane trees on the quayside.

Among the other characters who patronized that legendary bistro I recall a negro with a little redhead on his arm whom I once witnessed selling a pair of trampers for thirty francs, the price of a can of beans. This pair of lovebirds of indeterminate age used to go and sleep every night in an extraordinary and distinctly dubious cavity behind a grating on the riverside by the parvis of Notre-Dame, a place where every lowlife in Paris has spent at least one night at some time or another, even made love there, and hung up washing, which drips slowly down onto hunched figures below while rats of respectable size play in every corner. Nights to remember. But, to come back to that late lamented bistro, pretty much the only one the police would raid on a regular (and hence predictable) basis, I want to describe a hustle to which I never fell victim but the subtlety of which I still admire and would not mind benefiting from. A guy who stayed anonymous by using various pseudonyms always came in with bundles of clothes, especially women's underwear, that he offered for sale very cheap. And three glasses away down the bar there would always be a tearful old hooker who went into ecstasies over his wares and moaned about how desperately she wanted them. And every now and again some drunk, washed up there by chance or by poor navigational skills, would feel his heart melt and buy her a dress, or a skirt, or a corset, or a pair of woolen stockings, or a tit supporter and present the item to the whore, who would almost piss herself as she simpered and wiggled her rear end like a young hussy, and by way of compensation offered the gallant favors of the libertine kind on one of the few available banquettes. The guy would be delighted at first, but many a time he would spot his conquest slipping his gift back to the slyboots, who was now eager to make his escape and go off to start over somewhere else. It all ended in the inevitable donny-brook complete with broken glass and great shouting matches.

As for the aforementioned redhead, I saw her one night coming back to her man's side and telling him in the sweetest way, "I have just done two at fifty francs each." Words that must at least have contributed to the nation's moral decline and all but launched me there and then on a quest for the gratification that her quite relative charms might vouchsafe. But that's another story.

Latest news: the Levantine is now a sandwich-man, but he looks more like a corpse fished out of the Seine (not because he is bloated but because of his greenish complexion) than a hunk of bread split by three slices of *saucisson* (to borrow the phrase of a neighbor of mine, hereby duly acknowledged).

And now neon is invading the shops even on the darkest streets. In Rue de la Bûcherie there are still passageways and inner courtyards il-luminated by Argand lamps, dark lanterns, kerosene lamps and car-riage lamps that have to be sheltered from the wind by thick glass far more opaque than transparent, but they are merely curiosities. Bright-ness reigns supreme. Night in the city lasts just a few hours. Metal rods at white heat fray the vision, revolving on their axes before eyes blinded and blinking—quite unlike the pleasant solar gyrations of gaslight—and exposing the signs of exhaustion, deepening wrinkles, moist brows, worn faces, aching heads and cancer-ridden brains, so that peo-ple can no longer hope to find anonymous warmth and refuge along-side the filthy, timeworn and creviced walls, but must instead remain standing in uncertain equilibrium under the glacial light, prey to the sweet delusional obsession with cups of coffee and glasses of rum at a bar as golden as high-class dental work, because warm wood, so gentle to the touch, disappeared from public places long ago, while tables cov-ered with chilly galalith are hardly welcoming to the arms and cheeks of standing sleepers who long to get an hour's seated slumber for the price of a glass of wine.

At Les Cloches Saint-Séverin (until two or three years ago Le Tango du Chat), the clientele is still quite special, and includes several local

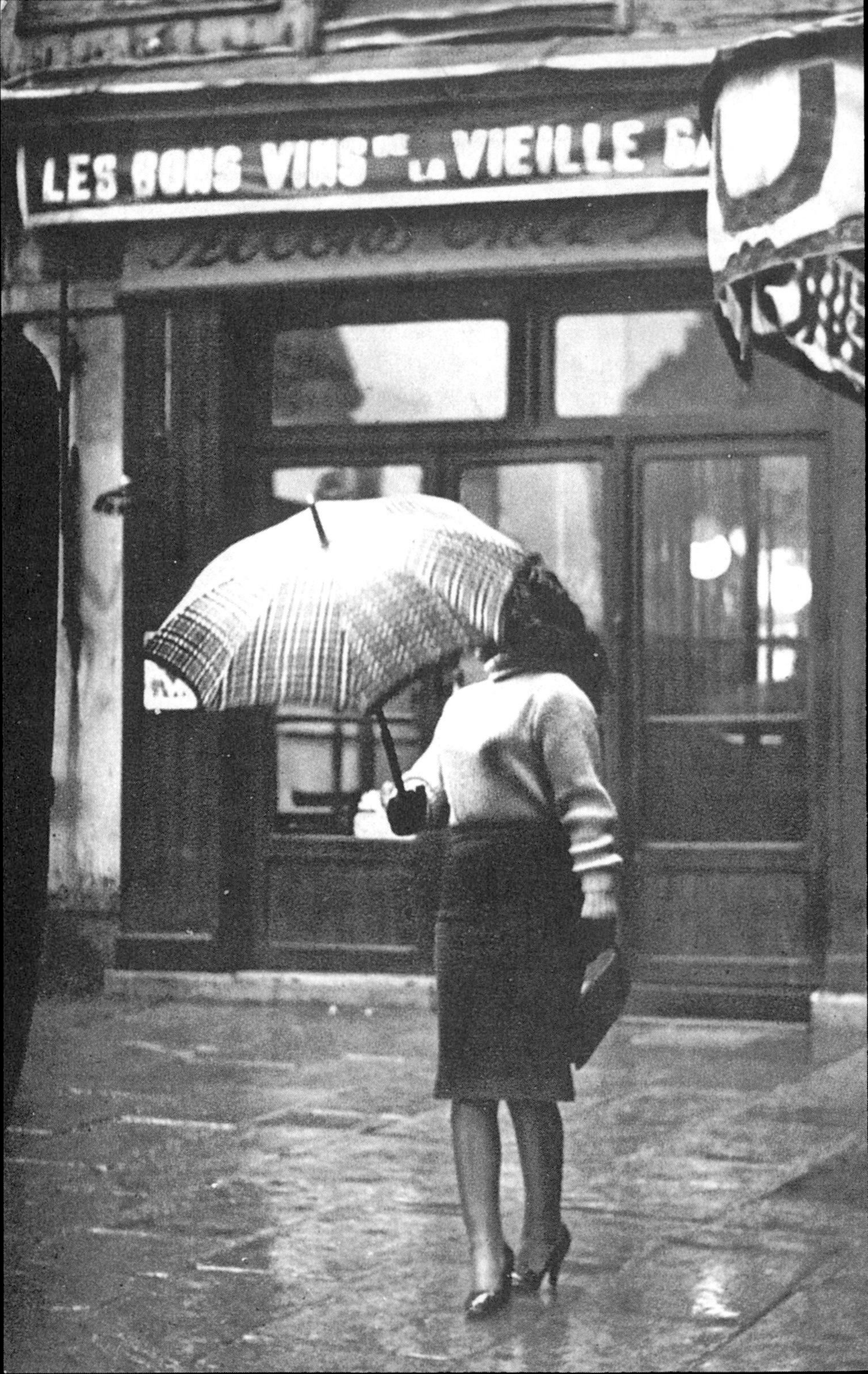
LES BONS VINS DE LA VIEILLE

characters, among them Robespierre, who is forever passing around portraits of the Incorruptible, his supposed ancestor. (And why not? After all, Edmond du Plessis de Richelieu, direct and authentic descendant of the Cardinal, lives in the vicinity of La Joliette and Rue des Fortins as an aristocrat-clochard who prides himself on his lineage, never eating his poor man's soup without a newspaper serviette about his neck, and unraveling his shirtsleeves to simulate frills and lacy cuffs.) Robespierre's specialty is sleight of hand, and he conjures at cafés, outside on the terraces or inside, wearing a top hat shiny with age and a tatty frock-coat; his tricks fail regularly, but he gets people to buy him drinks for his good intentions, a trait, incidentally, that is said to have caused him to sell his identity seven times in succession—a bizarre tale, long drawn out and in any case unverifiable. There is Robespierre, then, and Bakerman, the Ambassador, Coco—all practitioners of petty cons, ragpicking, small-time trafficking in junk, old iron, paper or bottles, if not actually fake cripples or panhandlers, and all invariably stony broke, but passing hours sitting with their backs to the wine barrels and the basins of fresh water used for soaking potatoes for frying in the rear of this combined bar and grocery, forever expanding its range of merchandise—liters of wine to take away, single smokes, bowls of soup, orders of fries—at reasonable prices but all too quickly consumed. On the front window a limewash sign offers to buy stale bread by weight, and this, along with the cornucopia of vegetables pilfered from Les Halles, is what makes the soup so thick and velvety. Nothing goes to waste.

Fortunately there are still a few bistros hospitable to our kind in the neighborhood, among them Le Petit Bacchus on Rue de la Harpe, whose back room is the meeting place and refuge of all the sandwichmen of the Left Bank, especially on Sunday afternoons—which means either that there is no work for them at that time or that they have let time go by sitting behind a glass—when other cafés are closed.

Among them too, and most important, is La Belle Étoile, located just where the extremely narrow Rue Xavier-Privas, which funnels all the clochards from the quayside, broadens out, an area that also crams

together Le Vieux-Paris and Le Salève, two well-known hotel-bars, as well as the aforementioned Attic of Bad Spells.

At night, life here has a slightly picaresque quality, with tippling and snoozing the dominant themes. All the laborers of the asphalt world congregate as brothers, members of a fraternity that, sad to say, is gradually disappearing, just as, in this nonetheless eminently plebeian sphere, the notions of family tradition, hustling academies, the employment of children, and tribal organization have all perished. The freemasonry of mutual counsel, however, has survived. La Belle Étoile is a public house wreathed less in glory than in tobacco smoke, but the lady friends of these gents do not shrink from coming down to chat, and the same goes for the tenants from upstairs, ambulant fruit-and-vegetable sellers, peanut vendors, artisans or metalworkers. But the roster is not complete without the old-timers, the park-benchers, loiterers, down-and-outers, and trash-can miners. Like Coco merrily downing his twenty half-liters of red per day (count them!), Pépère with his handlebar mustache, who carries an advertising placard, The Admiral, also known as Victor Hugo because he has whiskers like the poet's (when said poet was a grandpa), and a fine pair of flesh-and-blood Daumier characters—all of them drinking endless glasses of light wine before going off in search of soup at fifty or sixty francs in a tin can or a real laborer's dixie at Les Cloches Saint-Séverin, or else, at the back door of a nearby restaurant, layered mosaics of food varied enough to satisfy every taste and every gastronomic desire. None of this differs significantly from the usual doings at a fourth-category bistro. The affrays, however, are notable for the violence of the insults bandied and the quantity of glassware smashed, and occasionally a woman might be seen wiping off a little kid who has taken a big dump, the naughty boy, in his diaper.

Outside the door, the conveyances of all these splendid folk await: soapbox cars, vintage baby carriages, high-wheeled, or even wheel-less, like Coco's, which is also his home, where he curls up and sleeps the sleep of the just, even if it's something of a tight fit.

4

THE TRUE Maubert bistros are not the three modern brasseries that cater to provincials and janitors from nearby buildings, to night street sweepers and the *noctambules* who go slumming in Rue des Anglais, but rather the cookshops in Rue Maître-Albert, a dog-legged alley that outsiders avoid; they are invisible from the sidewalk and you enter from the passageway leading to the building's stairs by pushing open a door at random, feeling your way in the dark before stumbling down a single step into a room the size of a hen-house with a strictly family atmosphere: a counter barely big enough for a pair of lovers to stand at; an oilcloth-covered table where the owner's wife is peeling vegetables or putting bread in the soup or giving her newborn his bottle; and a double row of bottles: the five wines and apéritifs, including raki, that constitute the house's entire stock. There are more small fry in evidence than customers. And if you happen to have a drink with an old junkman friend whistled up from the street who has seized on the chance to knock one back and top up his one-liter nightly quota, the boss never fails to pour another, and when it comes time to settle up you need only produce your small change, twenty-, forty- or hundred-sou pieces, and just a few will do it (the franc must be defended, after all). At those prices, of course, you order another, and by the time you emerge, banging your pate on the beams, the night belongs to cut-throats, it is too late to get into the next dive along, whose door is long shut, and the street has completely emptied. Any drinking is going on upstairs. You go up to see. And perhaps for a quickie with the woman who lives there. Because that's the way the night ends, sometimes.

The cardinal times of day in the Maubert neighborhood are, first, the early morning, when all the indigenous old clothes and junk dealers trickle in with their cast-off wares attached more or less securely to their carts, though items are already classified, sorted, categorized and presented with the prize offerings to the fore; and, secondly, the evening, when coins are arranged on the edge of a familiar bar into little piles each of which represents the exact sum needed to order, taste and relish one glass of red.

Between these two high points in the day everyone is doing their job. Some pass out advertising flyers, paid by the hour or at so much per thousand (sheaves of said flyers get shoved down the nearest drain, for people in the street have the reprehensible habit of refusing to accept free handouts). Some are sidewalk artists using colored chalk (there is an anonymous tinker living in Rue Maître-Albert who creates works of art not to garner pocket change but as a vocation; having discovered belatedly and on his own that he was gifted, he procured a plane table, four drawing pins with which to attach a white sheet of paper to it, a black pencil, a razor blade, a soft eraser, a drawing-pen, and went straight off, following his nose, down to the Pont de l'Archvêché, where he surveyed Notre-Dame, with graduated rule in hand and raised to eye level, and fervently set about taking its measurements, determining that there were three-millimeter gaps between each niche and proceeding to draw three niches just that far apart, so that, after two days of dedicated work with his tongue hanging out, he had reconstructed the cathedral stone by stone, tile by tile, no doubt missing the odd turret or statue here or there—but people, he said, might well not notice this, and when he eventually realized that his paper was too small to include the spire and flying buttresses of the apse, he said no matter, I'll stick another piece on. Authentically naive art. To this character I am indebted at least for getting me to take a close look at our national church. Others are fly-by-night bookies, or river beachcombers, or peddlers of shoelaces and pencils—objects of little real interest that are merely covers, just sufficient to keep the wrath of the law at bay; still others are low-grade public entertainers— like poor Robespierre, whom I spotted yesterday huddled up over a sewer grid like a little heap of misery; or illegal porters on the platform when trains come in and at the exits from Les Halles; or collectors of inanimate objects; or hunters of stray cats like the simpering fellow who attracts his prey with a curled finger and sweet talk before swiftly snatching it up and stuffing it into a bag, for sale, if it is a fine specimen, at the Rue Brancion Sunday market (behind the bust of Monsieur Decroix, "promoter of horse meat"), or, if it is scrawny, to the first sap who comes along.

But all these fine-feathered specimens work only on their own timetable, blissfully ignorant of the device known as a timeclock, and have no greater ambition than to pay for the two or three 65-franc liter bottles that they will slowly polish off under the quayside plane trees as they lie on doubled-up newspapers or an old sack (comfort is the watchword!) with head delicately raised towards the mouth of a bottle and eyes half-closed in affected slumber but riveted on the spread legs of female tourists peacefully watching the Seine flow by. With the bistro activity ending early, each and everyone repairs to their den, their hideaway, their illusion of a home. The guys of La Maube go to bed with the chickens. Night falls over a tangle of empty backstreets prowled by none but wretched alley cats.

The inhabitants of the quarter are nothing if not diverse, ranging as they do from the model low-ranking government employee who leaves home every morning at a measured step on his way to the joys of work well done (in all fairness to Maubert I should add that this bird is fairly rare and in any case rapidly identified, categorized and roundly despised by his neighbors) to the Arab with a game leg who sells fruit and vegetables from his pushcart and the washed-up old hooker who sucks cock for a glass of wine. Not forgetting the Gypsy car stripper, the perfect housewife, the bibulous debonair retiree, the illegal, the family of carders, the Latin teacher, the Russo-Turkish cab driver, the homebody bartender, the hotelier-receiver, the raggedy crazy woman, the innocent kids, the firewood seller, and that's just scratching the surface. The whole throng makes up a splendid gallery of confirmed winebibbers who regularly frequent the same bars as another group, a little cuckoo, less sedentary, that of the clochards and vagrants, but who (like water in oil) rub shoulders without mixing with a third category of people, namely the North Africans, now firmly established in Rue de Bièvre and at the Restaurant d'Alger, on the corner by the quay. In winter, all the men lying flat on the gratings of the metro's hot air vents or crouching elbow to elbow in a circle around glowing braziers in so-called public places, and in summer all those in the shade of the poplars on the banks of the Seine or in the relatively cool back rooms of bistros seem to have been bitten by the tsetse fly and contracted sleeping sickness. I have seen guys who can sleep twenty hours straight without so much as a groan, or standing up with their head lolling back and forth over their glass as though on a spring, but most snooze on their folded arms, snoring and burping and drooling, oblivious to bustle, racket, fighting, screaming and shouting matches, and even the scrutiny of the gentlemen in blue. I remember two such impervious sleepers in particular: Petit Jean-les-Vappes, so named for having his head in the clouds even when he was not deep in dreamland, and Mange-Tout, who earned this moniker because he could dispatch any portion of couscous, no matter how large, without accompaniment— unless it was simply because he regularly spent his summers working at a pea-canning factory in Seine-et-Oise?* In any case, you had the feeling he might dispatch any Christian who happened to pass by in the same way.

But if Maubert, along with the vicinity of Rue de La Huchette, is still the citadel of Paris's ten thousand clochards, getting into it demands a little more cerebral arousal each day that passes, as food and lodging get harder and harder to secure. The late lamented Hôtel Pécoul, for instance, where a year or two ago one could still rent a place to doss by the hour, as timed by the taut-string system (the pleasant and healthy arrangement described earlier in this book), is now no more, ditto the hotel in Impasse Maubert where two or three "little cuties" well over the hill used to clack their high heels and smack their lips.

The truth is that there is nothing left for lovers of the picturesque to see. True, there is one remaining *bal-musette* in Rue des Anglais, complete with anachronistic décor and tables and benches riveted to

*The French call snow peas or snap peas *mange-tout.—Trans.*

the floor (just as customers are no longer permitted to serve themselves from the bottle in case of a brawl), *apaches* and bargirls on the payroll, costume acts, and *javas-vache* to a whistled accompaniment for the benefit of the last moneyed nocturnal romantics, but such people are obliged to pass quickly through the streets, race down Rue de Bièvre curbing any inclination to ooh and ah at the potbellied form of the buildings and not risk so much as a glance into the bistros. The owners no longer want them and the regulars want them even less, and would scream bloody murder and create mayhem if swarms of rich idiots intruded on their last strongholds, on the tranquility and congenial animality of their fellowship, provoking them by turning up their noses in disgust or else enjoying the show from the ancient buses that drift by in pairs—in search of what exactly? For as I say this place is dangerous, closed, as it were, to the public. Most of the cafés just mentioned are in fact Arab, and thus impenetrable places where French is a dead language and outsiders, meaning native French people, are unceremoniously tossed out by owners who will not serve them. Unless you have the open-sesame look, the eight-day beard, the hands crusted with dirt, cracked and bloody from fatigue, the eyes rolling up from sleeplessness, the shoes gaping like carp, if you fail to place your hand on your heart and offer the customary *salaam aleikums*, the men within will grumble. But still, what a fantastic sociability is here! You need only pass the frontier of these restricted areas, go down the little Rue des Trois-Portes, at the corner of Rue de l'Hôtel Colbert, take a probing look through the window to find oneself in the depths of Turkestan or at some Anatolian way station.

5

THE PERAMBULATOR is no longer the exclusive appurtenance of those nannies and maids of all work who adorn the public squares and are far from averse to sucking a little cock; rather, baby carriages belong typically to junk sellers, derelicts, and old-clothes merchants, each of whom has his own—and his own model: Trois-Quartiers 1934, Belle-Jardinière 1938, Samaritaine de Luxe, and notably L'Hirondelle (made by Cycles de Saint-Étienne), the most popular in the junk-dealing fraternity, low on its wheels, navy blue, flat-blade springs, deep interior a little more solid than a cardboard box, a false bottom over a cubby designed for toys but now serving as a safe, and usually no canopy, which makes it possible on big market days or for longer circuits to erect, atop the basic chassis, an elaborate, towering structure of wood, sacking, twine and paper to hold and protect the seller's ephemeral treasure from the elements as he trundles along with his bric-à-brac, disparate but of obvious value for anyone acquainted with scrap metal, the harvest of a night delving in trash cans followed by a first triage, along with his scant personal effects, his set of kitchen utensils, and a change of clothing, all ill-assorted items but adequate for a precarious and particularly an outdoor existence.

Manya was not part of the ragpicker world (where in any case a woman would find it hard to survive without shacking up with an old hand), yet her baby carriage was famous in the vicinity of Rue de Seine, for it was full of cats, a round dozen of them; the old Russian woman had a passion for them, collecting them, feeding them God knows how, teaching them how to live without the fears that haunt the perilous life of the alley cat, keeping the toms leashed with lengths of string,

babying the offspring, whose numbers and pedigrees she carefully logged, nurturing newborn kittens, which she would sort and keep in noodle boxes, and spending her afternoons and nights on her bench in Square Champion transforming her rickety old carriage into a tree full of howler monkeys, or into the sort of scraggy, stunted, leafless and skeletal tree often placed in chicken coops, as she engaged in a nice and polite kind of begging based on her need to sustain her charges. Manya has just died. No one knows where or how, under what conditions of deprivation, of hunger or cold (or even perhaps from a scratch from one of her guests, who like ship's rats can transmit the germs of murine typhus or Weil's disease to humans), although she certainly did not die after a drinking bout, because she never drank anything but a little watered-down milk. And no one will ever know what has become of her cats, probably scattered like a slow-moving flock of sparrows in the feline jungle of the Sixth Arrondissement. But as I write these lines the guy next to me is reading curiously over my shoulder with his tongue pulled out in surprise. He interrupts me politely to inform me with a self-important air that the cops found old Manya dead on the quay, doubled up in her carriage, limbs sprawled every which way, with her animals decamping and mewing disconsolately; and that beneath her, embedded in a clotted mass of old clothes and rags, was a thin wad of blue banknotes—a fortune. Another one of those!

How many must there be of these ladies (and they are ladies far more often than men) who amass money Lord knows how and do nothing with it but store it up, often secreting it deep in their most intimate regions in a little black bag dangling between their thighs or tight against their pudenda, held in place by a complicated system of laces and elastic bands whose positioning they check when satisfying their daily needs and when nature imposes its, well, monthly house-cleaning. I knew an old professional in Rue Quincampoix who kept hundreds and thousands of francs there, who would turn her back (and not out of modesty, you may be sure) to hide her treasure, which she slid up her thigh along with her garter belt before nestling it carefully between her buttocks; she would let herself be fucked fully dressed only, merely rolling down the tops of her stockings, with her ass clamped reassuringly around her little package quite unbeknownst, of course, to her client's prick. She was crazy! Like so many other crazy women who spend their evenings unpicking and sewing up the linings of their skirts and the hems of their corsets in order to prevent their clients getting so much as a glimpse—not, as once upon a time, of gold pieces, but of pieces of quality paper, folded, twisted, sweat-soaked, soiled and stuck together like rotting dead leaves. There may even be Treasury bonds or post office money orders, or, more romantically, love letters from a far-off youth, truly startling, about which one might be forgiven for saying that they have returned to the source. All these old streetwalkers claim (and why not?) to have enjoyed a gilded youth, to have been pampered, adored, loved passionately, kept in high luxury, to have been queen of this or that, or the supreme beauty of a fashionable brothel, and they love to prove these claims by means of old photographs of bathing suits, feather evening gowns, limousines and torpedoes, chauffeurs, and assembled domestics. What a descent into nothingness. The only consolation: a liter of red. What degradation. What decrepitude.

But things need not go that far. There are any number of fruit-and-vegetable sellers in Les Halles who continue to wander about with their day's takings, their purchasing power, in a vast pouch slung about their waist under a frilly black skirt. To get to their resources, these last remaining vivandières and fishwives in period costume must lift up their finery, which has three layers: one of them confided to me that they were in fact referred to, in order of exposure, as the modest, the naughty, and the secret.

Although baby carriages have become a tool of the trade, if not a habitat, for peddlers, all of them cannot boast such an asset, or have lost theirs during a night of bingeing, or had it stolen by some unscrupulous character, and so must make do with an enormous patched-up bag bulging at the bottom and gathered tight at the top, which gives it the look of a stomach, as they lug around their evanescent fortune and the ad hoc paraphernalia of their precarious life like a snail its shell. But such a bag's capacity is limited. A man who lives on hunks of bread and floury soup is scarcely inclined to shoulder more than twenty kilos,

whereas he can easily push along four hundred pounds of old iron or a hundred kilos of bundled-up newspapers so long as the weight is evenly distributed above the four wheels of a carriage. Stock in the second-hand baby-carriage business, however, must be forever going up. You would have to have the luck of the devil or be ready to wade in shit to find an old carriage, perhaps alongside a trash can, or in the shallows of a sewage farm, or, very rarely, on the rubbish tips of the Zone. Every owner keeps a keen eye on his own, even if he has more than one. But I have never yet run into a dealer in junk or second-hand goods with a sideline in spare parts for these contraptions, though a fortune could obviously be made by buying and selling and bartering and fixing them up. A word to the wise: all you need is the corner of a shed that you can lock up and the patience to drum up custom.

6

ACCORDING to an article by one Dr. Charles Fiessinger which I
came across in a back issue of the *Journal des Praticiens* while browsing
through a pile of old magazines upon which I was sitting, taking it
easy, in the depository of the Sauguets in Rue Saint-Fargeau, the ragpickers of Paris have enjoyed official status since Philip Augustus. In
other words, no Parisian profession could boast a more illustrious tally
of quarterings of nobility. The ragpicker was a person of standing. The
feeling of having his own position in the social hierarchy filled him
with a strong sense of caste. Mismatches were unknown in the profession. A ragpicker's daughter should marry a ragpicker. Marrying a grocer's son would bring shame and dishonor to her family!

So much for the history of the Paris of old.

And the good doctor, who is full of book learning, goes on to laud
the proverbial honesty of ragpickers, who, when now and again they
chance upon jewelry in the discards they collect, will move heaven and
earth to find the rightful owner. And he adds that, even though the
refinement of modern conveniences may not have made it into their
homes, their souls are pure, so they know true happiness. Politics leaves
them cold.

If so, why is "fighting like ragpickers" such a popular expression (assuming that "popular" refers to the common people)?

One need only read the newspapers, especially the "police blotter"
columns, to realize that not a week goes by without violence and mayhem in the workers' housing on the outskirts of the city. I am not making anything up.

Physical attacks swiftly executed are made inevitable by the particularly thin skins of people who live more like animals than like bourgeois, and whatever dear Dr. Fiessinger may say, their right-thinking virtues evaporate very quickly at the first whiff of alcohol. In my humble opinion it is not so much some caste feeling that makes these folk so touchy about their honor, but rather the countless glasses of red wine absorbed in one blessed day. The name Philippe-Auguste means nothing to any of them except a metro station and a few nearby dance halls, but what they do know, by contrast, is how to offload the few metal or paper objects of value that show up in trash cans. And should one of their daughters go up onto the fortifications to listen to sweet nothings from a Don Juan of an apprentice barber and get knocked up, the family council may rant and rave and lay into her, but this will not be for the shame of it, but because the dishes have not been done and because there might soon be another bambino in the bedroom to be fed and cared for. All pride swallowed—or rather, all such family and nurturing feelings washed away, as on any day, in a flood of booze—life goes on and traditions are lost. The sense of honor boils down for the men to a sense of having a pair of balls, and for the women to the need to get food on the table. Believe it or not. If you want proof, consider these headlines from a daily paper: "Drama in the Court of Miracles of Boulogne-Billancourt—Ragpicker Bludgeoned to Death after Night-Long Orgy with 'Jesus Christ'" And the next day: "Brutus the Terror of the Rag Grubbers Calmly Tells of his Crime."

I cite these print sources for the sake of the truth, and if I rely on press clippings, it is simply because I have unfortunately never witnessed such crimes myself.

As for our physician-author's evocation of the age-old ethics of ragpickers, here are some lines from *Détective* magazine: "In what remains of the Zone, between Paris and Saint-Ouen, Raoul, known as Flea-Beard, a sprightly sixty-year-old, lives in a shack with his sweetheart Marie-Jeanne, ten years his junior. Since the revenue of Flea-Beard, who describes himself as an itinerant vendor, is close to zero, Marie-Jeanne decided to keep their pot bubbling by means of 'gifts' received from North Africans whom she met in nearby cafés, but this did not

do much good either. So, being a resourceful fellow, Flea-Beard undertook to expand these operations and run the business from home. He invited one of his girlfriend's girlfriends to move in: Mélina, whose nickname is too racy to print here, even in Latin[!]. In short, the packman set up his cabin so well that all it lacked was a red light bearing a number to signal the location to customers. Business was beginning to pick up when the police arrived and arrested the trio."

7

STILL, such cases concern mere scavengers marginal to the corporation of bona fide ragpickers: small-scale junk dealers, occasional scrap-metal gatherers, car strippers, Sunday sellers, half-assed con artists—a tribe residing for the most part on the edges of Île Saint-Denis or in huts in the Zone, where the vast clan of beggars swarms and proliferates. As for genuine ragpickers, each has his own area, his own few streets to dredge, and they are, so to speak, more serious: they work incessantly (which already distinguishes them from the grubbers), rising well before dawn to harness nags that are not so famished as all that, leave home in the inner suburbs for their target neighborhoods, drag trash cans out onto the sidewalk themselves, tossing the lids aside noiselessly with a swift practiced motion, spreading out their tarps, hanging their sacks up on a lamppost or in a corner, poking about with hooks in the containers and carefully sorting their articles while ignoring the stench, hardly negligible despite the cold. Among them is a whole contingent of young people, a far cry from pathetic old men and women: lads and strapping girls, some of them quite attractive, dressed, naturally, in hand-me-downs. It is hard to imagine that these bin divers, filthy as they are to look at, could go to a flick on a Sunday, or play durak, or practice nudism at a swimming pool. But why not? Another myth that needs exploding.

This is a trade that pays. Many ragpicker families possess a horseless carriage—a lemon-colored convertible "torpedo," for example, for weekend picnics—or a detached house on the outskirts of the city.

The best example I know is that of an old loner who works like a slave for ten months a year, living in a shed at the bottom of a little

garden in Bagnolet and amassing piles of dough, which, come July, he changes into big bills before dressing himself like a prince and going down to one of the finest hotels in Nice, where he passes himself off as a rich industrialist, plays the dandy on the Promenade des Anglais and the ladykiller in the bar of the Negresco, and takes pretty girls dazzled by his extravagance driving around in a limousine. Once his vacation is over, he returns to Paris, hangs up his suits, dons his utilitarian old clothes, gets out his ragpicker's sack and hook, and goes off to work as fit as a fiddle. But he is a bad lot. An egotist. And he is never satisfied. Not content to make a reasonable round between dawn and midday, he eats into his own sleep by running all over the city scouting out nooks and crannies where anything convertible into cash might be found, peering over fences, noting likely locations, going back two hours later with his cart to load up everything, without finding or enquiring after an owner, and make off leaving no one the wiser. The fact is that wasteland, building sites off limits to the public, areas bordering factories, automotive graveyards, inner courtyards of buildings and the rubble-strewn Zone all offer gatherers of scrap metal a source, sometimes slim but never negligible, of money enough to buy cheap wine and plain country bread. The commodity is not in short supply. Pilot prices (as they are called by the professionals) are high, varying from one to three hundred francs the kilo, and sales are quick. The variety is endless, so a measure of expertise is called for. Items include aluminum sheet scrap, pots and pans, crank cases, foil, turnings and shavings; copper wire and scrap, red tinned copper, copper sheeting and shot; brass cartridge cases, mixed brass, non-mesh brass casings, rod ends, turnings from cast brass and brass-bar machining; tin turnings and scrap; lead pipes and lead sheet, lead seals for bottles and lead-battery plates; and zinc shavings, zinc covers and "scrap merchants' zinc." Collection is relatively easy. The trick is to find a reliable outlet without getting hoodwinked by wily fences who size you up and scoff at your goods to beat the price down.

Aside from its resale value, which is quite considerable, waste paper is a basic contributor to comfort in the lower depths, because its uses are legion, notably in the struggle against the cold, rolls of crumpled newspaper being perfectly impermeable to chill air. Little old men and women, concierges or folk living on three-hundred-franc-a-month pensions, are fully aware of this when they exclude draughts by means of paper, likewise ragpickers in their sheds and storerooms when they stuff it in openings and cracks.

Plumier, an old junkman with a remarkable experience of the underground life, has contrived to take maximum advantage of this, turning his foreshortened room in Rue de Bièvre into living quarters properly furnished with enormous bundles of newspapers, meticulously pressed, stacked, and bound with string, upon which he is able to perform every task, alimentary, culinary, or otherwise utilitarian, and even sleep, on a vast mattress of the same material reminiscent of a boar's wallow, with the paper hollowed out and compressed by his body, doubtless returning to its original state as a cellulosic paste and sticking to the floor, which is itself covered by a thick layer of disparate sheets of paper that he rucks up as he drags himself around. I have to wonder why all this has never caught fire, despite the extreme caution he exercises when extinguishing matches or lighting his petrol lamp. I have never been tempted to sleep or even spend an evening there. Furthermore, the ventilation of his hovel rivals that of a lion's cage, and the odor produced by Plumier's doings overwhelmed that of printers' ink long ago.

Although Plumier lives in paper up to his neck and feels fine about it, he dresses respectably in clothes of real fabric, albeit of dubious quality. I met one anonymous clochard, however, clearly of no fixed abode but nonetheless with a perfect knowledge of the possibilities of paper, who had designed a whole undergarment, covering even his arms and legs, out of newsprint held together with glue and string, reinforced at his joints and at his body's sharper points. Carefully tightened around his extremities by means of ingenious sewing, this strange costume, whose weak spots he must unfortunately repatch from time to time, though without replacing the whole thing, adheres to his skin and fuses with his body hair and allows him to stroll about town in the middle of winter seemingly clad only in thin canvas pants and a seaman's jersey, thus arousing admiration for his remarkable indifference to the elements, except of course for rain, which he flees like the plague, and for good reason.

SIX

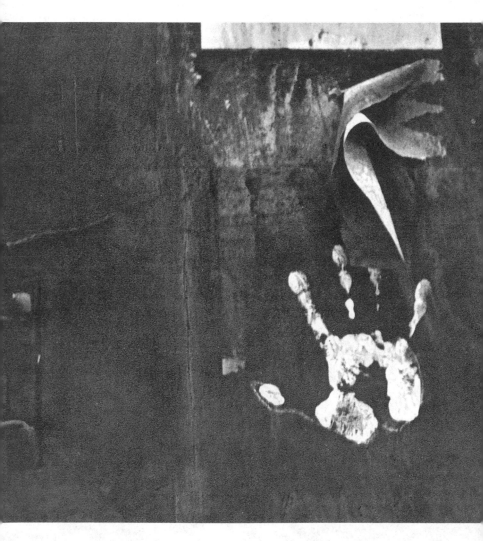

I

THE WINE warehouses of Bercy are a town in their own right. The gates, however, are always open and there is no trace of guards (indeed there is no sign barring access). And although this extraordinary precinct might seem like a bum's paradise, I have never seen a single one in there. Perhaps the cops keep a firm hand on vagrancy, but I have slept there several times without witnessing any kind of surveillance. Granted, I took elementary precautions, entering one or two hours before closing, slipping furtively between two warehouses, behind a cistern or a stack of empty barrels, curling up in a dark corner seemingly of no interest to anyone but me and full of piled-up crates and jumbled scrap iron and planks, giving up the joys of tobacco save during the chill just before dawn, holding the cigarette in the hollow of my palm and releasing the smoke in the slowest and thinnest of wisps, and then, when day came and the streets livened up, leaving nonchalantly, walking briskly towards the exit, going so far as to riffle through and busily peruse a sheaf of papers for the benefit of a watchman who did not give two hoots about my being there, or else passing a guard's box that was still empty, and voilà! I was out after another quiet night under the stars and five hours of sleep to the good.

But my greatest pleasure in Bercy comes from rambling about in the middle of the day, strolling down the little rustic streets paved with large cobbles that you feel under your feet and following what seem like tramlines until round a corner comes an exceedingly tall rail car; passing by houses that are simple farm buildings, their walls full of cracks and festooned with green creeping plants, beams with projecting hooks, gentle sloping tiled roofs, ogival double doors, short stone staircases with balustrades, and square windows with solid wooden shutters; and going around great pudgy broad-trunked trees beneath which the odors of dead leaves, mown grass, damp stone, and the schoolyard hang in the air, whereas elsewhere the nose is assailed by scents of full-bodied wine, corks, new barrels and rubber hosepipes. All around the dwellings and warehouses the luckiest children in Paris play and chickens cluck and peck. The streets bear fairytale names, including those of enough great vineyards—Médoc, Beaugency, Mâcon, Chablis—to summon a powerful thirst; nor are these streets in the normal sense, even in the eyes of the local authorities, who have dubbed them courts, alleys or closes: Cour Barsac, Couloir Deroche, Enclos Mâconnais (just as, across the river inside the Halle au Vin, you find Le Grand-Préau and Le Préau-des-Eaux-de-Vie—Great Court and Brandy Court). In point of fact this nomenclature is better, and certainly easier on the memory, than asinine plaques memorializing so many unknowns, benefactors of school budgets, donors for public urinals, founders of charitable organizations, and indeed genuinely great figures known to all from the earliest stirrings of reason, as for instance Victor Hugo, to whose name some municipalities have seen fit to add the words "French Poet"—just in case we needed reminding of this. But then perhaps we do: not long ago I overheard a fellow in a bar directing an interlocutor to an address on Boulevard Gambetta and adding helpfully that the name of the boulevard was spelled just like the name of the man in the school history books!

Anyway, here I am one early morning, cramped and bundled up beneath a little wall behind a tree. My mind is clear but my throat is furred and my movements are sluggish as I take stock of my situation. It is obvious that anyone passing by can see me, and therefore that I have been seen. So why in heaven's name did they leave me be? Could it be that in this citadel of good wine people respect Bacchic excess more than elsewhere, have taken me for one of their own and left me to sleep it off. Young cocks are practicing their reveille. The plane trees already have leaves. The first sparrows are pecking in the dirt. But, judging it prudent to go and appreciate the joys of nature a little farther on, I gather up my goods and chattels, head down the slope to the gates and leave. Unseen and incognito. A little car exits with me. Maintaining my innocent demeanor, I head for the Porte de Bercy and go down to the dockside, which is also closed to the public, but open to anyone who looks the part of either an angler, a glass worker, or a bargeman. In any case, here too there is no guard in the guard's hut. The full length of the retaining wall is punctuated by arched doors opening into cavernous storage areas where metalsmiths, coopers, or carpenters may be seen moving slowly about among piles of sacks, planks, barrels and hoops. Out on the quay the same orderly sorting of goods is proceeding. I smoke a cigarette and chew the fat with a rather prepossessing fellow. The wafting scent of Beaujolais is receding. Time to start off again. But I don't have a penny in my pocket. And I am famished. So after a couple of hours dreaming in the hazy sunshine and paying a visit to the guys wetting their lines I decide to cross the water and, by way of the Rue Watt tunnel under the railway lines, go behind the Magasins Généraux d'Austerlitz and up Rue Nationale to my friend Marc's grocery. There I can count on a full breakfast in the country style of old, café au lait and buttered bread along with an understanding smile from Marc's wife, a rarity among such women, who so often revile those who put their hand to nothing and live like "parasites."

Thus restored, I go off to for a nap in the grass down by the railroad line that parallels the outer boulevards. In Paris there are several abandoned stretches of track like this where no train has run for an eternity, as for example between Pont National and the Maison-Blanche station, at Porte de Montmartre, at Porte d'Aubervilliers, by Rue de la Haie-Coq (this last is unserviceable): all rubble-strewn and grassy trenches where you can easily walk, camp, cook your grub on a discreet fire and sleep soundly. Naturally the hard part is gaining access, for there are always railings, but there are holes in them, bent or broken bars, places where the fence has been forced, which you have to know about, and wide enough to let someone through, and once through you slide down on your backside, then follow the tracks for a few hundred meters before settling so as to avoid being noticed by any bicycle

cops curious enough to peer through the opening. At Porte d'Ivry, in particular, the line passes through a deep cutting with luxuriant vegetation, and the embankment on the side opposite Rue Regnault offers any number of hiding places. On one summer night I made love there with a wench from the modern housing nearby. I can no longer recall her face but I do remember the smell of the earth, the texture of the branches and leaves, and how the steepness of the terrain obliged me to take certain precautions to prevent the pair of us rolling down onto the tracks.

Following a refreshing sleep, I quit my den and go wandering in the Thirteenth Arrondissement, fertile territory for picking up useful tips, peppered as the area is with homeless shelters, dispensaries, soup kitchens and charitable institutions, notably the Nicholas Flamel shelter in Rue du Château-des-Rentiers and the Salvation Army's Le Corbusier skyscraper, known as La Maison Blanche, in Rue Cantagrel. You can go into the local bistros with empty pockets, tiny rooms sometimes gray (like Chez Louis, in Rue Chevaleret), sometimes pink (like the café on the corner of Rue Oudiné, now closed for unknown reasons). Which is exactly where I run into an excellent troupe consisting of three hirsute individuals and two old streetwalkers, among them Godillot, Le Boucher, Eugène, and La Minette, all of whom doss under the Pont d'Austerlitz and are at present putting away liters of red in the company of young guys from the Zone, the sort of anachronistic *roman-feuilleton* characters now met with only on the fringes of the metropolitan area, lean and jumpy, features sharp as a knife-edge, mean and arrogant expressions, thick sideburns, peaked cap pulled down to their noses, espadrilles for footwear—Romanies, Gypsies like the ones you see sometimes in Les Halles by the flower pavilion gathering armfuls of lilies and rat-tails which they use to pass themselves off as vendors but which only their women actually sell near Paris's *portes*. There has never been any marked rapport between them and me. Not that they despise me, not at all, but they are wary, and in addition I am too young (and not of their milieu) to trail after them. Despite my credentials, namely my vocabulary, my general attitude, my haircut and clothes, they direct not a word to me without some very good reason.

And to my great regret, there are times when I don't understand everything they say, because they talk very fast in their own lingo, which I daresay is a mixture of Romany, Arabic, Yiddish, Hungarian, and terms of their own cant whose meaning likewise escapes me. But none of this prevents us from dealing the cards, drinking light red wine and smoking imported cigarettes together. The boss is snoring on his chair. By eight in the evening I am completely soaked all over again. God help me!

Old Michel has been out bumming enough small change for a large country loaf, and since the soup hour is long past we have made do with that. Now the group breaks up, the Zoners going their way and the old-timers theirs. I seize the moment to hurry back to Marc's place (no doubt because of being drunk already) to get two seventy-franc liters from him on tick, then rejoin my raggedy companions under the Pont d'Austerlitz; they too now have liquid refreshment in hand, don't ask me how come—probably one or other of them still had a couple of banknotes on him and got the café owner to turn them into wine. You never know quite what to expect with these birds. In any case we are soon comfortably ensconced on the corner of Quai de la Gare in a grassy cul-de-sac behind the travelers' café that occupies the sidewalk; and we are well protected from the elements, as we settle down for the night, by walls on three sides, as likewise from aggravating tourists by the proximity of a shipyard. The presence of the Salvation Army barge just fifty meters away gives us ammunition if challenged, because it is easy to tell the cops that we arrived too late to go on board.

As for the various doings of that spring night I have but fragmentary and hazy memories. As we all sat around a cheerful fire built from scraps of lumber with half-empty liter bottles between our knees, the rumble of our conversation quickly turned into personal monologues, so that before long each of us forgot the presence of the others and fell captive to our own digressions. Except, that is, for Godillot, who needed to let off steam and picked a fight with poor Le Boucher, who was not up for it, and stumbled about on his gams as his adversary, seriously lit, got to his feet and threatened him with a bottle and tried to throw him in the river. I have no idea what became of Le Boucher,

because at daybreak he was gone. As for Godillot, despite a few good kicks to his legs he did not deign to open an eye. The women for their part had seen nothing. When I awoke I was lying on a board up against the wall with a thin trickle of water running down my neck. And a wicked hangover. But a little splash from the Seine would surely fix that. Leaving the two empty liter bottles for my friends, who would have a use for them, I went to take a look around the barge. Low in the water, white and green, it was much more reminiscent of the floating dwellings of the "de luxe Bohemians" at Port du Gros-Caillou than of its fellow barges permanently tied up nearby, linked to terra firma by flower-bedecked gangways, enhanced by little vegetable gardens and noisy barnyard animals, and inhabited by the perfectly sedentary. The Salvation Army was alert to the need for decoration, and even though its guests might be flea-ridden its vessel boasted rose bushes climbing a painted wooden lattice. You almost expected to see deckchairs, parasols, and a majordomo on the bridge. As for the interior, there was a vast rectangular room with columns, and camp beds arranged with geometrical precision and covered by striped woolen blankets in lively colors. Not at all what you imagined a shelter to be like.

2

PARIS'S last *guinguettes* are vanishing along with the last poetic traces of the *belle époque*, and the tourists can only go into raptures, and myself only smile, when round some corner you come upon a bistro with a little yard in front festooned by wisteria or an old garden at the back and an ancient well in the middle of it bordered by geraniums. Do the Paris guidebooks include the Cour de Rohan in their picturesque walking tours? I don't know, but for myself I cannot overlook it. It is the capital's most beautiful romantic efflorescence. None of the sad remains of the great centuries of the past, the grand townhouses turned into business offices; all the lofts and attics serving as depositories for the archives of trading companies, filled to the rafters—and their skylights blocked—by mountains of dead files, account books, inventories, balance sheets, by cubic meters' worth of bundles of dossiers covered by layers of dust as solid as congealed grease that no household duster could remove but that would have to be scraped off with a kitchen knife, dossiers from which invoices, carbon copies, customers' letters handwritten on sheets as thin as cigarette papers have fluttered out, the entire mass now worth just forty francs a kilo (what a pitiful last gasp for all those ill-paid minor servants of the Republic!); all the inner courtyards, farmsteads and stables turned into garages, workshops, and warehouses; and all the surviving details preserved in corners, in timbering, in lintel decorations, or on the fronts of massive *portes-cochères*, square, thick, studded with enormous nails, and padlocked, that are scattered all over Paris for the delectation of *flâneur* poets and lovers of old stones and anecdotal history—none of these, I say, can match the Cour de Rohan, so well sealed off from the shabbiness of civilization and the din of the traffic by a long, austere, rather Jesuitical street on one side and, on the other, by the souk-like Cour du Commerce: an oasis of visual exhilaration closed at night thanks to unscalable railings which to my deep regret have always prevented me from sleeping and dreaming there, at the bottom of the stone stairway, by the lip of the well, and in the restful light of the carriage lamp, obliging me to settle for a chat with the bookseller who is lucky enough to have his shop on the corner of the house with the gable.

Bistros with arbors and greenery-draped bowers persist in Paris, but the elaborate frames are invaded by dry rot, disintegrating into damp dust, tottering, wormeaten, yet miraculously rescued by lovers and collectors of old wood. As for the wisteria, it continues to cling on like a tangle of old pieces of string. There are watering holes of this kind near the various *portes*, in the interior villages, on the Buttes, and even in the heart of the Île de la Cité.

At the corner of Rue de la Colombe and Rue des Ursins (the former Rue d'Enfer, or Hell Street, as per an old inscription on a large stone in the wall) is Chez Desmolières, the last *bouchon** in the center of the city, covered with leafy creeping plants like some Robinson Crusoe's cabin and packed full inside with a startling assortment of ancient rustic artifacts—bird cages, stools and low tables, postcards pinned up beneath a clock with an upside-down face, a deep-red plush easy chair at the end of the counter, comfortable despite its threadbare arms, empty lead-ringed bottles, would-be humorous drawings on the walls, along with a view of the Seine. Add the look of the owner, clad in an immense buckskin, who has just finished rinsing glasses in a large basin meant for vegetables, and now vanishes like a caveman into dark rooms below ground level. The clientele is typified by local *petits rentiers*, domino players, and big talkers with little to tell. Now and again tourists pass by, if only by sheer happenstance (this little street is fortunately off the official circuit); they cast an astonished glance inside but dare not approach the arbor, for they are intimidated by the feeling of intimacy, of privacy. Yet another bistro that will soon close, business being bad.

---

*A *bouchon* is a type of restaurant, characteristic of Lyons, formerly serving hearty fare to the silkworkers of that city.—*Trans.*

3

LEAVING the banks of the Seine as night falls, just as the cold is preparing to alter familiar landscapes, I head for Rue Visconti—a narrow corridor itself destined to disappear shortly to make way for a main North-South traffic artery—and go up to see my pal Bob Giraud, bookseller on Quai Voltaire and the canniest of connoisseurs of Paris's social fantastic, as I noted in my dedication to this book. Climbing, groping my way up one of those amazing staircases that snake through the houses of the oldest sections, I use up my last matches, no flight having the same number of stairs as the next, and orientation being subject to rapid change, widening my eyes in vain against the darkness, and knocking haphazardly at the first door I bump into.

My visits to Bob were never disinterested, for aside from the liter of red on the table at all times, I was bound to glean new leads about the underground life of Left Bank neighborhoods, bound, too, to peruse the finest collection of documents, books, and photographs of plebeian Paris, and hear the latest stories concerning our shared acquaintances among the rag grubbers, vagrants and extraordinary characters who people the riverside. Sitting in the warm, relaxing for a moment or two, with plenty of whole cigarettes close to hand and a glass of red wine at my lips, I would let him tell me about his latest discovery, which on this occasion is a tattoo market held in a nondescript bistro in the leatherwork district (no kidding) that he went into by chance, or rather for the purpose of drinking a glass of Beaujolais. This is the only place in Paris, he informs me, and I fully believe him, where tattooed human skins are traded out of an enormous officer's trunk or evocative pirate's chest and displayed so well cleaned, tanned, stretched,

framed, or delicately pinned to a board like frog's feet mounted by an anatomist, that you have to lean over and touch the material with your finger to make sure that this is not wrinkled animal hide but genuine patches of skin taken from a fellow human. An astonishing collection, with tattoos ranging from tiny triangles composed of three mystical points to large pictures, masterworks, erotic scenes, copies of naively picturesque paintings, not forgetting the whole gamut of epithets, invective, declarations of love, details of incarceration or military service, and the commonest motif, which is the sexual organs in full flower. The source of this bizarre merchandise? First of all the morgue, where crafty employees detach strips of skin from corpses on their way to the potter's field; and secondly the dissecting rooms of the École de Médecine, where opportunistic students operate with speed and discretion. Business is brisk. As for the customers, they are merely peaceful collectors, lawyers, former big noises in the police force, medics who use their purchases for coasters, and bookdealers who use them for bindings (there are some kooks, seemingly, who turn them into gloves, tobacco pouches, lampshades, and so on).

Naturally enough, in this bistro (whose name I cannot give for the good reason that Bob keeps it secret, and in any case…), the talk is all shop. And a good number of tattoo artists come in to take care of "small jobs." I am referring to those specialists who undertake to remove tattoos that have turned out to be ill-advised, as for example the slogan "Mort aux Vaches!"—"Death to the Pigs!"—which the cops have not yet digested despite their long acquaintanceship with this kind of courtesy, or the insignia of prisons or brigs that mark a man as indelibly as any collection of personal memorabilia, and who strive, in exchange for a flood of red wine or for cold cash, to eradicate these adornments in an expeditious manner and by more or less painful means involving the application of the back of a red-hot spoon directly to the flesh, which sizzles, followed by a vigorous rubbing with a handful of coarse salt. And it is also to this bistro—which I am sure I shall find my way to one of these days—that hard cases supposedly come to see how much their skin, quite literally, is worth, and ready to trade part of their living hide for a few thousand-franc bills, or even, for that matter, to part with their entire epidermis provided that the proceeds be given to their widow after their inevitable demise. But these are all just tall tales, because it is in fact impossible to remove the skin in this way—and the same goes, between you and me, for its tattooing.

4

IN SUMMER, the Arab cafés, or more precisely those home-country cafés where everyone except perhaps the owner is North African, quickly—and curiously—come to be much like *guinguettes*, just as gay and noisy though less peaceful, and in many neighborhoods they are almost the only places to have dooryards or corners of patios that a potted plant can transform into a garden. The entertainment hardly varies. The record, always the same one, revolves on the turntable of a phonograph whose sound is so relentlessly metallic, throbbing, scratchy, ear-piercing—in short so strident that the racket must drive even the most tolerant neighbors to distraction. But the music is rapidly overwhelmed by the voices of men. You simply have to have been present (not incognito, but sure to keep your wits about you) on one of those garish nights when they chant, sing, keep the beat, shout, scream, clap their hands and stamp their feet to the obscene rhythm of a belly dance performed by two or three naked women, washed-up or maverick streetwalkers (usually from Paris, sometimes fake Gypsies, because here as everywhere in France genuine Ouled-Naïls are few and far between), women finding their own pleasure by pleasing their men, their imposing curves hardly voluptuous save in a kind of nostalgic way; as the shouting redoubles, the dancers stagger, the smoke becomes thicker, smelling of mint from the tea and of kief, sweat pours, shirts come off, belts are unbuckled, drawstrings untied, the gramophone needle skids, you can hardly see anything, the heat and the humidity are suffocating, and bodies clinch. Meanwhile the people across the street stay behind the barrier of their windows peacefully smoking their evening pipes and watching through the glass. They are at the movies.

Often, however, women are absent and it is two or three young adolescent boys (or seemingly so) who mime voluptuousness. Satisfaction is no less general, but fights erupt more easily, the first blow becomes a hail of blows, the boss tries to close his shutters, and you need to crouch in a corner, because the presence of a Christian is a powder keg, a prime target, and your marveling at the social fantastic is suddenly replaced by sheer terror, the best course being to make yourself inconspicuous and be sure to present yourself sideways to the nearest enthusiast so that he cannot grab you by the lapels and charge you head down.

The Arab places on Rue Nationale and Rue du Château-des-Rentiers are low-ceilinged rooms, oddly devoid of an ordinary bar and furnished only with wall benches and long trestle tables on each side, where customers gab, of course, but have to wait, if they can afford to buy a drink, while the boss goes to fetch glasses and bottles of beer from his back room. What is more, there are often fewer drinkers here than guys with a bowl of gray frothy water in front of them, getting a free shave from a volunteer barber, because all these Arabs can effect a first-class Mongolian haircut. I always wonder in what classification—perhaps invented for the nonce—the fiscal authorities place this kind of waiting room of a bar, and whether the owner pays for a business license, and, if so, what category.

As for the bistros around La Goutte d'Or and La Chapelle, you are assailed from the moment you walk in by the smell of kief, which the men puff sitting silently on banquettes against the cracked plaster walls, regularly taking a sip of water or tea to chase the smoke, and making no attempt at concealment as they crumble up their dust-gray pastille and mix it with tobacco produced in pinches directly from their pockets, then carefully deposit the mixture on the corner of the table and spread it out on three Job Noir cigarette papers ("Special"), stuck together in a triangle and rolled into a cone with a still-intact Gauloise butt serving as a filter. The pastilles are usually prepared by the boss himself in his lair by placing cake between two sheets of cellophane and pressing it with a lukewarm iron before cutting it up. And when the owner does not supply the dope, it will be a regular customer, standing permanently behind the bar and accepting contributions, little deals at seventy-five francs for a heap of powder—enough for two spliffs, so putting paradise within reach of every purse.

The façades of the city's flophouses are just that—façades: the décor is identical everywhere on the fringes of Paris, in Saint-Ouen, Clichy, Saint-Denis, La Chapelle, La Villette, Aubervilliers, or, on the other side, in Boulogne, Billancourt, Gennevilliers, Gentilly, and so on. The names likewise are much of a muchness: Hôtel du Nord, Hôtel du Sud, Hôtel de l'Ouest, Bellevue, Saint-Ange, Sans-Souci, L'Étoile d'Or, Hôtel du Croissant, Hôtel d'Orient—commonplace names, trite on their face, but capable of rapidly acquiring a specific significance, of signaling an intention or serving as a magical, exotic, equivocal, ironic, or tragic inscription. These are hotels with ground-floor windows shuttered and a usually inaccessible "office." They seem like short-time hotels whose hookers ply their trade in plain sight of kids on their way home from school and playing at marbles on the same sidewalk, and all the girls know all the kids and smile at them and tousle their hair—more affection quite likely than the poor tykes get at home. Houses of joy, then, in front, but in the back what is sold is sleep. Down a hallway you come to a courtyard, or a succession of courtyards, with lean-tos, sheds, rabbit hutches, scrap-metal stores, disused outhouses, doors dangling from broken hinges, menacing places day and night where johns rarely venture, preferring to cruise along sidewalks and down sidestreets; further back still are blind alleys, entryways, dead ends, passages that were once vegetable gardens piercing through streetless blocks of houses, and sometimes a tree—God only knows what it is doing there—perpetually bare and dry as a bone amid piles of refuse encroaching everywhere and combining over years into the hard-packed dirt underfoot or filling the cracks between battered paving stones and miraculously sustaining shoots of grass. I say that sleep is sold here because the hotel owners, who regard Arabs on principle as cattle to be milked or slaughtered, exact an enormous amount of key money (as much as several thousand francs) from tenants of a room with a folding bed and a bidet renting at twelve hundred francs a week,

while at the same time hiring it out in the daytime for fifteen-minute tricks; then they keep the tenant for just a couple of weeks before evicting him on some stupid pretext, drinking, noise, homosexuality, or lack of cleanliness (all of a sudden the man finds his room key gone from its hook and his clothes in a heap at the bottom of the stairwell), and moving on to their next victim. A black market in sleep. An Algerian, be he a lathe or milling-machine operator or a peanut vendor, has no choice but to lay his bedding in some corner of the courtyard or go down into the cellar and join the tribe of the penniless, as in Nanterre, or La Plaine Saint-Denis, or Gennevilliers, where the largest group of North Africans in the Seine department is holed up.

5

IN RUE du Château-des-Rentiers, just by the Nicolas Flamel shelter, is a municipal fumigation center which is the workplace of Martini, a tough guy who can put up with anything, including the immediate downing of a liter of the apéritif wine that earned him his nickname. Martini has the least fun-filled of jobs and when he invites me, as he does regularly, to accompany him to work, he warns me—and this is what makes me turn him down—that it will nauseate me and put me in urgent need of cleansing my stomach with a good dose of dry white wine, because according to him, and I am inclined to take his word for it, it is truly unappetizing and you need to have a cast-iron constitution and call frequently on Dutch courage, because habituation and insensitivity come only after long years of experience, something to which most workers are unwilling to subject themselves, preferring to sacrifice their pension and go and look elsewhere. Being close to two shelters, and run by the City of Paris, this laundry is responsible for cleaning the clothes of the homeless, and every evening, as soon as a cohort of derelicts has been mustered in an observation anteroom, they are asked to strip naked and hosed down with cresol disinfectant, after which the fumigators come with wooden pitchforks to pile the men's clobber up like manure before tossing it into steamers for treatment out of sight but not beyond the sense of smell, which takes a big hit, for the tattered garments are rife with the piss, vomit and like minor accidents with which dozens of habitual winos have "soiled" them. And even when they have been removed from the tubs the operation is far from complete, because the rags are steam-soaked, twisted, rumpled and tangled up and must be sorted, identified by function, and wrung out before being hung up to dry on frames. For my part, all I know of shelters is the aspect familiar to the boarders, and, whatever my interlocutor may think, I would rather remain in ignorance of the aspect familiar to the staff.

But Martini has more than this to tell, because he also adds variety to the joys of his profession by performing home disinfections, meaning that he fumigates the dwellings of the sick and dead in the neighborhood, and so great is his experience in this regard that he claims to know, from the moment he enters a room, whether a stiff is a victim of cancer, tuberculosis, syphilis or some other disease, and this on the sole basis of the smell impregnating the walls. None of which, however, is especially surprising. Close acquaintanceship with someone who works at Lamy-Trouvain, the funeral directors, is all that is required to learn in intimate detail just how corpses are washed and their strategic orifices stoppered. But what fascinated me in Martini's stories was his description of certain lodgings that he had been obliged to enter, generally those of old men and women who had died in a state of incredible physical deprivation amid surroundings of hellish darkness, fetor, and terror, not to mention those of suicides, their ends becoming apparent long after the fact by virtue of telltale odors escaping from beneath their doors, as for instance in the case of a beautiful young woman asphyxiated three weeks previously whose rear end was swarming with worms of various girths.

It is hard to reckon just how many such human beings, out of resources and breathing their last, who expire in secret, go to ground in their hole to *watch themselves die.* You would have to consult the police logs, comb through the newspaper police-blotter columns, and create your own files.... As a rule three anecdotal lines of type is all they get, and some not even that. Woman paralyzed and too weak to call out gnawed to death by rats on her wretched bed, sensing, hearing, seeing and then feeling and suffering their presence, enough to make the eyes themselves scream. Woman invalid accidentally suffocated in her closet, collapsed and slowly rotting in piles of clothes, hat-boxes and brooms. Vagrant dead of cold under sacks and planks of his hutch at the back of a vacant lot, a wrinkled, bearded scarecrow of a man that

memory's gaze can never erase. Mad musician dead of starvation and pride in his attic, in bed and well tucked up beneath the gutters and geraniums at the window. Fat blonde girl with squint slain by her own hand and a set of knitting needles with which she was seeking to kill her "sin."

And all of them, fast approaching the last moments of clarity, trapped between six impenetrable walls, contemplating their lodgings: roosts, maids' quarters, huts, garrets, lean-tos, cabins, or venerable bourgeois apartments (inhabited by old ladies decked out in faded finery, adorned with jewelry, gold, and face paint, and haunted within by the memory of their *very last* bowl of clabbered milk), city interiors shamed by layers of grease, slowly settling dust, long-disused furniture crammed together, dirty dishes as sticky as flypaper, old family documents, academic pictures and portraits, and, visible in the empty space at each corner, the immense bareness of the floor. And the only genuinely *present* features are the door you would like to burn, the wallpaper you would like to shred, and the silence you long to chase away.

But death and dire poverty are hardly requirements for running full-tilt into the horror of some living quarters. A multitude of single and solitary people (and couples too) dwell in inhuman holes: street singers, ragpickers, failed artists, and all the invisible tenants of old houses in old neighborhoods, sleeping, snoring, guzzling, drinking, dragging themselves blindly from one end to the other of a dismal room without windows or even a fanlight (at best a pane of glass in the ceiling, sealed tight by time and dust and occluded by refuse, mud and pooled water), and obliged to leave the door open from time to time in order to see clearly enough for a little needed sewing. Take a look around Rue Visconti, Rue Brisemiche, Rue Hautes-Formes, Passage de l'Avenir, or Passage de la Trinité....

See also: Court of Miracles.

As for the well-known legend of woolen socks and mattresses stuffed with banknotes, Martini had nary a word to say.

6

ON THE fringes of Saint-Germain-des-Prés there are still bistros unknown to intrusive outsiders which to my mind are far more interesting than all the others in the vicinity combined. Take all the *bougnats* and bars of Rue des Canettes, where life is a far cry from the hoitytoity, so-called literary world, as likewise from the petrified religious one, by both of which they are surrounded. These places are frequented only by *petits rentiers*, tradesmen, workers, and old men and women ripe for the hospital who roost at close quarters in the paunched and mansard-roofed houses of Rue Guisarde. A café clientele, in other words, whose conversation does not go beyond the weather forecast, crude politics, the rigors of getting enough food every day, and the latest (but not too malicious) gossip about the neighbors, while diversion is confined to dominos, belote, yellow dwarf and manille, and consumption never tops three glasses. I can claim to have slept, if not stayed, at the most unpretentious hotel on Rue des Canettes, Old Jules's place, and its remarkable tranquility, created by a combination of respect for silence, accumulated exhaustion, and nugatory finances, I found all the more miraculous in view of the fact that less than ten meters away the corner *café-tabac* was raising a diabolical hullabaloo whose echoes were nevertheless unable to get past the intervening bakery and reach our ears. The hotel's immense lobby is still a paradise for a scribbler in search of a haven of peace where he can cover pages with writing without any pressure to re-order after getting a cup of coffee in the morning and letting it stand all day long.

But the most exciting dive is La Chope, in Rue du Four, which is open by four in the morning and immediately filled by a tribe of rag-pickers who have kept the dress and look of the slashers of popular novels: three-decker cap, bristling side whiskers, tight jacket, bell-bottoms. Where do they spring from? I have never come across them anywhere else, but I have seen them coming in from the direction of Grenelle. I strongly suspect them of being foreigners. And you should see their women in flowing Gypsy dresses! It is hard to get to know them. You would have to find out the exact route of their round of trash barrels. They must have nags and carts somewhere around. They say not a word as they slug liters of red from the bottle; silent types, all of them. Nobody offers to buy them a drink. They treat nobody. They cluster around the stove, whole families, with occasionally a couple of snotty brats who stare at the other customers and to whom you are tempted to toss a coin. And every time I have watched out for their arrival or planned to follow them as they left, something has always distracted me from my urge to know more, a pal buying me a glass, the boss serving his round on the house, a drunk to show the door to, or a big talker to listen to. Today I am sidetracked by Ali, a mischievous little old Arab as skittery as a squirrel, who puts his basket of peanuts down on the table and orders me a coffee and gives me a packet of the legumes for me to shell. The stove snores, crackles and farts, as compla-cent as we are as we bask in its warmth. Ali begins telling me about his wanderings in the South of France. Like me he has worked for "the Catalan" near Béziers during the wine harvest, dragging tubs and tuns of grapes along behind him, sleeping in his own room, assigned him by the kindhearted grower and equipped with a real camp bed and a per-sonal kitchen range, where he could cook his beans and eat the melons that he picked in the garden in plain view of the boss, choosing the most appealing, then using the tip of his knife to cut out a little square opening in the skin, lifting the fruit to sniff the interior, checking the color and, if not satisfied, using his thumb to delicately replug the hole and proceeding to the next one; and he had tomatoes galore for the traditional sauce and the assorted hors d'oeuvres that only the Arabs know how to prepare from next to nothing, making them the finest of cooks for building sites and farms.... In the course of an evening Ali would put away his allotted three liters of *clairet*. After twenty days of work he earned enough to leave, flush with the same number of thousand-franc bills—the wherewithal to get him to Marseilles and buy him a full case of watches to sell to foreign tourists on local beaches, in accordance with a complicated, meticulously developed plan that was highly lucrative, because peddling packets of peanuts brought in next to nothing and it was simply a cover, a respectable occupation in the eyes of the police—though in fact the police were not taken in, and merely shrugged and moved him along with a knowing smile when he produced his hawker's license, which was in perfect order. On this occasion Ali has made enough to come up to Paris with the passing notion that he might sell carpets in the cafés and at metro exits or go up in the summer to the Normandy beaches to offload the contents of suitcases full of knickknacks, medallions, bracelets, pendants, and religious objects that visiting zealots from Lisieux would be dumb enough to buy at knock-down prices. Go for it, I say, you are right my son, take their shekels, drive them crazy and deafen them with your fake whining and stick to them like a limpet until they buy your entire stock, take them for all they've got, they do you enough harm on the side with their colonialist missions and the living conditions that their pious souls refuse to see. Whereupon Ali crinkles his eyes contentedly and nibbles his nuts. He is not a Communist, and doesn't even read *L'Algérie Libre* (which I do), but he acquiesces, trusting, so to speak, in what I say. Ali is the most appealing figure in the neighborhood. But he will never read these words.

Meanwhile, in La Chope, daybreak brings in more people and the local garbage men make their appearance. The general conversation centers on a dramatic incident overnight: around five in the morning, a pair of English *demi-mondains* showed up after the bars in Rue de l'Abbaye had closed and the woman, quite drunk, let herself be pawed at length by a group of clochards of the finest stamp, while the husband remained virtually impassive, under the impression perhaps that this was a quaint Parisian custom worthy of a note in his diary, and the guys went on quite shamelessly kneading the opulent female's rear end, indeed warming to the task, the boldest groping beneath her skirts and feeling her up, the shyest, an extraordinary pint-sized fellow holding a shopping bag, hardly daring to put his fingertips to the bare flesh of her upper arm, and others tickling her feet. There was nothing erotic about all this; it tended rather to produce wild laughter. The woman wriggled and flapped, asking in her mother tongue for an explanation from her husband, who was footing the bill for drinks all round, as everyone took turns on the banquette and proceeded ever more vigorously, with a certain Victor trying to open her well-filled and deeply cloven bodice and everyone laughing till tears rolled down their cheeks; from time to time the Englishman received friendly claps on the middle of his back or his shoulder, which made him overbalance and splutter and prompted him to offer dignified observations with upper lip stiff and in broken French until he at last made up his mind to get to his feet, take his wife's arm and escort her by a zigzag route to the exit, apologizing in the most well-bred fashion for leaving such congenial company so abruptly.

7

LEAVING the Saint-Merri neighborhood behind, the dallying walker pays no heed to the cheap picturesqueness of the architecture, but punctuates his progress with stops at bistros that resemble waiting rooms, birdcages full of chattering girls, street corners where everyone calls everyone sweetheart, and gatherings on the edge of the sidewalk; he goes down Rue des Lombards, halts for a glass on the corner of Rue de la Reynie (which the locals, who like to simplify, call Rue de l'Araignée, or Spider Street), and emerges into the nameless plaza formed where several streets collide—namely Brisemiche, Aubry-le-Boucher, Saint-Merri, Pierre-au-Lard, and Geoffroy-l'Angevin—an intersection crossed surreptitiously by Rue Quincampoix, which runs by decrepit houses before continuing its obscure path, like a knotted rope, on the far side. The bistros facing the most beautiful row of tumbledown dwellings in Paris, fissured under the sun like overripe fruit, are largely patronized by Arabs, now busy in the market area sorting out items for display on their carts, and local ragpickers who have finished their day at ten or eleven and intend to spend the afternoon getting some shuteye in basements or in the shops below street level that are so typical of the whole area. And a few carders and mattress-makers who also work at ground level, with the door of their windowless stores open and welcoming to a good number of people who go into the rear to sleep on bales of wool and straw. (A handful of women mattress carders still work under the arches of the Pont Neuf in the summer, but the tradition is on the wane everywhere.)

On the other side of this crossroads is a women's shelter, some sort of prefabricated structure stuck behind a wall but designated in very large, red-painted letters: BELIEVE IN GOD AND IN ME (the *me* in question remaining modestly anonymous). Next door is a dealer in old papers (buy and sell—no barter), his walls covered with prints pinned up with great care. On the sidewalk archetypal drunks croon their solitary songs. Our peripatetician has almost reached Rue de la Grande Truanderie. And by now Rue Quincampoix is the almost exclusive preserve of junk dealers and rag grubbers, the exception being a few Arabs in their lairs and their little brothels. There is no trade for whores here unless they are old hundred-franc hookers who do not even trouble to stand and wait for custom but instead go right into the back rooms of cafés, circulate among the patrons, state their terms *sotto voce*, then go out again with as much ease and nonchalance as their sisters from the Salvation Army touting their illustrated magazine.

Somewhere on this street, in a corner, you can still read the odd inscription MADAME ADAM—FRESH LEMON ZESTS. But by crossing the "Topo"—Boulevard Sébastopol—and reaching Rue Saint-Denis, the alert walker finds himself among the kind of whores he is used to. The entire right side of this sperm-drenched street is lined with cafés where from four in the afternoon until the middle of the night there is a ceaseless mingling of streetwalkers, pimps, tough guys, young gangsters, owners of regional bars, and reliable meal-tickets whose tastes and visits depend on their whims. But despite what this list might suggest, life here is quite calm, and voices are rarely raised except for those of cardplayers declaring *tierce* or *quarte*, belote being the great palliative for the misery of the times. And the girls get into it. You sit them on your knees. You play and make comments, drink like a trooper, have a little dinner with the boss at a table in the back, occasionally welcoming the gentlemen from police headquarters on Quai des Orfèvres and chewing the fat with them, or sharing a round with the civilians. Everyone gets on well and has little desire to change such a satisfactory state of affairs.

The finest fillies in the area are to be found near Porte Saint-Denis, clustering at the small intersection where Rue d'Aboukir, Rue de Cléry and Rue Sainte-Foi come together, a place where scarcely anyone goes save customers and the odd resident. Any stranger who wanders through by chance is accosted and shoved smartly from one girl to the next and has a devil of a time making his escape. There is old Margot baring most of her splendid large breasts, Muguette so tall and lithe with her world-weary expression, and Juliette who laughs hysterically when she is doing her job. A familiar scene.

8

MUCH LESS familiar is the series of backstreets and dead ends that give off Rue Saint-Denis like herring bones. First comes Impasse Saint-Denis, a narrow trench coming to an abrupt end which at first seems uninhabited and which serves above all as a storage place for itinerant fruit-and-vegetable sellers. Next, Passage Basfour, leading into Rue du Palestro, a stamping-ground for dawn streetwalkers, the early birds at work from five in the morning, rubbing their eyes along with the market porters. These are the same girls—more numerous than the long-horned hand-trucks mustered in ranks along the street—that you see trolling Passage du Ponceau and Passage Dubois.* There is one alley, though, known as Passage de la Trinité, which at nighttime acquires a gothic death-trap atmosphere: a dark corridor lit by the greenish glow from a single starved streetlamp, and not even straight so that you might be assured of a clear exit, but crooked, twisting its way through a succession of silent courtyards. But halfway down this long canyon is the entrance to a hotel where I have always vowed to bunk for a few very cold, snowy, windy and rackety winter nights. Unfortunately, I have never done more than walk through the place, all the sleepable corners being "private," long occupied and defended tooth and nail by old-timers. It was also the scene for me of an amorous disappointment. I stupidly took a young pickup into this terrifying rat's nest for an unmentionable purpose, but the poor thing was so panic-stricken that she slipped from my grasp and hightailed it, deaf to my urgent entreat-

---

*Probably Passage du Bois de Boulogne, which is off Rue du Faubourg Saint-Denis just north of Porte Saint-Denis, also known, since 1930, as Passage du Prado—*Trans.*

ies. A truly phantasmogorical setting, and I recommend it to all seekers of a frisson and all patrons of the Grand Guignol.

If you ferret about, you will find that the whole of Les Halles and its dependent neighborhood are full of such sinister alleyways, baneful for the incautious night stroller but a boon to those sleeping rough. Off Rue Saint-Martin, in particular, are several mysterious narrow passages where human life huddles immobile in the corners—bulging forms, under piled-up cardboard boxes and rags, that you could stumble over without them stirring; where animals, greatly varied in size but always startling, chase after one another, mangy cats and rats as long as a man's foot; and where oozing gutter water trickles down the crumbling walls on either side. Among them: Impasse Clairvaux, Passage Brantôme, Rue du Maure, Passage de La Réunion, and, notably, Rue de Venise, location of Hôtel de l'Arrivée (you can say that again!), that great dumping-ground of a retreat for all the city's cripples, crutch-borne, beggars, street singers, drunks, game-legged, sickly Kabyles, blind men real and fake (one of these last, famously, worked so hard at aping this lucrative disability that he wound up as blind as a bat), and legless—the skaters whom you no longer see in little crates on wheels using the palms of their hands like flatirons for propulsion. It is a sign of the times that they now travel by Dupont motorized wheelchair. But they still sleep under old sacks just inside *portes-cochères*, taking up slightly less room than their cohorts. (A legend much retailed in the bistros of the southern part of the Zone tells of a bogus skater, in a wooden soapbox in this instance, a slightly nutty fellow, or at any rate slightly touched by Jesus, who, not for profit but by *vocation*, being convinced that he had lost both his legs, would haunt the inner suburbs, choosing steep streets and stationing himself at the bottom, not begging but simply waiting until some charitable soul hauled him to the top of the hill by means of a rope, whereupon he would thank the good Samaritan, then turn away quickly and let himself roll back down the slope at top speed screaming wildly and nearly breaking his neck several times over.)

SEVEN

I

So here I am with fifty francs in hand and a rainy afternoon in prospect as I make for the nearest bistro to do a little writing, sit down with a *café-crème* in front of me, go through all my pockets in search of notes scrawled on scraps of paper and rack my brains for shreds of sentences committed to memory last night. I am composing a book from fragments, organizing it bit by bit, not even chapter by chapter or paragraph by paragraph, but by things glimpsed and flashes of memory, which explains and I hope excuses its especially cascading form, its digressions, its repetitions and omissions, the sole causes of which are the fact that in my ramblings I might go three times down the same street and stupidly ignore a fascinating alley; the fact that the writing is subject to the whims of the weather, of hotel rooms taken for the sake of an entire night of scribbling down and revising accumulated recollections and impressions rather than for the sake of a feather bed and white sheets, of park benches where one is rarely left in peace, or of the back rooms of cafés, though certainly not those of the so-called literary variety—which are simply salons, talking shops (far from the last of the species) for chattering and wasting your time—but rather of so-called people's joints where nobody is used to seeing customers writing anything down except a message on a postcard or the belote score. And every time I am queried by the boss, a waiter, a whore, or a fellow imbiber I am forced to answer that I am taking care of my correspondence. Happily, my look protects me in many surroundings from the wounding label of intellectual or, even worse, of existentialist—a word distorted to the point of caricature by the obvious idiocy of utterer and recipient alike.

The *vie de bohème* is a great thing—so says, or thinks, or laughs, or sneers the grown-up. Ironically or bitterly—it depends on their degree of socio-marital fulfillment.

Bohème. The term is now completely blunted and has no meaning, for it covers too many misunderstandings, too many incompatible ways of living, and refers to too many disparate individuals, including genuine vagabonds who take the notion of freedom as their only serious value, to be preserved at all cost and exercised to the maximum, but also including all the dumb rich kids in Saint-Germain-des-Prés who affect to be starving to death, subscribe to a corrupt and corrupting romanticism, dragging themselves around with dirty feet (not to mention the rest of their bodies), haggard, with pale eyes and leonine hair, only to depart at four in the morning, leaving the café where they have been sitting all night long with an empty glass before them engaged in sterile conversation, walking three hundred meters until, out of sight of their little friends, they take a taxi home, to the paternal abode, where a hot bath and a cozy bed await them. Little shits! On this subject there is too much that might be said, or yelled. But it would be to no avail, because I have to wonder who, between Odéon and Rue de Rennes, is most to blame for the regressive form of life in which they wallow: is it the petty (and not so petty) bourgeois in their procession of American cars and the gloriously plumed and distinctly mature wild fowl on parade, or is it the pathetic boys and girls whose entire personality boils down to layers of dirt and carnivalesque American dress?

But, as I say, *la bohème* also includes true vagabonds, notably foreigners, students, painters, writers, or simply the long-haul wanderers that you run into on the outdoor terraces of brasseries on Boulevard Saint-Germain or in Montparnasse, seated at a table or standing at the counter, or at fairs or fleamarkets or the old-iron market—wherever the show is in the street, along with the chances of survival for another day. Americans, Germans, Englishmen, Scandinavians. Very few French, for the French are elsewhere. Never any South Americans, Africans, or Asiatics. Once I met a Greek. You find these people too around the rich neighborhoods, the Champs-Elysées or Opéra, because they come to Paris armed with the same information as most tourists and readers of Maugham or Gertrude Stein, and because (unless they are in dire need of solitude) they find compatriots there more quickly, or, for those who do not receive occasional remittances of dollars, pounds, or florins as a last sign of their former status, because they can more easily find temporary protectors, who still exist though they are now rather rare and tend to belong to the freemasonry of homosexuals, as indeed do many of these intellectual wanderers, whether by inclination or for reasons of convenience, for their style of life, as judged by criteria of grooming, indigence, cleanliness, instability, and inability to buy drinks or rent a hotel room, has little appeal to women, whereas the frequenting of cafés, the ease of striking up a conversation, and the dynamics of nocturnal conviviality involve them swiftly in ephemeral yet honest encounters with men. The sensitivity that is the hallmark of such vagabonds demands more from human relationships than a woman's caress.

I talked about this with Alex, a German drifter from Barcelona who, beginning at some prehistoric stage of his life, had rambled all over Western Europe, but had been haunting the streets of Paris since he was thirteen (he was now forty-five), stopping only long enough to sleep for a few hours on a park bench or the floor of a friend's room, climbing into a real bed no more than once every couple of years, spending his days and nights inhaling the *Zeitgeist*, observing passersby; he was always silent, opening his mouth only to drink from the Wallace fountains, nourished by metaphysical entities or considerations, obviously quite irresolute, never really knowing if he was hungry or tired but letting himself bounce about, borne along not only by events but by the slightest breath of air, with his immense silhouette, black beard, astonishing miniature haversack slung over his shoulder, and of course knowing everybody, every last corner of the town, every hideaway, every night walk voluntary or otherwise, and prone to standing for hours on end at the curbside, motionless, head down, expression soulful, and answering the question I asked him on finding him in this stork-like posture by saying simply: "Oh, I had a marvelous

dream last night." A protean character, Alex, whose only ambitions were to be head cook on a cargo ship or pianist in a brothel.

As for another character, a young Danish or Norwegian vagabond who was camping, quite literally, in Paris, I never knew his name. He always lugged with him an old rucksack with no frame, limp, washed out, and festooned with dangling strings, in which, apart from his tent and blanket, he kept a quite adequate selection of weekend camping gear, including a kerosene stove upon which (after a daily and thorough forage in Les Halles—for scraps of food, naturally) he would manage to heat up a hodgepodge meal or at the very least some tea. For a time he set up house at the end of Impasse des Peintres off Rue Saint-Denis, where I found him one evening and shared his meager rations. He had been in the city for seven months and was not yet tired of Paris—on the contrary, he had not explored more than a tenth of it and had chosen to spend the rest of the winter and wait until spring to go on the road again. For several nights in a row after that I came back to join him, bringing my share of food and if possible a few liters with which to introduce him, while giving him the latest leads on underground Paris, to the joys of tying one on with cheap red wine, for he drank or used to drink nothing but milk or *cafés-crème* in the bistros; avoiding, for once, the close company of the garrulous old clochards who sleep and do their business behind the Church of Saint-Leu, we would squeeze ourselves between sacks filled with shredded paper, light our pipes with powdered tobacco (the ground around here having of course been swept clean of every last butt), and take it in turns to recount our adventures, which did not fail to educate us both. In the continual clear light that blesses Les Halles, I contemplated his chiseled Nordic peasant's puss and his bulky stooped build. Just now he had come in from Austria, having spent a couple of months in Vienna in perilous but thrilling equilibrium on the fringes of that amazing city, then crossed the Tyrol and the Alps on foot—in high summer, admittedly, but I tipped my hat to him. And his face creased with delight when he recalled the days a couple of years earlier when he worked as a fisherman in Lofoten, as a log-roller in Sweden, and as a woodcutter in Finland before getting into trouble with the Riga police as an "illegal" worker and going down to Germany. His dream now was to set off for Australia. In short, here was a vagabond in the grand manner who had for the moment exhausted the vital resources of old Europe, whereas I was still captivated by the social fantastic of the continent's capital cities. I concealed my writing ambitions from him, so he failed to understand my specifically urban wanderings. I was on my way, in fact, to sharing his point of view, but said nothing. God only knows where he is today. The last time I saw him, he was tackling the difficult task of producing drinkable java from a handful of grounds he had found in a trash can.

2

INEXHAUSTIBLE Paris.

Having crisscrossed Paris in every direction, been tested by its pores and innards, one is bound to be acquainted with its external aspect too, its everyday face. But you have only to push open a door, go down an alleyway, or enter a courtyard to encounter the offbeat, the fantastic: the startling sight of an old well with chain and pulley buried in ivy, a manufacturing trade you would never have thought of, or a secret passage through a building into another world of farmyards with ancient paving stones, hay lofts, carriage houses, wooden balconies with washing hung out to dry, or an odd character following his own path quite oblivious to city ways, living a full and joyful life of idleness.

Idleness has much to be said for it.

As old La Puce the ex-con was wont to say, "Listen, son, I've hit fifty and I've never worked in my life, and as you can see I am in perfectly good health. I get drunk in the normal way, and I am properly dressed." La Puce ("The Flea") was the genuine article: a denizen of the Mouffetard neighborhood and the leather district, where he was to be seen wandering all one winter long with a heavy bag that could no longer, in view of its gaping corners, really qualify as a suitcase, into which he stuffed not the usual sartorial and culinary paraphernalia of the itinerant bum but instead a startling array of items that he would spread out on the bar with an initial air of mystery that captivated the customers and the boss and kept every eye on him: a potpourri of ecclesiastical vestments and decorations, including (going by what I can remember of my first communion) chasubles, maniples, lace surplice sleeves, everything ragged and stiff, four or five kilos' worth, with cheap thread

unraveling and glass beads whose buttercup yellow was largely overwhelmed by verdigris, and old La Puce, beard wagging and breathing
fire, would poke about in the pile with his fingers and rage in veiled
terms against clerical mumbo-jumbo while telling his followers (read:
anyone who would listen) how he had pinched the stuff during a fashionable wedding in what he called a "saint-christy" into which he had
wandered in search of a crust of bread and where he had immediately
been attracted by this great bulging valise which he imagined must be
full of valuables—a set of dessert spoons, for instance, complete with
tart server—or else blunt instruments in precious metals used as props
at Mass, only to discover, three kilometers away and two hours later,
that all he had was a priest's dress-up. Swallowing his disappointment,
he tried to sell his booty by the kilo to his Jewish pals in Rue Charlemagne, but they had his measure and sent him packing, after which,
in desperation, having no clue what to do with this unoffloadable treasure but loath to junk it, he sought to use it as collateral against bar
bills and hauled it around with him everywhere, laying his head on it
to sleep and blowing his nose on the lace in a spirit of vengeance and
anarchy. At last, in a final irony, having abandoned bag and contents in
a café on Rue de Chevaleret, he was nonetheless nabbed by the cops
and given shelter from inclement weather for a six-month stretch. And
this notwithstanding his vigorous protestations to the effect not that
he denied the theft but that he had a horror, dating from his very ten-
derest years, of being locked up and having his needs met against
his will.

3

Truth is stranger than fiction, we say. And this holds good in Paris as much as anywhere. The city is obviously a realm of the offbeat. What can you say about a clochard with a monocle pushing a wheelbarrow? Or a whore walking the street with a dog on a leash? Another soliciting in cock-of-the-rock-orange shorts? A bistro in Grenelle patronized by Russians and Arabs, an impossible combination which the owner handles by drawing a chalk line on the floor to keep the two groups apart? A café frequented exclusively by the deaf and dumb? A barge named *Gérard de Nerval*? A beautiful Negress who lives in the crate-return depository in Les Halles and fixes her face every hundred meters using her reflection in the gutter?

My dear friend Célestine from Montparnasse, also known as Coquillette, as Spaghetti, and as La Poivrade, is another one who risks public notoriety, with the newspapers mentioning her from time to time when they have nothing else to give their readers to chew on except the latest police raid and the names of those hauled off in the last paddy wagons of the night—Célestine, with whom I have had the good fortune to kill not a few bottles at the *bar-tabac* on Rue d'Odessa, Célestine, who, to the initial astonishment of the old listener to tall tales that I am, complained about still being out of jail. "Because you see," she told me, "when I am outside I have nothing but friends, who buy me drinks, and then I get drunk, ruining my health, and anyway I hate red wine." (She usually drank three liters a day.) "I'd sooner be in the can, at least it's nice and quiet there, nobody picks a fight with me or tosses me out like they do in these stinking bars where I get no respect, I'm an honest woman, mark you, a housekeeper by profession,

but there's no work anymore, and then I have no man, monsieur, so I'd rather be inside, up at La Petite-Roquette, where they know me, they like me quite a bit, I have girlfriends, and I earn my bread. Another one, okay? I make straw hats, and when I get out I have a real little nest egg, you might say I have a bank account at La Roquette, they pay me two *livres* a day"—her voice rose sharply—"and then all of a sudden they've had enough of me, the idiots. For two or three days now I've been trying to get myself picked up but nothing works, they just refuse, can you credit that? And that's not all, sweetheart, did I tell you I have a total of twenty convictions—and three hundred and twenty years of restricted residence, not bad, wouldn't you say?" I *would* say— and I signaled the waiter to call a halt, because we were both listing dangerously at the bar. It seems that she once tried to slit her wrists while imprisoned—perhaps so as not to be let out. But my rather few female acquaintances in the neighborhood have been unable to confirm this. What I can say is that I found her one night raising hell on Boulevard Montparnasse, firing up the cops, berating them, telling them just where they could go, and working at full throttle (literally) to get herself thrown into the slammer. Quite a girl!

It was this same bistro that the fish-tank man, swallower of frogs, used to visit from time to time (though I have now lost sight of him too). Smack dab in the middle of the rustic Place d'Aligre, with its ancient market for old clothes and old iron alongside its pinnacled bell-tower, he would first attract a crowd of good folk, bellowing out his patter to housewives and old-timers ready to be amazed by a show they had already seen twenty times. He would then dip a saucepan (capacity one hundred centiliters, he would claim, turning it round to show its depth) into a bucket full of water and drink the contents, then repeat the procedure a second and third time, until he had swallowed five liters, which swelled his belly with no apparent trickery, at which point, with his tight paunch swinging to and fro, he produced little frogs one by one from a jar, stroking them, talking to them, petting them before raising them in turn to his mouth and pushing them in with his thumb, and there! Each one disappeared with a little moist sound. The fellow would inflate first one and then the other cheek,

seeming to chew, and swallow, the eyes of the crowd following the movements of his Adam's apple with great interest. He repeated the trick until all five animals had gone down his gullet raw, as the kids in the audience shuffled with impatience and the women nudged one another. The artist made the rounds, holding out a begging bowl and rattling the coins, which poured in (after all, everyone has a little loose change in their pocket—well, perhaps not everyone . . .), then, returning to center stage, he would raise his eyes heavenward, twirl his hands, give his stomach a swift tap, belch enormously and, from a mouth suddenly full, gently draw out by its back legs one of the hapless and tailless batrachians, holding it up between his fingers for inspection before returning it to the jar. Continuing the same pantomime, he resuscitated the four other ranidae, which were in all likelihood almost done for. After duly checking his critters for signs of life, he announced the finale, the human fountain, and, leaning back and taking each ear between a finger and thumb, he sent a perfect jet of almost five liters of fluid straight to the bottom of his pail.

4

PARIS'S cohort of colorful characters, whose appearance marks them off sharply in the eyes of all general-issue individuals, is not, however, made up solely of good guys, "amusing" eccentrics, and free and lively spirits whose company reassures you about world progress and the bonds of friendship: it also includes rotters, sadists, vicious lunatics, perverts, busybodies, voyeurs, and rapists. And then there are the goggle-eyed types who stand and stare at you blankly, who turn to look at you at the urinal, halting your stream instantly and obliging you to do up your fly and walk five hundred meters to the next *vespasienne*, where you may or may not be able to revive your arrested urge to piss.

Sexual perversion is boundless, especially in Paris, where neat and clean civil servants have been known to place a large hunk of freshly-baked bread on the strip of netting at the base of the slate slab in one of the aforementioned booths, then come back for it a few hours later and take it home in a state of high excitement; an object that seems repugnant even to my dulled sensibilities is thus fated to be further polluted in ways one shudders to picture.

It is very hard to sleep in the woods in Paris—in the Bois de Boulogne or the Bois de Vincennes. This is a real shame. Even in winter, when the cold reduces the glare of public lighting. You cannot spend the night because *they* are there: should you lie down peacefully on the grass, musing, stargazing, there will always be some guy all in gray lurking around, pacing back and forth near you, then stopping, getting out a cigarette, wasting the last match in his box and coming over to ask you for a light. Piercing blue eyes—nothing is more hair-raising than his gaze, blank, somehow too direct, hollow, haunted by the impossible. And you pull out all the stops to make him understand that you are not here for pleasure (hardly!) but to grab some horizontal. You have to threaten to rob him of everything he has on him, to beat him up, or even to kill him before he reluctantly moves on. After the dinner hour, any number of these individuals race down to Porte Maillot wheeling their bikes up the avenues or round the lakes, or walking slowly down the paths, eyes wide as they peer into the half-darkness, familiar with every clump of bushes, and, stopping the moment they spot a couple on a bench or lying on the grass, circle at a considerable distance, and approach as stealthy as Indians, passed masters in the art of creeping silently over dead leaves and fallen branches, then hiding behind a tree and treating the lovers to a sentimental but attentive gaze, tightly focused on their wandering hands, picturing the contours of their bodies and striving to interpret the shadows. And you never know quite how to categorize them, because the same fellow who at five in the afternoon hangs around the gates of the boys' high school at La Muette may well turn up a few hours later, at nightfall, pestering a woman on foot by the Bois de Boulogne, walking alongside her, making obscene propositions, grabbing her ass and frightening her into running off and leaving him with her handbag, which he has snatched. I know these bastards, having chosen to live for a good while behind the Longchamp waterfall with two or three vagrants of my stamp, and to get a good sleep we were often obliged to move far away, at least as far as the last remaining real thicket.

5

PARIS vécu—"Real-Life Paris." Such is the title of a set of hundreds of postcards sold in massive numbers before the War of 1914, picturesque images full of life, of teeming streets and folk standing on their doorsteps, groups happy or unhappy but always looking straight at the photographer under his black cloth—naive photos to be sure, but realistic, capturing the moment when a coachman raises his whip, or a beautiful woman hitches up her skirts, or an old rattletrap slows to turn a corner. Another series illustrated small trades and their practitioners: anachronistic characters who lived from hand to mouth and were none the worse for it, the last sidewalk strollers and *flâneurs*, traveling musicians, courtyard singers, barrel-organ players, ambulant clothes dealers, peddlers of jumble from cleared cellars, flower girls, knife grinders, tinkers, china repairers, chair-bottomers, model-sailboat renters in the Jardin des Tuileries, dog groomers on the quays, mattress-makers under the bridges, bird charmers in the squares, and a sprinkling of characters known in and inseparable from their neighborhoods: Old Charles, Mother Louise, The Viscount, and the like; and scenes of Les Halles: vivid snapshots of the swarming crowds, the medley of vegetables, the horde on the market floor, the bustle and uproar of Rue Berger, the clogged mass of horses and carts, and, here too, a host of vanishing figures, women selling fries or fresh produce, costermongers with their pushcarts, soup kitchens set up in the open air alongside the market halls—three enormous cauldrons heated by braziers that attract clusters of vagrants, beggars, war-wounded, cripples on crutches, idled workers and old women all warming their hands and scorching their faces. *Paris vécu:* Paris as lived. Or as it *was* lived: today all you can find by way of a card to send to your country cousin are views of the "four monuments" (government whorehouses) or panoramas featuring the Eiffel Tower, "Paris by Night," or Napoleon's Tomb. A Paris as dead as a doornail but still standing on its historical foundations.

6

WHAT A mute yet vibrant rebirth transforms this city—these streets, sidewalks, houses, lampposts, shady nooks, trees, urinals—once it is no longer covered, as with a skin, as with a crust, by people swarming larvae-like into the great machine of wage-labor—when, with night, it comes back to life, back to the surface, washing off its filth, straightening its back, scrubbing itself down, singing its silent song, lighting up its darkness. It stretches, relaxes, takes its ease, spreads out before me, the solitary walker, the stroller from elsewhere, free to explore its diverse extremities, thrilled to get lost in its labyrinthine immensity, turning at any corner, leaving a boulevard at the first street on the left, returning to the river, crossing it, tripping along, whistling softly with a cigarette butt between my lips. Darkest night. Three or four o'clock on a winter morning, the gas lamps on the backstreets are out, the trees in the parks carry on growing, the benches creak, vapor rises from the *vespasiennes* and the drain grids, a thousand million houses are just one house, an enormous flat barracks covering kilometers as seen from the city's hilltops, the stones are cold, the cobbles gleam, and I settle by the curb of a square in a dry gutter, my eyes level with the street, and meditate, dream, forget to draw on my cigarette end, and, crossing my legs in the lotus position, put my ear to the great seashell of the city, whose canopy covers and whose lowing lulls me.

I am in Paris. The fact is a blessing in itself. How many times, with my face buried in straw in some barn, or my back lashed by the rain on the high road, have I longed for such a moment? Yet how often too shall I dream now, spending the night on a park bench with an empty

belly and chilblains on my fingers, of the sun of Spain or the brothels of Antwerp? So goes the vagabond's life.

Now that I have written this book, which is to say passed two or three hundred nights crisscrossing Paris, making countless visits to countless bistros, penciling notes on toilet paper, sniffing the air in search of some rock to crawl under, scanned the gutters for small change, and moved heaven and earth just to survive here, well, I've had enough.

As might probably be said of any great human conglomeration, Paris is indeed an extraordinary caravansary for those who know how to live there and see things from a particular point of view. But it is suffocating. There is less and less oxygen. Less and less chlorophyll. A vast horizon of stone, *where no dew falls at night.*

OTHER NEW YORK REVIEW CLASSICS

For a complete list of titles, visit www.nyrb.com or write to:
Catalog Requests, NYRB, 435 Hudson Street, New York, NY 10014

* *Also available as an electronic book.*

RECEIVED APR – – 2016